Mount

A Mountain Man's Adventures

Arlen Blumhagen

Untreed
Reads

Mount; A Mountain Man's Adventures
By Arlen Blumhagen

Copyright 2017 by Arlen Blumhagen
Cover Copyright 2017 by Untreed Reads Publishing
Cover Design by Ginny Glass

ISBN-13: 978-1-94544-758-7

Also available in ebook format.

Published by Untreed Reads, LLC
506 Kansas Street, San Francisco, CA 94107
www.untreedreads.com

Printed in the United States of America.

Also by Arlen Blumhagen and Untreed Reads Publishing

Mount II: The Next Adventure

Mount III: The Adventures Continue

The Killings in Boulder Valley

"Green Beans & Murder" (part of the Untreed Reads anthology, *The Killer Wore Cranberry: A Second Helping*)

The Christmas Pony

Foreward

Howdy folks. The name's Mount. My given name at birth was Thaddeus Beauregard Battner. Now, my pa's name was Christopher and my ma's name was Sara. How the hell they came up with Thaddeus Beauregard plumb mystifies me. I never did get around to askin' them about it before they passed on. I guess the reason I never asked was cause they never called me Thaddeus or Beauregard. Oh, Ma may've used Thaddeus a time or two when I got her real riled up over something, but as far back as I can remember it's always been just Mount. It started out, I was told, as Our Little Mountain Man, but it's just been Mount as far back as I can remember. As I grew, and grew, and grew, it became obvious that I was gonna be one mountain-sized mountain man. Ma and Pa both being rather considerable, I guess it was just natural that I'd be big as a danged ole cottonwood. I finally quit growin' at around six and a half feet. Cause of my size other folks took to calling me Mount too, short for mountain. Truth be told, there's a couple of lady folk down at the Rendezvous who, with just a bit of a blush blooming in their cheeks, call me Mount for a whole other reason, but those stories ain't for tellin'.

Pa decided he was picking up and coming out west around about 1815, the best I can figure. He'd heard about a couple of gentlemen name of Lewis and Clark who had led a military expedition to the Pacific Ocean and back. Pa had heard stories of the Lewis and Clark trip, the adventures they'd had and the incredible beauty of the land, and just decided it was someplace he needed to see. He came, he saw, he stayed for the rest of his short life.

Pa knew it was gonna be a hard trip crossing the country headed west, and an even harder way of life, especially since he was dumber than a pile of buffalo shit when it came to living off the land. I think one of the reasons he and Ma survived was that he was a smart enough man to realize how dumb he was, and took that fact into account. I reckon "simple" and "careful" best explain how they traveled. They mostly ate the grub they'd brought with them. Supplies included plenty of dried meat: bacon, salt pork, and jerky. They also had vegetables such as potatoes, carrots and beans; according to Pa, lots and lots of beans. There was rice, wheat, and flour for making hot cakes or mush. Pa learned how to hunt by trying and failing over and over again. Lucky for him and Ma they didn't have to rely on Pa's hunting skills or they would've been danged hungry. As for danger, about the only real threat they ran into was in crossin' the rivers and streams they came to. It was early spring and the water level was still fairly low so the crossings were possible, but still put quite a scare into them. Neither Ma or Pa could swim. I don't remember any stories of near drowning, so being scared must've been as close as they came.

He was attracted by the totally untamed west, the unknown and the undiscovered; the challenge. Locking horns with Mother Nature and defying the elements sounded not only dangerous, but adventurous and exciting. Being the son of a general store operator in St. Louis, adventure and excitement were things sorely lacking in my pa's upbringing. He was in his early twenties and knew if he was going west it was time to go. With his mind set on leavin' he faced the task of telling his lady friend, Sara Mae, goodbye. Years later Pa's eyes still lit up like a full moon as he told me how he nearly burst with joy when his Sara informed him she'd be going along.

"You can barely take care of yourself in the middle of St. Louis, you wouldn't last a week in the wilderness." Is how Pa said she explained it. Ma said she just couldn't picture living life without him. Ma and Pa got hitched about a week before leaving St. Louis, Ma bein' a proper lady and all.

Together, with nothing more than a couple of horses to ride, one horse to pack all they owned, and a whole wagon train full of hopes, and dreams, they crossed the country from St. Louis to the Rocky Mountains in the northwest; and found themselves the most beautiful spot in all the world.

Their families made it real clear they thought both of them were plumb crazy for going. Pa admitted to me there were a few times during the trip that he figured they were probably right. It was a mighty hard road, and a danged miracle that a greenhorn and his young bride even survived the trip.

But they did survive, and Pa found that special place near the foot of one of the smaller ranges in the Rocky Mountains. There's a fairly large creek that Pa named the Sweetgrass, running past the cabin and down to the Yellowstone River about a mile away. The mountains are a couple miles back behind, rising up in all their God-given majesty. The mountains give way to the rolling foothills, pine covered, green, and lush; the dark green pine forest here and there broken by a stand of aspen or birch trees, standing out in different colors depending on the time of year. The foothills then roll on down and open up into the most beautiful valley meadow a person can picture. In the springtime, when the world is reborn, that meadow is plumb full of wildflowers in bloom, butterflies showing off, birds flying and singing, and the like, all spread out under the biggest, bluest sky you can imagine. It'll all bring tears to a grown man, and that's a fact.

Back then the land didn't rightly belong to nobody except the Indians, buffalo, and grizzly bear. Pa built a right nice log cabin, with a small corral for the horses, and a tilled vegetable garden; worked with a shovel Pa had traded for. There was plenty of game to hunt, once Pa figured out how to hunt it. There were also plenty of vegetables from Ma's garden. With Pa trading animal pelts and hides for anything else they needed, my folks built a wonderful and special life in those mountains.

A direct result of that special life was me. Ma and Pa figured I was probably one of the very first white children born out west, since they were one of the very first white couples to make that move. We didn't have any neighbors, only a few Indians ridin' by now and again. Mostly they were friendly, and if not, they were very respectful of Pa's flintlock rifle.

Twice a year, in the spring and fall, we'd pack up the horses with Pa's furs, pelts and hides and travel for about a week south to Fort Granger where they held the Rendezvous. Rendezvous was a gathering of settlers, mountain folks, and Indians for the purpose of trading goods, having numerous competitions such as horse races, foot races, wrestling matches, or sharp shooting; but I think the main purpose was raising hell. Rendezvous could last up to a month, although we normally stayed for only five or six days. Pa would trade his hides and furs for coffee, sugar, flour, salt, and the like.

That gathering was about my only chance to be around other folks; there were even some kids, mostly Indian, near my own age. Now kids bein' kids, we tended to get into all kinds of mischief; stealing food, stealing liquor, stealing a peek at the ladies that entertained the men at Bell's Place. Hell, watching the adults, we figured that causing mischief was the main purpose of Rendezvous. As I got older the trouble we got into got more and more interesting; fist fighting, getting drunk and rowdy, and spendin' some time with those ladies at Bell's. Yep, I've always enjoyed Rendezvous—visiting, trading, and mostly just raising hell.

On the way home after every spring and fall get-together, when I was a youngun, Ma would bring out a peppermint candy cane she'd gotten for me.

"Now if you're careful, you could make that last all the way home, you know," she always told me, and I knew she was right. The candy cane lasted about two miles.

Ma was a schoolteacher back in St. Louis, and was downright serious about giving me an education as I grew up. We spent hours sitting beside the creek doing school work when it was good weather. When the weather was bad, and during the winter, we'd sit huddled by the fire to do our studying, using the fire for heat and light. Ma made sure I learned my reading, writing, and arithmetic. I've gotta admit, over the years, all three have come in mighty handy a time or two.

I guess I've always been a storyteller. When I was small enough to walk under a snake's belly I was a storyteller. Of course back then I hadn't lived a whole lot yet, so I had to make up most everything. But as I've grown and had some livin' under my belt, and a few adventures I've survived, my stories now are, of course, the gospel truth. Well…mostly.

Chapter One

It all started about four years ago when, mid-winter, Pa left to check his trap lines along the Yellowstone River and never came home. Bein' the way of the mountains, Ma and I, in a way, expected it to happen someday. Although not awfully surprised, we were mighty grieved and missed Pa something powerful. Ma never was the same after Pa was gone; it was like a part of her had gone with him.

I spent the better part of a month following Pa's trap lines and scouring the country looking for some sign, but saw nothing. Whether he was set upon by hostile Indians, tangled with a grizzly bear or mountain lion, or slipped and fell into the river and drowned, I guess we'll never know.

Like I said, Ma was never the same. She spent most of her time sitting and staring off down the valley like she was expecting Pa to come home. After grieving for a little over a year after Pa was gone, Ma gave up on waiting and went to join him in that happy hunting ground beyond the sky. I don't rightly know if she had a sickness of some sort or if it was just her broken heart, but in the end she just kinda shriveled up and passed on real quiet like. I buried her on the hilltop by the giant cottonwood, so she could keep watch over the cabin and her garden down below.

Over the next year or so I just kinda existed without really living. I hunted for food, ate when I had to, drank when I had to, slept when I had to, and spent a lot of time wondering why and pondering the ways of life...and death. That whole time is kinda hazy to me now. After an awful long time wandering in that fog it finally started lifting a little and I realized that life was just gonna keep going on after all, so hell, I might as well join back up.

In all my born days I'd never been far from the mountains. Other than going to Rendezvous, I did all my traveling in the mountains with Pa, hunting, camping, and setting trap lines. I'd listened to my folks talk some about St. Louis, and how life had been there. They didn't talk about it much, but it sounded to me like a whole lot of people in an awful small space, with lots of noise and confusion. In fact, it sounded scary as hell.

I figured both Ma and Pa probably still had family in St. Louis, and I felt like it was just the proper thing to do to let their families know of their passing. Since I didn't figure I could count on any of them to be stopping by the cabin any time soon, the only other thing to do was to pack up my bedroll and traveling gear onto Skyhawk, the Mustang pony I'd traded for, and travel to St. Louis; I just needed to figure out where the hell St. Louis was.

Pa and I had done a whole lot of campin' out and living off the land so I was confident that I'd be okay on the trail. Having no idea what was in store for me in the months to come, I was even excited about my adventure; and knew that I was doing the right thing. As soon as the snow melted enough to travel in the spring of 1841, I started out for St. Louis. My trip began by going south to Fort Granger for two reasons. First, it was the only place I knew how to get to, and second, I was hoping that Captain Lancaster, who was in charge at the fort, could give me some directions to St. Louis.

I'd made the trip to Fort Granger twice a year most of my life, but that spring was the first time I made it alone. I figured I could make the trip with my eyes closed; turned out I barely made it with my eyes wide open. The afternoon of the third day I came out of a long narrow ravine to find myself facing a large pine covered hill with a valley running up both sides. I remembered the place; I just couldn't remember which valley we had taken in the past. I'd always just followed Pa. Luckily, as I sat beside a small spring having a bite to eat and pondering which way to go, three young Indian braves rode up coming from the west. One of the braves was a feller I'd known from past Rendezvous. Turned out they were headed to Fort Granger themselves and I was able to ride along. I didn't bother telling them that I was lost when they found me.

When I got to the fort I found Captain Lancaster and inquired about directions to St. Louis. "You need to head northeast until you meet up with the Missouri River." Captain Lancaster told me. "Then follow it until you come to a big city. That should be St. Louis." How could I go wrong with that?

Actually, the trip out to St. Louis turned out to be by far the easiest part of the whole damned adventure. Once we'd found the Missouri and knew we were on the right trail, Skyhawk and I took it real easy, traveled at an easy pace and just enjoyed being out amongst God's creations. The good Lord sure enough knew what he was doing when he created this land of ours. The rugged, majestic Rocky Mountains will always be my home and my most beloved part of this country, but even when I got away from the mountains and was traveling across hundreds of miles of plains and prairie, it was still beautiful in its own special way. As far as your eyes can see, and in those parts that's a long danged way, there is...well...nothin'. But somehow it's still beautiful; endless miles full of sagebrush, snake grass, and wildflowers.

Not long into the trip I saw a herd of buffalo stretched out on the plains so vast it took me a full day to ride past it, and that's the truth. Once I got away from the foothills and into the prairie lands the deer and elk pretty much disappeared. There were mostly just buffalo and antelope. Once I moved on into the desert prairie lands even the buffalo disappeared, but there were still antelope; millions of antelope. Now, I've eaten buffalo, deer, and elk my whole life, and enjoy one just about as well as the other. Not only do I not like antelope meat much, but you gotta work awful damned hard to get it. One particular day I lay in a little hollow in the ground for nigh on to three hours until I could get a shot. I won't shed a tear if I never eat antelope meat again.

I did have one rattlesnake meal along the trail. Skyhawk was working a steady trot across the prairie and I wasn't even half paying attention when he suddenly quit going east and headed straight north. I continued headed east without the benefit of a horse. To make a bad situation worse, as I was flying through the air I saw the reason for Skyhawk's distress; a large prairie rattlesnake was coiled on a flat rock. The same flat rock I was about to land on!

I can't explain it folks. I don't know myself how I did it, but I swear on my momma's grave that in mid flight, touching nothing but air, I twisted and somehow changed directions; not much, but enough. I landed maybe two feet to the left of the rock where that snake was sunning himself. Now two feet to the side was way better than right on top of, but still plenty close enough to get snake bit. So when I hit the ground I didn't bother to take the time to get up, I just started rolling; all the time waiting to feel those fangs latch on! After rolling over a rock or two and a big sagebrush, I jumped to my feet and stood ready to run, jump, or spit, whatever needed to be done; but the snake was still on the rock. He was still coiled up for business, but didn't seem to be concerned about me anymore. There were several other rocks spread around to use for weapons so I had rattlesnake for supper. Snake isn't my favorite meal either, but it sure did beat the hell out of antelope again.

Then there was the afternoon that I built a little, and I repeat little, fire under a tall ponderosa pine to warm up some grub while waiting out a bit of a rainstorm. It'd been a downright hot day, and the little sprinkle cooled it off real nice; so nice that I dozed off sitting up against the tree, beside the fire. Well, seems that while I slept a breeze picked up and whipped my little fire up and into the dead under branches of the pine tree. I woke to my world on fire. Thought maybe I'd died and woke in the pits of Hell for a second or two, until I remembered where I was. The tree burned, but the rain kept the fire from going anywhere, and I learned another important life lesson. Actually a couple, I'll be picking my tree more carefully, and I won't be going to sleep with a fire burnin'; that last one my Pa had taught me, I obviously just needed a little reminding.

The trip east took around two months. Now I ain't gonna bore you folks with a day by day account of my journey to St. Louis.

Nearly getting snake bit and burnt alive were the two most exciting things that happened. There were a couple of violent spring thunderstorms that I rode through; and one so powerful I was forced to take cover among a small stand of cottonwood trees that lined the river. There were also a couple of anxious moments crossing streams that joined the Missouri and there were three days that I was watched from a distance by a small band of Indians; it was hard to sleep at night waiting to see if they were going to attack. Most of the trip was filled with easy traveling, where each and every sunrise welcomed a new day full of new experiences filled with new sights and sounds. I'd highly recommend traveling in the spring if you were to ask; even the ugly is prettier in the spring.

I saw a whole passel of wild flowers I'd never seen before, and some I'd seen before, but never in those colors. Or maybe one day it'd be the gnarled remains of a tree standing all alone out in the middle of nowhere. Each day was something new and exciting. And the sunsets in the prairie! They're a whole different critter than the sunsets in the mountains. Now don't get me wrong, a Rocky Mountain sunset is one of the most beautiful sights God placed on this here earth, but the colors tend to stay in the west near the horizon, sometimes bleeding onto nearby clouds. A prairie sunset takes over the whole damn sky. The colors kinda spread across the clouds like a runaway grass fire. On the other hand, without clouds for a prairie sunset, you don't get much of a display. It's light, it gets darker, and it's dark. A mountain sunset doesn't necessarily need clouds to show off.

One day I came upon a couple real nice homesteads built close together along the river, and I figured I was getting close. At the first of the places I had to stop out front and take a few minutes just to take it all in. I'd never seen such extravagance! Those folks had built a house that a whole damn Indian tribe could live in. Then, behind it a hundred feet or so, they had another danged house! Why the hell they'd need two houses is a mystery to me, but there it was just the same; and it was all surrounded by a fancy white fence.

Late afternoon that same day, as I was travelin' easy, just like every other day, I came up over a little rise, just like every other rise, and there she was! Spread out below me in this little hollow, St. Louis! I have to admit I wasn't as impressed as I thought I'd be. It just wasn't as awe inspiring as I had figured it to be, but still more buildings, people, animals, and ruckus going on than I'd ever seen before. It was like three or four western Rendezvous going on all at the same time.

As I approached down the main road into the city I was met by a hard-looking man packing one of them fancy new Colt six-shot revolvers. It was holstered but the stranger's hand rested on the grip.

"Howdy partner," I called out. I put on a big smile hoping he'd see how friendly I was. "You the official welcoming committee for St. Louis, are ya?" I'm thinking I musta looked one hell of a sight. I had trail dust covering me in layers, and that was with taking a dip in the river every few days. The way I looked and smelled, I could see how this feller could have been a bit cautious, but instead of looking scared or nervous the guy just looked a little confused.

"Where'd you say?" he asked.

"St. Louis," I said, and pointed back over my shoulder, like that'd show him right where I'd been. "I came clear from the Rocky Mountains out west."

"Don't know anything about any rock mountains," he replied, "but I do know St. Louis, and this ain't it partner. This here is the American Fur Company's western trading post. St. Louis is nearly 300 miles east of here." Sure enough did explain why it'd looked so small.

Turned out this feller, name of Jim Ferguson, who came out to meet me was a right fine gentleman. I looked like six and a half feet of ugly having a bad day and smelled like the wrong end of a buffalo, and he still invited me back to his home.

Now his wife, Mabel, she wasn't quite so understanding at first. She saw us coming and met us at the front door with a broom that she wasn't intending on doing any sweeping with.

"What in tarnation you bringing home now James?" She looked at me like I was the very devil himself and she was preparing to spread some gospel with that broom handle. Mr. Ferguson had quite a time talking some sense into that lady. She finally came around, and after washing most of the dirt and smell off in a nearby pond, clothes and all, Mrs. Ferguson allowed me to come into her home, and I have to say, treated me right nice. She fed me some sort of soup/stew that just may have been the finest eating I've ever had. It was chunks of chicken mixed with several different vegetables in a thick broth, and it was all seasoned straight from heaven. Mabel served it with fresh baked bread and huckleberry jam. After eating way more than is healthy for a feller, and then having a couple pulls off a whiskey bottle, I slept like a baby. I did have to pull up a chair to the bottom of my cot for my feet to rest on. Next morning, after a breakfast damn near as good as supper had been, I was plumb eager to get back on the trail.

One thing Captain Lancaster failed to tell me about was that the Missouri River emptied into the Mississippi River before gettin' to St. Louis, and I had to cross the damned thing. I'd crossed several small tributaries that emptied into the Missouri along the way, but nothing Skyhawk couldn't wade across; still being early in the spring and all.

Neither of my folks had ever learned to swim. When I was just a youngun, they decided I needed to know how. We had a mountain man friend named Buck Nealy. Ole Buck knew how to swim although he couldn't remember how he'd learned. So, Buck, during a summer visit, got the task of teaching me to swim. Now, Buck figured it wasn't so much teaching a person to swim as just giving them the opportunity. His thinking was that everybody knew how to swim deep down inside, some folks just didn't know they knew. He gave me my opportunity by dumping me into the deep fishin' hole down on the creek. I damn near drowned before I was able to catch hold of a willow branch and pull myself out. After that I worked on teaching myself. Over the next couple years I spent a lot of the summer down at that fishin' hole and got so I could do a passable dog paddle. Dog paddling across the creek is a hell of a long ways from swimming across the Mississippi River. Swimming the Mississippi wasn't something I was looking forward to.

As it turned out I didn't worry nearly enough. Skyhawk, bless his heart, paused for only a second on the bank. I picked a spot where the slope into the river was gradual so we could walk in slowly. When his feet left the ground Skyhawk panicked for just a second, his eyes flashing and his nostrils flaring, then he realized he could swim, and he settled down. The Mississippi, being the Mississippi, was wide and to the eye appeared to be moving slow, so I was surprised at the pull of the current when we got into it. Then, just as Skyhawk was really getting the feel for swimming, his front hooves hit some rocks that were the outer edge of an underwater gravel bar. His feet stopped moving, his knees gave way, and Skyhawk tumbled head first into the river. Don't know why the hell a person would try to hang on to a horse that's going underwater, but that's just what I did. My hands locked down on the saddle and my legs clamped down around Skyhawk's middle, and I hung on! Skyhawk sorta rolled onto his side up onto the submerged gravel bar, with me still in the riding position. I'd gotten a pretty good breath before we went under, but by the time I'd bounced three or four times with a horse on one side of me and a pile of rocks on the other, I was in bad need of some fresh air. On the upward side of the next bounce I kicked myself free of Skyhawk, twisted to get my legs under me, and kicked for the surface. It didn't take long to get there seeing how, squatted down like I was, the surface was only about six inches above my head. I stood up on the gravel bar panting like an old dog; the water was up to about my chest. Again I was surprised at the power of the slow moving water. I planted my feet wide apart and leaned back against the current and looked for Skyhawk. Seems all he was waitin' on was for me to get the hell off his back. Skyhawk was twenty feet downriver, and thirty feet closer to the far bank, and was swimming like he'd done it all his life.

So there I was. Standing on some slippery, slimy rocks in the middle of the Mississippi River, my legs were spread wide and I was leaning back against the push of the water. And I'll admit my knees were shaking a little too. It wasn't much further to the far shore than it was back to where I'd come from, and the far shore was where my horse was headed, and where I needed to be. It didn't look like Skyhawk was coming back for me; in fact he was nearly to the bank; looked like it was up to me.

I lifted my feet up off the rocks and let the current take me. By staying in a sitting position with my feet pointed downriver, I was able to keep my head above water and sort of control where I went with my hands and arms. I floated for maybe a half mile, while I slowly worked my way towards the bank, and tried hard to keep hold of my fear and not let it turn into all out panic. I knew panic would kill me. Finally, I felt mud underneath my feet. I got my legs under me and scrambled the last twenty feet to dry land.

"Hallelujah! Thank you Lord!" I sent up, between gasps. I figured I might as well pray since I was on my knees anyway; trying to catch my breath. I think the being scared was more of a hardship than the getting myself out of the river. I looked and saw Skyhawk a couple hundred feet away grazing, so I spent the next little while sitting on the bank of the Mississippi contemplating the joy of still being among the living.

It took about two more weeks to get to the real St. Louis; I figured around two months total since I'd left my cabin. The traveling between the American Fur Company and St. Louis was easy, with a dirt road to follow and farms and folks on a pretty regular basis all the way. There were more than a couple of places where I had to stop and stare; spending a few minutes in wonder at the splendor of it all.

9

When I did finally get to St. Louis, early one afternoon, there was no mistaking it for anything else. Folks, this mountain man had never even imagined there could be that many people and that much chaos going on all in one place.

As I sat there atop Skyhawk and stared in awe and some fear at the city before me, I'll admit I almost just turned around right there and then and hightailed it back to my mountain cabin. But I came for a reason and damn it all, I was set on getting it done. I took a couple of deep breaths to calm my nerves, worked up my courage, nudged Skyhawk with my heels, and rode on into the city of St. Louis, Missouri. I should've gone home.

Chapter Two

Now folks, I been face to face with an Indian trying to take my scalp. I been face to face with a grizzly bear trying to take my whole damned head off. I been ankle to face with a timber rattler long enough to use as a lasso. Was I scared? Damn right I was! Every time! But I swear, not as scared as I was that day riding into the confusion and calamity that was St. Louis. As I rode down that main street; oh yeah…I found out that roads are called streets when they're inside a city…I just couldn't believe there could be so much going on all at once. I swear I was so busy gawkin' at everything all around me that a couple times I plumb forgot to breathe and nearly fainted out of the saddle. The street I brought into town kept going straight ahead until the buildings on both sides seemed to meet off in the distance. And every few hundred feet or so there was another danged street running north and south too! And when you looked down any of those side streets they were filled with houses that met off in the distance. I couldn't believe there were people that lived in each and every one of those houses. Hell, I didn't know there were that many people in the whole damned world!

Just on that main street alone there were people in the street, on the boardwalk beside the street, between the shops, in the shops, hell, even a couple on top of the shops. There were horses for riding, horses for packing, and horses pulling wagons; little wagons, big wagons, even wagons covered with canvas. There were dogs and cats running around everywhere. I swear I even saw a pig strutting down that street like he owned the whole damn works. One thing there wasn't was any other mountain men. Wearing my old deerskin britches that were so thin in the rear that my backside was threatenin' to play peek-a-boo, and my four- or five-year-old deerskin shirt, I stood out like a rainbow trout trying to run with a buffalo herd.

Skyhawk and I wandered down the street in a daze for a bit trying our best to stay out of the way. It took awhile, but when I finally started thinking again, I could only wonder where a feller would even make a start to find someone in all this mess.

Having no idea what to do, I was still simply taking it all in when I saw it. Right there beside something called a telegraph office was a sign I recognized from Fort Granger. The sign said saloon. Wasn't sure if I would find out anything about my grandpa's store in there, but I knew it was a damn good place to start lookin'. I hitched Skyhawk to a post out front and went in.

Along one side of the biggest danged room I'd ever seen was a bar that had to be forty feet long, with probably forty men leaning up against it. The rest of the room was full of tables and chairs, and I swear there was a feller's butt in every chair. Not knowing what to do I just kinda ambled up to the end of the bar and was just watching all that was happening when the barkeep feller came up to me.

"Whiskey?" he asked.

Well now, I hadn't thought about it, but that did sound powerful good. "Why, yes sir, thank you," I answered, proud that I'd remembered my manners. He poured some whiskey into this little glass and set it down in front of me. I picked it up and drank it down in one swallow as there was just barely a mouthful. Well I wanna tell you folks, whoever mixed up that batch surely knew what he was doin' because that whiskey burned from tongue to gut. Now folks, I've had my share of whiskey, probably had my first drink when I was just a teenager, but I hadn't had a drop for a long while, and I commenced to coughing and choking like I was gonna keel over right there and then. My eyes were tearing up. My throat was closing up. It must'a took a full two or three minutes before I could take a proper breath and my eyes cleared enough to see. There were a few curious stares, but nobody seemed to be paying much attention to me, which I was damn glad to see; but that barkeep was still standing there looking at me.

"That'll be a nickel," he said, with just a touch of a snicker in his voice.

Now, I knew about money. They used it instead of trading sometimes at Fort Granger. Yes sir, I knew what money was, but I sure as hell didn't have any! I told the barkeep that and he got all kinds of worked up. He was yelling and carrying on so that I couldn't even understand most of what he was saying. Some words I did catch were "freeloader," "bum." and "drifter." Well now, that barkeep's outburst had gotten everybody's attention, and it seemed everyone in that saloon was staring at me like I was some sort of bad news. Part of me wanted to just turn around and get the hell outta there as fast as I could, but the pride in me rose up and couldn't be convinced to leave.

"Now hold on there, friend!" I said. "I ain't none of those things you're spoutin'; now just calm down a damned minute! I didn't know you'd be wanting money or I wouldn't of taken the glass. Hell, I thought you was just being neighborly." Well now, that got everybody in the place to laughing and whooping it up like they'd never heard of such a ridiculous notion.

Not quite everyone was laughing. That barkeep didn't see anything funny in being taken for a nickel. It took some doing, but eventually I got enough of my story out to convince him that I truly wasn't trying to take advantage, and we worked out a trade. He put me to work behind the bar washing dishes and stocking shelves in return for some food and a little more of that ass kickin' whiskey. After a few more sips I was able to swallow it down with just barely a shudder.

As it turned out that barkeep feller, Harold Pearson by name was pretty understanding of my situation. He was also smart enough to figure that having a mountain-sized mountain man around could be a damn handy thing. I got a place to sleep, which was a cot in the back room that I shared with five or six rats and a flying bug of some sort that was nearly as big as the rats. I got a meal twice a day and a stall for Skyhawk out back of the saloon. And I got all the whiskey I could drink...when Mr. Pearson wasn't looking. What Mr. Pearson got was a danged ole slave. He had me packing whiskey barrels, beer barrels, and boxes full of wine. I was stocking shelves, washing dishes, taking care of customers, polishing mirrors, and even mopping the damned floor. It didn't take but two days for me to decide this city life wasn't my cup-a-tea as they say. I needed to find my folks' families, give them the news I came to give, and get the hell out of here; the sooner the better.

My Pa's name was Christopher Battner, and as I said his Pa, Fredrick, ran a general store somewhere in this mess of a city. I started asking the customers as I waited on them. Problem was most of the customers were the same fellers every day. By noon of my second day I'd done asked everybody in the place with no success. On the third day my luck changed.

Shortly before noon, this gentleman I hadn't seen before came walking in. It was obvious that he wasn't one of the neighborhood fellers. He was all dressed up in these fancy duds like he was going to a funeral or somethin'. He had a disgusted look on his face as though he could barely tolerate being that close to the rest of us; like maybe he was afraid the poor was gonna rub off on him.

"I'm looking for some men." Mr. Fancy Pants stood a few feet inside the door and spoke loudly to the whole room. "I have several acres of land south of town that needs cleared. Pay is fifty cents a day." Probably two dozen men lined up to take the job.

While he was interviewing the men, signing some up and sending some back to their seats, the gentleman seemed to be taking stock of the saloon as though he was trying to decide something. I guess he was contemplating whether it'd be safe to have a bite to eat or not because when he got done with the men he walked up and took a stool at the bar. When I went over to help him I got a whiff of flowers or some dang thing. After I'd gotten him a glass of beer and gave Mr. Pearson his order for a sandwich I started up a conversation with Mr. La-dee-da. Turned out St. Louis had a poor side of town and a well-off side of town. I'd entered on the poor side. The fancy feller, Mr. Travers, was from the prosperous side. And it turned out that Mr. Fredrick Battner's general store was also on the wealthy side of town.

Mr. La-dee-da Travers sure as hell wasn't gonna be seen in town with the likes of me, but he was nice enough to give me directions. He said my granddad's store was about twenty minutes away; took me over an hour to find it. I rode through the city trying to follow Mr. Travers' directions, sometimes forgetting what I was doing I got so caught up in seeing all the things I'd never seen before. I started out on Market Street for a ways, turning left on Seventh Street. I followed Seventh Street for what seemed like miles to Hickory Street, gawking left and right and all around the whole time. I was plumb amazed at not only the size of that city, but also the fact that every place I looked there was something going on. There were wagons everywhere, plus dogs and cats and even farm animals roaming the streets; and for every animal or carriage I saw there musta been a dozen people. They were riding and walking and running and strolling; I even saw more than a couple of fellers staggering. They were headed north or south or east or west or somewhere in between. After an hour of riding and gawking around I finally stood in front of my Grandpa Battner's general store there on Hickory Street. I knew it was the right place because the sign on the front said "Battner's General Store."

Chapter Three

I was nervous as a long tailed cat in a room full of rocking chairs walking into that general store. Not knowing what to expect, or how I was gonna be received by my Pa's family. One thing I sure wasn't prepared for was to see my Pa standing there behind the danged counter helping a little ole lady purchase fabric of some sort. My shock was short lived, as upon a second glance I could tell that this "Pa" was a tad bit shorter and a little bigger around than my Pa had been, but the resemblance was close enough to be uncanny. I'd been so intent on finding his folks I didn't even give a thought to maybe Pa had some brothers or sisters. I thought back to my growin' up, and as best I could remember he'd never talked about any. When the lady at the counter finished her business and walked away the feller behind the counter looked up and our eyes met. I'm not sure if he saw Pa standing there or maybe himself, but he made this funny sound and grabbed for the counter cause his legs got all sorta wobbly. Thinking an introduction was in order, I walked right up to that feller, stuck out my hand, and started talking.

"Howdy, name's Thaddeus Battner, but folks just call me Mount. My Pa was Christopher Battner. I'm guessing you'd be his brother." The feller behind the counter just stood and stared.

"I came all the way from the Rocky Mountains out west to find my Pa's family," I explained. "Have I got the right place?" That feller took a couple deep breathes and his legs firmed up a bit. He took my hand and started shaking it.

"I'm Joseph Battner," he said. I saw tears welling in his eyes. "My God, I haven't even thought of Christopher for nearly twenty years."

He looked down at the floor as if suddenly ashamed. "Christopher and I weren't on speaking terms when he left." After a short pause he looked back up at me and a smile slowly pushed the sadness aside. "You, my boy, are the spitting image of Christopher, maybe even a little taller. You sure are a big one aren't you?"

"Yes sir, I reckon I am at that," I replied. "And you look enough like Pa that you gave me quite a start when I walked in here. It sure is a relief to find you." It was my turn to look down at the floor for a couple seconds. "I'm afraid I'm bringin' bad news."

Chapter Four

Turned out there weren't a whole lot of my folks' families left. My Grandpa Battner had passed on years ago. It seems Grandpa drank a bit; seems he drank a bit all day and a bit all night. The two boys, Christopher and Joseph, were the only children they'd had. Grandma Ella Battner was still alive, if that's what you want to call it. The store had living quarters in back and Grandma Battner sat there in a rocker and stared out the side window, except when she was sleeping, which was most of the time. I swear the good Lord was just a little boy when that woman was born. When I told her of her oldest son's passing I really didn't know if she understood a word I said, or even if she heard. But as I sat there wondering, a single tear rolled down her cheek. It's hard to explain how I felt. I can't say I enjoyed that moment, but that one tear made the trip worth the effort somehow.

Ma's family was even more depleted. Both of her parents, Jean and Samuel Ricks, had died years earlier during a malaria outbreak that had killed hundreds in the area. Ma had a brother and sister who could be dead or alive as far as Uncle Joseph knew. Both had left town as soon as they were old enough; just a couple years after Ma had left. Uncle Joseph said this was due to the fact that Sam Ricks was a mean ole bastard who liked to beat on his wife and kids. I don't remember Ma ever saying anything, but if it's the truth I'm glad the bastard is dead. I wasn't about to try tracking Ma's siblings down. Uncle Joseph promised to pass on the word about Ma if he ever saw either one of them again.

As far as I could see my work in St. Louis was done. I'd made it there and contacted what family I could. Meeting Uncle Joseph has nice and all, but I was ready to head for home as soon as possible.

Uncle Joseph and I stayed up most of the night. Me sharing stories of Pa and his exploits; fighting Indians, grizzly bear, and now and then Ma. Uncle Joseph shared a large jug of moonshine.

The next morning, late the next morning, I was helping stock some shelves for Uncle Joseph in exchange for some provisions I wanted for my trip home. The front door opened and this feller walked in. I didn't like him.

Have you ever noticed how some people just kind of fill up a room when they enter it? This man was tall, well dressed, and slightly overweight, but it doesn't have a danged thing to do with size. It's just their presence overpowers everybody else's presence somehow. Sometimes it's in a good way, and sometimes it's in a bad way...shoot, I don't know if I'm makin' any sense to you folks, but this man was one of them kinda folks, regardless; in a real bad way. He stood inside the door for just a second before he saw Uncle Joseph behind the counter.

"Joseph," the feller shouted across the room. One word, and I liked him even less. The way he barked out just that one word I could tell this gentleman was a swollen-headed, arrogant son of a bitch. He started across the room like he owned the place.

I'd only spent a few hours with Uncle Joseph, but one thing I'd noticed was that he had many of the same qualities Pa'd had. One of which was a whole passel of pride. He stood straight, talked proud, and seemed ready and able to handle pretty much anything. So I was truly surprised when, as that feller walked across the store, I watched the pride and self respect Uncle Joseph had, seep out of him like air from a leaky balloon. His shoulders slumped and his eyes dropped to the floor like he wasn't good enough to meet the gentleman's gaze.

"Hello Mr. Worthington." Uncle Joseph sounded like a slave talking to his master. "How are you sir?"

Ignoring Uncle Joseph's inquiry completely, Mr. Worthington stepped in front of a husband and wife coming up to the counter, and announced. "I need a few things, Joseph. Just load them into my wagon out front. I'll be back in half an hour." With that he lay down a list as long as my arm and walked out.

The offended couple paid for their few things and left the store arguing whether a wealthy person's financial standing should give them the right to be downright rude if they wanted.

As Uncle Joseph and I filled out Mr. Worthington's considerable list and hauled it all out to his wagon I heard his story. His pa, Mr. Andrew Worthington Senior, and before that his grandpa, were among the founding fathers of St. Louis and the whole danged state of Missouri. As such, the senior Mr. Worthington became one of the richest men in those parts. Then along came Andrew Worthington the Second. Not only his father's son, but the only child the Worthingtons were to be blessed with. As a result, the child grew up as one of the most spoiled human beings ever placed on this earth. He could do nothing wrong and had never been told "no" to anything.

A desire to take things that didn't belong to him got a young Andrew Worthington the Second into trouble several times while he was growing up, but the accusers always seemed to have a change of heart, along with a large bank deposit, and never pursued the matter. In short, Mr. Andrew Worthington the Second grew up to be an obnoxious, egotistical bastard; just like I'd figured him to be. He was under the impression that he owned the world and everything in it. He also grew up as one hell of a smart businessman, according to Uncle Joseph; doubling his pa's already large fortune.

When Mr. Worthington came back for his wagon he nearly rode off and out of my life with nothing more than, "Put that on my tab Joseph." He hopped up on his wagon, even moved ahead a few feet, then seemed to see me standing there for the first time.

"Who's the big guy helping you out, Joseph?" he asked as if I wasn't standing right there.

"That's my nephew, Thaddeus Battner, sir," Uncle Joseph answered. "He came clear from the Rocky Mountains to tell me my brother Christopher has passed. He'll be heading back home tomorrow."

Again Mr. Worthington just about rode away. He started. He stopped. He just sat there on that damned wagon starin' straight ahead for what seemed like the longest time. Then, even worse yet, he turned and began starin' at me. Watched me like a hawk while I moved some sacks of feed from a supply shed to out front of the store. I should've run for cover when he got off that wagon and walked over.

"I'm not one to mince words," he started. "I would like to hire you to guide me and my family. I have recently become aware of unprecedented financial and business opportunities available on the Pacific Coast, specifically the Oregon Territory. I would like you to guide us out west over the Oregon Trail to the Pacific Coast where I plan to meet up with a business associate of mine who is already in the area. Tell me, what would be your recompense for such a service?"

I was not impressed with Mr. Andrew Worthington the Second's "greater than thou" attitude. I was not afraid of him, or in awe of him, or under whatever damned spell seemed to affect Uncle Joseph. And I sure as hell was not confused as to my answer.

"No thank you, Andy," I said, with just the touch of a smile. "First off, I ain't a guide; just a mountain man. Second, I'm going back along the Missouri River to the Rocky Mountains, the way I came. And third, I don't have any re…recom…pense, whatever the hell that is." I put my hands on my hips, stood up extra tall, and waited for what I thought was going to be quite a show.

Now a couple things had just happened that'd never happened to Mr. Andrew Worthington the Second before. First, he'd been stood up to and told no. That alone was gonna take some to sink in. And, even as a boy, he'd never, ever been called "Andy." It simply wasn't proper.

I stood there with hands on hips waiting for the storm. I think I saw damn near every emotion there is passing through that man's eyes. He just stood there for a couple full minutes and I think he was so confused, that for the first time in his whole pampered life, he didn't have the slightest idea what to say or do.

"I will thank you to call me Mr. Worthington," is what he finally managed to come up with. He turned around, climbed up on his wagon, whipped the horses, and hurried away down the street. I turned to go back into the store. There was Uncle Joseph standing in the doorway. I ain't ever seen a bigger grin than that man wore! He was smilin' from ear to ear and head to toe.

"Yee-haw! My boy, that was the damndest thing I ever did see!" he fairly shouted out. "You just told ole Mr. Worthington what for, but good! You and me are gonna get drunk tonight. Yee-haw!" We did. If only that would've been the last I was to see of Mr. Andrew Worthington the Second.

Late the next morning, I got all my things together in a bundle and tied onto Skyhawk. I gave my blessings to Grandma Ella; she thanked me by nodding off to sleep while I was saying my goodbyes. I thanked Uncle Joseph for everything he'd done and told him I was pretty sure I wouldn't be comin' back to St. Louis any time soon, but he was always welcome in my cabin if he ever found himself wandering through the Rocky Mountains with no place to stay.

I worked my way back across town to Pearson's saloon where I'd left the rest of my belongings. Mr. Pearson and a bunch of the regular crowd were there.

I'd been saying goodbye for a couple hours and was actually getting fairly close to leaving. I'd even made it outside to the boardwalk.

"Mr. Battner."

Mr. Pearson and a couple of the fellers were wantin' to buy me one more whiskey, and one of the men had a story he thought I should hear about the time he was in the mountains some damn place I'd never heard of.

"Mr. Battner!"

I was trying to explain to Mr. Pearson, and the rest, that it was getting late and I needed to get going if I was gonna make any miles at all before having to set up camp for the night.

"Mr. Battner! Excuse me!"

It took three tries before I realized that "Mr. Battner" was me. Hell, I'm just Mount; Thaddeus'a time or two, when Ma was up in arms, Snake Eater by some Indian friends cause they saw me cook up a rattler one night in camp. But I've never, ever been Mr. Battner.

I turned, and there was my good friend Mr. Andrew Worthington the Second. About as quick as I realized who it was I forgot all about him again due to the fact that he was mounted on the most magnificent horse I'd ever seen.

"Mr. Battner, I'd like a couple minutes of your time."

He was a palomino quarter horse. He was one of the biggest horses I'd ever seen and without a doubt the most beautiful. That horse had to stand 17, maybe even 18 hands high. His body was a golden brown that seemed to glow like a gold nugget shinning in a creek bottom. His long mane and tail were a lighter shade of the same golden color. And all you had to do was look into his eyes to see he was an incredibly intelligent animal.

"Mr. Battner, I want to talk to you!"

Damned if I hadn't gotten so wrapped up admiring that horse that I'd completely forgotten about the horse's ass sittin' in the saddle. Mr. Worthington dismounted, tied his amazing steed to the hitching post and walked over to where I was standing. The rest of the folks from the saloon moved away.

"Mr. Battner, now I know you turned down my offer of employment as a guide yesterday," Mr. Worthington said. "I've come to try again to convince you. I am prepared to pay you whatever you require."

Now I'll admit I did enjoy seeing the great Mr. Andrew Worthington the Second humbled just a little bit. He still had the stink of a very wealthy man of privilege, but it was obvious he understood that I didn't give a damn about such things. Although this fact changed the way I felt about Mr. Worthington a small bit, it certainly didn't change my mind. I didn't think. Damn, what a beautiful horse.

"Well now Mr. Worthington, I live in a cabin in the mountains. I hunt or grow all my food. Anything I can't hunt or grow I trade for with pelts, furs, or animal hides. So you see there just ain't a whole lot that I need," I answered him; fully intending that that would be the end of it.

"Mr. Battner, it is absolutely vital that I get to the West Coast as soon as possible." You had to give him credit, when Mr. Worthington the Second got stuck on an idea he was determined as a bull stuck on a red shirt. "In the next few years I believe there is going to be a virtual human stampede out there, and I intend to be there, prepared to help all those folks with the things they are going to need. As far as I know you are the only man presently in St. Louis with the knowledge and experience to guide me out west." He paused and looked around. "I assume you'll be spending the night since it's nearly seven o'clock already. Reconsider my offer. I'll be at the boarding house up the street until mid-morning. You can get a hold of me there if you change your mind."

Mr. Worthington turned, walked back and started to untie his horse from the hitching post. I swear folks, I had no intentions of doing anything other than standing there and watching that man ride out of my life forever.

"I want your horse!"

Who said that? Mr. Worthington turned and stared at me.

"Excuse me?" He couldn't believe it was me talking either.

"I didn't say anything," is what I meant to say. What came out was "I'll do it...for that palomino you're riding."

"Now let me get this straight." He came back up on the boardwalk; it was obvious he couldn't believe it. Hell...I couldn't believe it. "You won't take any amount of money, but you'll guide me and my family to the West Coast for ownership of this horse I'm riding, is that right?"

I truly meant to say "no." "Yep, that's right." Who the hell had took over control of my mouth to say all those stupid things? "Mr. Worthington you don't understand. Probably the most important thing in a mountain man's life is his horse. A good horse can mean the difference between life and death. A wagon full of money...well, that means I've got a wagon to use after I unload it."

As though he was afraid I'd change my mind Mr. Worthington hurried back, untied his horse, mounted up, and started to leave.

"We have a deal Mr. Battner. We'll be here around midday tomorrow," he said. "We leave right after that." And he rode off.

What the hell had I done? Had I really agreed to guide a family of city folk across damn near all of the country...for a damned horse? But what a horse he was. I walked into the saloon thinking, not about what the future held, but about the most incredible horse I'd ever seen.

Chapter Five

I didn't get a whole lot of sleep that night. Mostly laid on my cot in the back of the saloon with my feet hanging over on a chair and stared out the little window over the ice box. The window was clear as a foggy day but I could sorta see a couple stars shining through, and I was wishing I was a thousand miles away.

I was up early. And I'll admit that I was danged close to packing up and taking off a couple times. Forgetting Mr. Worthington the Second and his family, forgetting that beautiful palomino, and just getting far away as fast as I could. Unfortunately, I was raised different than that.

Now it's true that a horse like that is far more valuable to a mountain man than any money, but at this point it was a matter of honor too. I'd given my word; and a man ain't any better than his word. I sure as hell didn't care what a bunch of St. Louis city folk thought of me, but I did have to live with what I thought of me. Seemed I was stuck haulin' those folks across the country; like it or not. Hell, I didn't even know what family Mr. Worthington had. Was I guiding him and his wife, or was I guiding him, his wife, and a whole damn herd of kids? I didn't know. Please Lord...not a herd of 'em.

All morning I was more nervous than a jackrabbit in a wolf pack. My mind was racing this way and that way. I was dreading what was to come; yet I was excited and anxious. I was ready to get going; yet I didn't want to start. I'd certainly prefer to head back to my cabin without them; yet I was awful curious to meet them. Mostly...I guess...I was confused as hell as to what I wanted.

About the time I figured I was gonna go hog-wild crazy from the waiting and thinking and thinking and waiting, the waiting was over. I came out of the saloon for about the thousandth time and looked up the street and here they came. Mr. Worthington was out front, on my soon to be horse, followed by a canvas covered wagon pulled by two horses with two horses tied to the back on long lead ropes. There was a lady on the wagon along with a teenage boy driving the team and a big ole hound dog sittin' between them.

"Mr. Battner." Mr. Worthington nodded curtly. "I trust everything is in order for our trip."

I smiled up at him. "Well, if by 'everything in order,' you mean is my bedroll strapped on my horse...then yep," I replied. We needed to get something figured out right up front. "Mr. Worthington we need to discuss this name business. Now, if you want to be called Mr. Worthington then that's okay with me, although it sure is a mouthful every danged time I want to say something to you. But I'm Mount. I ain't Mr. Battner or even Thaddeus, if you don't mind. I'm just plain ole Mount."

"Very well...uh, Mount." He was so high society that even using a person's first name was considered improper; using a nickname damn near choked him. And he sure wasn't going to give me permission to be so bold as to use his first name.

By now the wagon had pulled up. "I would like you to meet my family. This is my wife, Sandra Worthington, my son Andrew Worthington the Third." Who else could he be? "And that's our dog, Red." Mr. Worthington dismounted and without another word went into the saloon.

"Hey there young feller." I tipped my hat to the boy. "Howdy ma'am." She was beautiful. She had skin that looked like the porcelain dolls Uncle Joseph had under glass in the corner in his store, beautiful but awfully fragile looking. I thought *wow she's pretty*, followed immediately by, *she ain't making it clear to Oregon*. Her hair was long and glossy black. It fell over her shoulder and the end was banded nearly at her waist; during the trip, passing between two full breasts. Her eyes were a deep, dark walnut brown, the kind of eyes a man can get plumb lost in.

With an effort, I turned to the young man. He was a good looking kid of around thirteen or fourteen. Looking into his eyes I saw a gleam, or maybe a twinkle. The boy was excited about the adventure we were about to embark on. It didn't look like growing up in his privileged lifestyle had knocked the boy out of this kid yet. I was happy to see that. Mrs. Worthington on the other hand looked like the last thing in the whole world she wanted right then was to be doing just what she was. She looked at me like I was a bad memory.

"Are you really a mountain man?" The boy couldn't hold back any longer. "You really fight Indians and wrestle grizzly bears and tame wild horses and kill rattlesnakes and…"

"Andrew Worthington mind your manners!" Mrs. Worthington interrupted. "You don't badger Mr. Battner with questions like that."

"Oh that's okay ma'am," I said. "The boy's just curious is all." I turned to the youngun. "Well Andrew, yes I am a real mountain man. Born and raised in the Rocky Mountains. As for all that stuff about fighting and killing, well let's just say I've done what's needed done when it's been needed." The boy sorta cocked his head to one side and looked confused. I smiled. "I'm a bit of a storyteller, and since we're gonna be together for the next few months we just might have time for a tale or two." I took the time to scratch my head. "I will tell you…as of yet…I haven't wrestled a grizzly. I did take a six point bull elk down best two out of three once though." I winked at the boy. He still looked a little confused, but smiled back.

"Mr. Battner," Mrs. Worthington spoke up. "I have a couple of questions if you don't mind." I looked back to the lady. This time I saw a strange combination of determination mixed with fear in those beautiful brown eyes. "I was wondering about meals. What will we be eating on the trail? Who will be preparing it?" She paused just long enough for me to open my mouth to answer. "What about sleeping arrangements? What do we do when we have to use the toilet? Is there a real concern about wild animals? What about Indians, are we going to be attacked? Just how long are we going to be out in this God forsaken wilderness anyway?

And what about...." By now she was talkin' so danged fast I couldn't keep up.

"Whoa, there ma'am." I had to interrupt her, I was afraid she was gonna faint from lack of air; far as I could tell, she hadn't taken a breath for a while. I was trying my damndest not to laugh. And I was real tempted to tell her to "mind her manners," but I didn't.

"Now, you need to slow down there a little Mrs. Worthington. It'll take me the rest of the day just to answer what you've already asked." She smiled a small embarrassed smile. Damned, but she was a pretty woman. "Now first off, my name's Mount. No Mr. 'Nothin,' just plain ole Mount." Looking at the boy I added. "That goes for you too." He looked happy as can be. "Now let's see...let's start with food. I've got some coffee, a little pot to brew it in, and a tin cup to drink it out of. I have about a pound of jerky from my Uncle Joseph, and I have a little salt. Now I don't know what you folks have in your wagon, but I figured everything else we'd find on the trail."

Her eyebrows arched up on her forehead and her eyes got a little bigger. "We have pots and pans and the like but as far as food goes we have only the basics. Salt, sugar, flour that sort of thing, for when we get to Oregon. Can you really provide three meals a day for four people off of the land?"

I couldn't stop a little burst of laughter. "Well now ma'am, I don't remember promising anyone three meals a day, but I reckon I can come up with enough wild game and edible plants and such to keep the four of us from starving to death. As for preparing it, I figure there'll be plenty of chores to go around. We'll all four have plenty to do." I couldn't help myself. "You do know about chores don't you Mrs. Worthington?"

I was glad to see the lady had some fire in her. "I assure you Mr. Battner, that I can do whatever is needed of me! Don't underestimate me sir!" The "Mr. Battner" and "sir" were like slaps to the face. Her eyes were now filled with determination and anger. She crossed her arms under her breasts and nodded briskly…as she added. "I will pull my own weight."

I didn't think that was the proper time to point out she was gonna have to do a hell of a lot better than that before we got to Oregon. She couldn't have weighed one thirty even if she was holdin' a twenty pound saddle.

"Well ma'am I think I believe you…now; and keep that attitude, you're gonna need it, and then some, before we get where we're going." I hoped my new found admiration for her showed in my voice and the encouraging smile I tried to give her. "I'll make you a deal ma'am; if you'll call me Mount I'll make a point of not underestimating you again, okay?"

I watched as, not just her eyes, but her whole posture softened. "You have a deal Mr. Batt…uh, I mean, Mount. It may take me a while to get used to it." She actually smiled. It may have been a rocky start but I was pretty sure I was gonna become friends with the boy and his ma.

"Now, getting back to some of your other concerns Mrs. Worthington, I assume you and the boy will sleep in the wagon. Mr. Worthington and I will sleep wherever we lay our blankets." I wanted to be honest to a point, but I didn't want to scare anybody. "As for the wild animals, they mostly don't want anything to do with us any more than we want to mess with them. And the Indians are mostly the same way. Of course that's not sayin' we couldn't run into a riled up grizzly or a band of young Indian bucks full of whiskey courage. In either case we'll just have to deal with it when, and if it happens. And I'll be danged if I can't remember what else you was asking about?"

"The toilet, Mr. Battn….Mount," she said. "What do we do when we need to relieve ourselves?" Her cheeks got a little pink.

"Oh, you're talking about pissing and shitting." I didn't even try not to laugh; the look of shock on her face was pure comical. Young Andrew was doubled over on his seat holding his stomach and rockin' back and forth, but not making a sound. Mrs. Worthington's cheeks went red as a cherry in the fall.

"Mr. Battner!" No "Mount" now. "I'll thank you not to speak so vulgarly in front of either me or my son. We are not...mountain...people."

"Well now Mrs. Worthington." I was still smiling. "I believe your husband made the decision that you are gonna be mountain folk. There sure as heck ain't a St. Louis in Oregon. And if 'shit' is the worst you or young Andrew hears from me between here and there, we'll all be damned lucky. Now, to answer your question, most of the time it'll be the other side of the wagon." I swear I actually heard her gasp. "Unless there's some trees or a handy bunch of willows or juniper bushes, cause there sure ain't any of those fancy chain-pull commodes you have here in the city. I've got an awful nice two-holer outhouse out back of my cabin in the Rockies, when we get that far." I could tell by the fearful look on her face she was not even slightly impressed. Mr. Worthington came out of the saloon with whiskey on his breath and what looked to be five or six bottles in a box that he stored in the wagon.

"Soft tissue paper, Andrew," Mrs. Worthington said rather anxiously. "We need more soft tissue paper before we leave." She paused and looked at me a moment. "And maybe some more food."

Chapter Six

It musta been an omen of some sort I reckon. We hadn't gotten but five miles out of St. Louis on the road back towards the American Fur Company trading post, when we had our first trouble. There'd been spring thunderstorms off and on the past few days and the road was pretty sloppy. As long as the wagon stayed in the packed ruts it was okay, but outside the ruts there was six to eight inches of mud, fit only for a pack of pigs. I was riding out front when suddenly I heard one hell of a ruckus behind me.

"No! No! Left! Go back left!!" Mr. Worthington was yelling from behind the wagon, which somehow had gotten outta the ruts and was slipping down off the right side of the road into about a five foot deep ditch. The two horses tied on behind the wagon were running, sliding and side-stepping like crazy, tryin' to keep their footing. I thought for a second the whole damned wagon was gonna roll, but it didn't. It slid to a stop with both rear wheels off the road and half buried in mud. The front wheels were still on the road but also half buried. The dog was running from the front seat to the rear of the wagon and back again howling like a crazed coyote.

"What the hell are you doing...damn you boy!" Mr. Worthington appeared about to burst. "Red...no!" The dog quit howling but kept roaming back and forth. Mr. Worthington turned back to where his son sat. "How the hell could you let this happen? What's wrong with you?"

"I didn't...I mean...they just...I don't know." The boy was crying. His mother sat beside him with her arm over his shoulder and not a lick of color in her face. She looked scared enough to faint dead away.

"You don't know? How the hell can you not know? You were responsible for driving the wagon weren't you? This situation is all your fault!" Mr. Worthington had his horse up beside the wagon and was leaning in towards the driver's side of the seat. Mrs. Worthington was starting to get a little color back in her cheeks, but I was surprised when I noticed that she'd taken her arm away from around Andrew's shoulders and had even moved away from him to the other side of the wagon seat.

Now folks, I didn't like the way Mr. Worthington was bad mouthing his son, and I sure couldn't see any sort of good that was likely to come of it. On the other hand, it wasn't my kid, my wife, or my wagon. What right did I have to butt in? Absolutely none!

"Now hold on there Mr. Worthington," I butted. I brought Skyhawk up close enough so I didn't have to holler. "I ain't sure what happened here, but seems to me maybe we should worry about getting the wagon back on the road rather then wastin' time laying blame. Besides, the boy's just a boy trying to do a man's job."

"Mr. Battner, I'll thank you to mind your own business!" Mr. Worthington turned on me, his eyes and nose flaring wide. "I am quite capable of dealing with my own son!" Turning back to the wagon, and the boy, he said. "Now do you think you can drive out of this mess or do I need to do it for you?"

I couldn't believe he thought anyone was gonna just say "giddy-up" and two horses were gonna pull that wagon up outta that muddy hole. City folk!

"Mr. Worthington." I began. "I don't think..."

"Hey-ya!! Get up there!" Young Andrew suddenly yelled, and started whipping those horses with the end of the reins. "Hey-ya! Go, go on!" Those horses spooked, and started off down the road which started that wagon sliding sideways, halfway in the ditch, plowin' through the mud and it would've rolled sure as hell if it hadn't been for one quick thinking mountain man.

I rode up front and grabbed hold of the reins right at the horses' necks. "Whoa there!" I yelled, and moved Skyhawk in front of them so they'd stop. I jumped down, took the reins from the boy, and stood there ankle deep in mud and mad as a bee's nest at everybody. I was mad at Mr. Worthington, for the fit he'd thrown over a simple accident. I was mad at the boy, for trying to force the wagon up and outta the ditch, which damn near made things a whole lot worse. And I was mad at Mrs. Worthington for not standing up a little more for her son. When Mr. Worthington started yelling I expected her to defend her boy like a mama bear protectin' a cub. Instead, she slid away from him and seemed to try her best to disappear. This lady, who earlier had been ready and willing to let me have it, obviously wasn't nearly as enthusiastic about standing up to her husband.

"Now just everybody calm the hell down!" My anger was already starting to melt away. Being raised such a peaceful sort, I never have been much good at stayin' mad. I tried to hold on to a little of my anger. "Mr. Worthington, you need to stop your damn yellin'. Boy, you need to do absolutely nothing, until I tell you to. And you…" I glared at Mrs. Worthington and realized I didn't have a damn thing to say. "You keep that dog quiet!" It was all I could come up with and didn't make a lick of sense cause the dog hadn't made a sound since Mr. Worthington yelled at it.

Surprisingly nobody said anything; all three of them just sat where they were and stared at me. Mr. Worthington was so mad he was ready to explode, but knew it wouldn't help. It was like a burr under a saddle blanket for him to let anybody else be in control. Now, if I only knew what I was doing.

I studied the situation. "Okay now, here's what we're gonna do." I hoped I sounded more confident then I felt. "First, we'll untie the horses from the back, then harness that big palomino up in line with the other two up front. Then I'll get on one wheel, you and Mrs. Worthington will get on the other, and we'll have Andrew lead the horses straight across the road to pull those wheels up and out of the ditch. Once the wagon's back on the road we can work it around and back into the ruts."

I looked up from the wagon. Mr. Worthington was looking at Mrs. Worthington. Young Andrew was looking at his Ma too. Mrs. Worthington was looking down at her feet. Until now I hadn't paid much attention to how any of the Worthingtons were dressed. As I followed her gaze down I realized the problem; Mrs. Worthington had on a light blue dress, white stockings, and white shoes that didn't even have any damn toes in them. I ain't kidding! This lady was prepared to cross the entire width of this great country of ours wearing shoes missing the toe part. She looked from her shoes to the muddy road, to me, and back to the muddy road, then back to her shoes again.

"I reckon you should put on whatever boots you brought along for sloppin' around in the mud." I already knew from the look on her face that she didn't have any. I tried to hide my smile. "And you might want to put on some britches so you don't get that pretty dress all dirty." The look on her face started to change. First it went to nearly shock that I would suggest such a thing as a lady wearing pants, and then I saw that mix of determination and anger boiling up again.

"Mr. Battner, I assure you…" She started to crawl down off the wagon. "I don't need to dress like a…a farm girl to do whatever is needed of me, now or in the future!" On her last word she jumped the last couple feet and landed with one foot on the edge of the road and the other in the ditch and proceeded to fall over backwards and roll to the bottom.

I'm guessing this was the first time in her whole life that she'd been muddy, and boy-howdy was she muddy! She had mud from head to toe, and one of her fancy shoes was buried in six inches of mud up on the edge of the road. To her credit, except for a surprised shriek when she fell, Mrs. Worthington didn't make a sound. She rolled over, sat up, and glared at me with fire in her eyes. Then she proceeded to walk over behind the wheel on her side of the wagon; wipin' mud off her face as she went. She was still a beautiful woman, but she didn't look so much like a porcelain doll anymore.

Sometimes a feller, no matter his age, just knows to keep his mouth shut. That was one of those times; right then that lady was more dangerous than a wounded mountain lion. "What are you three waiting for?" As bad as we wanted to laugh the three of us men folk didn't so much as crack a smile. Andrew and Mr. Worthington dismounted, I untied the two horses, hitched that big palomino up front, and we each took up our positions at the other wheels. Luckily my plan worked first try. Andrew led those horses across the road and we hauled on the wooden spokes of the wheels, and sure enough that wagon rolled up out of the ditch and back on the road just like it was suppose to. Another few minutes to work it around facing the right way, ten more minutes to unpack the mud from the wheels and around the axles, and we were ready to go.

Mrs. Worthington then had Andrew fetch a bucket of water from the river which was about a hundred yards away, and she disappeared into the wagon for what seemed like at least an hour. When she came out the mud was all washed away. She had on a fresh dress and another pair of city shoes, but these, at least, were leather and had the toes covered in them.

The trip back to the American Fur Company trading post, after the little tussle with the wagon, was damn near pleasant. The road dried up and there were farms now and again, which gave Mrs. Worthington a chance to use a proper outhouse instead of the other side of the wagon, although by the time we made the trading post she'd gotten used to doing what she had to do, where she had to do it.

"Now don't you be peeking Mount," she warned me the first time she had to go when I was hanging around by the wagon. Mr. Worthington and Andrew were down by the river trying their hands at fishing. I was at the fire ring cooking up some jackrabbit I'd shot that morning.

I thought about it for a second before I answered. "Mrs. Worthington, you are a mighty fine looking lady, and I hope I haven't offended you by saying so. Hell, I'll even admit that if you was down to the river havin' a bath, I just might be tempted. But watching you do what it is you're about to do just doesn't interest me a bit, and that's a fact." I didn't feel the need to mention that I saw her peeking out under the canvas of the wagon that morning as I was pissin' in the bushes.

As the days passed we sort of settled into a routine. After the first couple days, and I was fairly sure the three of them could be left alone for a while, I started hunting in the morning, usually getting up and out before sunup. Jackrabbits, squirrels, and fish were all plentiful. We also bought fresh vegetables and fruit from the farmers. By mid-morning I'd usually be back with enough food for the day.

Mr. Worthington mostly rode behind the wagon and tried to seem important. He always looked like he was watching for something. What it could have been I don't know. Andrew drove the team, and didn't once let the wagon slide off the road again. Mrs. Worthington mostly rode beside him. Now and then she would get down and walk a ways, but with those danged city shoes she couldn't go very far. The Worthingtons didn't like a lot of things that came with traveling; the heat of the day, the cool of the night, the scrounging for food, using tall sagebrush as an outhouse...but they adjusted better than I thought they would. We had an awful long ways to go, and things were just gonna get harder.

I guess it was bound to happen sooner or later, especially since Mrs. Worthington and I had talked just a couple days earlier. The day had been damned warm and we were all in need of a break. Mid-afternoon, we came across a nice section of river with lots of trees and willows and a meadow filled with grass and wild flowers. I decided to set up camp early and rest up till the next day.

It was a couple hours after we'd stopped, and all three Worthingtons were off on their own. I'd gotten the fire going good and took a stroll along the river to search for some edibles for supper. As I bent to pick some morel mushrooms, I saw movement through the willows off to my left. I was instantly alert, but didn't see anything else. Slowly I stood and moved quietly forward. There was a small, still pool off the side of the river, and Mrs.

Worthington was just stepping into it. She was naked as the day she was born, but had grown up considerably. As soon as I saw her I told myself to look away and just go about what I was doing. I didn't listen. Mrs. Worthington was easily the most beautiful woman I'd ever seen. If it makes any difference, I did feel guilty as hell as I stood and watched. It just ain't right for a man to be ogling another feller's wife, even if that feller is an arrogant, feelingless bastard like Mr. Worthington. I had several more opportunities on the trail to watch Mrs. Worthington bathe, but I always walked away; always…after that first time.

We made pretty darn good time on the trail considering. I figured we were making around fifteen to twenty miles a day. Mr. Worthington seemed to be in some kind of all fired hurry and wanted the rest of us to catch the fever, but we were just fine traveling at a nice easy pace. After several days of listening to him complaining that we were "going far too slow," I stepped up real close to him, stretched up so I was about a head taller, leaned into him a little, and politely pointed out. "You know Mr. Worthington, hurrying or not, it's gonna take us several months to get out to Oregon, and I really think it's a good idea for you to relax and enjoy the trip so the rest of us can too." I could tell he was deciding whether to argue or not. I backed away from him a bit, and gestured toward the wagon wheels. "Besides, a wagon can only roll so fast for so long before things start breakin'." After that he seemed to ease up some, and we all enjoyed the trip more, for a while.

It took just under two weeks to get from St. Louis back to the American Fur Company trading post. We got there mid-afternoon and went straight to the livery stable. As I was helping unhitch the horses and get them settled, the Worthingtons went across the street. Mr. Worthington went into the saloon and Mrs. Worthington and Andrew went into the general store.

After the horses were taken care of I went on across the street to the saloon. Mr. Worthington was at the end of the bar with a bottle of whiskey talking to the owner. Turned out he was making arrangements for them to spend the night in a room for rent in the back. He looked up when I walked in, then looked away again like he didn't know me. Mr. Pearson, back in St. Louis, had paid me a few dollars before I left, so I stepped up to the bar and had myself a taste of whiskey. After a few tastes, I came out of the saloon and headed back to the stable. I noticed Mrs. Worthington and Andrew going into the wagon with their arms full of packages. I went to check on the horses and to spend some time admiring that magnificent palomino that would be mine if I ever got these folks to Oregon.

Coming back out to the street I was just in time to see Mrs. Worthington climb down from the wagon. I looked once, then twice to make sure it was her; I had to smile. She was wearing a heavy denim shirt tucked into a pair of britches, the fancy lady kind mind ya, with the puffy legs, but still britches. The bottoms of the britches were tucked into a pair of leather boots. I'd tell her later that real cowboys put their pants on the outside of the boots; to keep the snow and mud and such out.

The Worthingtons had steak dinner in the saloon. I caught a couple of fish and cooked them over a little belly fire down by the river. The Worthingtons then went into their room to their beds to spend the night. I slept in the stable with the horses.

Chapter Seven

Next morning I was checking over the wagon, smearing a little grease on the axles, and wondering if it was gonna make the trip. I was surprised, hell I was plumb shocked, when Mr. Worthington came in and asked me to join the family for breakfast in the saloon.

Turned out he wanted to talk me into changing my plan of goin' back along the same route I'd come east on. He thought, and of course his family agreed, that we should follow the newly developed Oregon Trail. As hard as it was, I had to admit that, after my cabin in the mountains, I didn't rightly know how to get to Oregon. And I also had to admit, it made some sense going to Oregon following the Oregon Trail. After two helpings of flapjacks, with bacon and eggs, I let him talk me into it.

The Oregon Trail it was gonna be! The saloon proprietor had a hand-drawn map of sorts. According to it the next sign of civilization we'd see was Fort Kearny. If the barkeep could be believed, it'd be about a month's travel. That's a month figuring everything goes well. I wouldn't be telling you folks this story if everything went well.

After a little scouting I found where the trail started; you headed to the northwest from the American Fur Company. It was being called the Oregon Trail, but turned out it hadn't been traveled much. Hell, ole Seven Fingers Slim could've counted, on his short hand, the times it'd been used. In other words, it wasn't much of a trail yet. The traveling was about to get considerably harder.

We got started from the Fur Company early afternoon. It was a beautiful spring day that made it a pleasure to leave the buildings and the people behind and head out across the plains. The wildflowers were in full bloom and the sun blanketed the whole scene with a soft golden glow. It was warm but not hot. I noticed Mrs. Worthington and Andrew staring off into the plains and enjoying the beauty, same as I was. Mr. Worthington was riding out ahead of the wagon lookin' straight ahead like he'd been on this particular trail a thousand times before.

The next few days we spent kinda getting into our rhythm. We switched horses from the harness to the lead ropes behind the wagon every other day. The hound dog spent most of his time nose to the ground roaming through the prairie and chasing anything that he could scare up, and catching very little of what he chased. The landscape changed to more rolling hills, with some trees now and again alongside a creek or stream. Then it'd change back to flat prairie land, then back again. It was mid-spring, May according to the calendar that city folk put so much stock in, so food and water were plentiful.

Mrs. Worthington and the boy took turns driving the wagon. They both spent a lot of time walking when they weren't on the reins. Both could walk for miles at a time now that their muscles had toughened up a bit, and now that they had real boots. Several days out I noticed Andrew, and not for the first time, watching his Pa and me on horseback with a wistful, 'I wish I could' sorta look. I waited until Mr. Worthington was a good piece ahead of us, then I rode up close beside the wagon.

"Hey Andrew," I said. "My butt and back would sure enjoy that cushioned seat and back rest you got up there. How about you sittin' Skyhawk and me riding the wagon for a few miles?"

I thought that boys eyes were gonna pop plumb out of his head! "Can I really?" he exclaimed! He looked hopefully to his ma. "Can I?"

"Oh, I don't know Andrew," Mrs. Worthington worried. "You haven't had very much experience on horseback."

"Ahhh Ma, please!"

"Mrs. Worthington, it ain't my place to interfere." I interfered. "But, seems to me, out here on the plains would be a danged good place to learn."

I sat up beside Mrs. Worthington with the reins to the team in my hands, and even though it'd been just an excuse so the boy could ride, that wagon seat with its cushion and back rest felt mighty good; and sitting up there next to Mrs. Worthington was kinda nice too.

I wasn't enjoying my ride nearly as much as that boy though. The stirrups didn't adjust short enough so I took a couple pieces of rope from the wagon and rigged something up so Andrew could ride. He sat up in that saddle like he'd been riding every day of his life. The only giveaway was the grin on his face that stretched from ear to ear, and never faded.

"Thank you Mount." Mrs. Worthington too was smiling. "I don't think I've ever seen him so happy. He looks like he was born to ride." Well almost.

Mr. Worthington was a quarter mile ahead but had stopped and was waiting for us to catch up. Andrew, feeling confident, nudged Skyhawk with his heels and moved up into a trot. It took him a little to get the rhythm but soon was doing fine. Ole Red was running beside them, his wagging tail and dog smile showing that he was enjoying himself too. Another nudge with his heels and Skyhawk took off at a full gallop. Andrew wasn't quite prepared for that and bounced in the saddle three or four times, each time a little higher and a little more to the side, on the next bounce he took flight, and landed several feet to the left of the trail and bounced again three or four times ending up on his stomach.

"Oh my God! Oh my God! My baby!" Mrs. Worthington screamed and started to stand up on the seat beside me. I pushed her back into her seat with my right arm and rein whipped the horses with my left. I pushed the horses as fast as I could, an icy cold stone suddenly in the pit of my stomach, and a cold sweat on my brow. "Mount, how could you let him get on that animal?"

We watched Andrew try to get up and fall back to the ground rocking back and forth. He couldn't seem to get his legs under him. We pulled up in the wagon and Mrs. Worthington was off the wagon before it stopped and ran to her son's side. I reined in the horses, threw the lock on, and jumped from the seat to the ground, rolling my ankle, and limped around the wagon to join her.

The first thing I noticed was the look on Mrs. Worthington's face as I hurried to kneel down beside her. It was a combination of fear, relief, anger, and several other emotions mixed in. The next thing I noticed was that Andrew was rocking back and forth holding his stomach in fits of laughter.

By the time Mr. Worthington rode up the three of us were sitting there beside the Oregon Trail laughing to beat hell, like falling off a horse was the funniest damned thing that could've happened. Red ran around in circles yapping and enjoying the whole thing.

"What the hell happened here?" Mr. Worthington demanded. "Andrew, was that you on that horse?"

Andrew looked up at his dad with tears in his eyes from laughing, but his smile disappeared fast. It was Mrs. Worthington that answered.

"Now you just take it easy Andrew Worthington." It appeared Mrs. Worthington had found some backbone, and she had a "don't mess with me" look in her eyes. "Andrew was simply practicing riding, something he should know by now. He got going a little too fast and…." She couldn't stop a snicker. "….and just bounced off, that's all." The three of us took to laughin' again as we remembered the scene.

"And who told him he could ride that horse anyway?" Mr. Worthington was looking at me. Only one thing was in his eyes, anger.

"I did of course! I'm his mother aren't I?" Mrs. Worthington didn't miss a beat. "We have a long way to go before we get to Oregon. Andrew can be a fine horseman by the time we get there if he's allowed to practice."

"We'll fix those stirrups up better Andrew." I felt like I should say something. "Once we get them right I'll teach you how to hold your weight with your legs so you don't bounce."

"Thanks Mount." Andrew turned to his pa. "I'm fine Pa. I really am. It was fun!" He looked at the ground. "It'll be more fun when I don't fall off though." Even Mr. Worthington smiled a little. "Can I continue to ride Pa?"

Mr. Worthington pretended to ponder for a piece, but I think he knew it'd already been decided. "Yes, I suppose it's probably a good idea."

"Thanks Pa!" Andrew jumped to his feet and started for Skyhawk who was grazing a few feet away. He stopped and turned to me with a questioning look.

"We got us a saying in the mountains, Andrew," I said. "When you get bounced off your horse, the only thing to do is get right back in the saddle."

Andrew smiled, turned and headed for Skyhawk again. He stopped, seemed to stand and think for a few seconds, then turned back around and looked at all three of us. He looked afraid but determined.

"And there's one more thing." He looked at me, then over at his Pa. "I want to be called Andy." He said it, real quick like. You could tell he'd wanted to for a long time. I think I heard Mr. Worthington actually gasp. Andy looked at the ground. "The kids at school called me Andy. And I liked it." He looked up at his Ma with big sad calf eyes. "Would it be okay?"

There was a tear on Mrs. Worthington's cheek that I don't think was left over from laughing. "Anybody that can take a fall from a horse like that and come up laughing and asking for more, deserves to be called whatever he wants...Andy. I'm proud of you."

He looked at me. I laughed. "Well I reckon a feller who wants folks to call him Mount sure shouldn't have any say so in what anybody else wants to be called. Andy rolls off the tongue easier anyway." I said that last part not looking at Mr. Andrew Worthington the Second. "And you can ride Skyhawk any time you want, Andy." He smiled a tremendous smile.

He looked over at his pa, and once more his smile faded away. Mr. Worthington was disappointed, I think, that his son would want to be so informal. But once again he knew the issue had already been decided.

"I suppose you're old enough to decide what you want to be called." He wouldn't even look at Andy while he said it. Then he rode off up the trail. Andy stared after him with a hurt look in his eyes for all of ten seconds or so, then his eyes lit up, the smile returned, and he headed for Skyhawk. He mounted like a cowboy and spent the rest of the day in the saddle. The fastest they went was a trot.

The country we were traveling through changed again from fairly flat plains to rolling plains that were cut more by streams and had more stands of trees, which were nice for making camp. The scenery got prettier as we went too, from flat plains covered with wild grass and sagebrush, to rolling plains covered with wild grass, sagebrush, and flowers; here and there some juniper bushes. As for the trail, it changed every few feet or so. Sometimes the wagon wheels were following ruts a foot deep, sometimes it was nice and flat and smooth, and sometimes the damned trail plumb disappeared, when the ground got hard as granite and wouldn't even take a track.

The wagon got bogged down in mud and water a couple of times while crossing streams. The dirt around these parts is called loess, and it's just barely heavier than air. When it got wet, and a couple feet deep, it turned into one hell of a mess. The horses had a hard time trudging through it; the wagon was nearly impossible.

As long as the ground was dry the going was pretty steady. Day after day we made our way across the loess plains. Somewhere up ahead the Platte River was waiting, and it should lead us to Fort Kearny. As long as the weather held we'd make good time; as long as the weather held.

Chapter Eight

Till the big storm hit we'd been fairly lucky as far as the weather was concerned. We'd had a couple of squalls pass by, those spring thunderstorms with a little lightning and a nice hard rain that'd last only three or four minutes; just enough to wash everything down real good and clean, and make the world smell like…well…like after a spring rain.

The morning of the storm I'd been out huntin' since before sunup. When I got back to the wagon about half an hour after daybreak, with a small red deer I'd snuck up on at a watering hole, the Worthingtons were just starting to stir. Andy had become a pretty fair hand at fire tending and had the campfire burning good. The sky was still a dark nighttime blue off to the west, a mid-morning sky blue above, and "goodmorning to ya" yellow off to the east. There wasn't a cloud to be seen from horizon to horizon.

After a breakfast of fresh venison back strap and the last of the oven baked bread we had, we packed up and got back on the trail. We'd been crossing a long, dry stretch of plains. There hadn't been as much as a creek crossing for a couple days, and the landscape had gotten pretty barren. Around noon the clouds started to build in the northwest.

Mid-afternoon Mr. Worthington was riding out ahead of the wagon a half-mile or so; as had become his habit. None of us missed him any. Andy and I were on horseback, Andy riding one of the spare horses bareback with rigged up reins. The boy had become a damned good rider. Mrs. Worthington was driving the wagon. Off to the northwest and a bit closer than before, the clouds were getting darker and meaner lookin', but seemed to be moving real slow. Red, usually off running and sniffing, came and wanted Andy to help him up into the wagon; where he sat on the seat beside Mrs. Worthington sniffing the air and now and again howling at the clouds.

Now folks, here's what I know about the weather; it does whatever the hell it does and you deal with it; then it changes. I don't know for sure, but I think maybe the fact that the storm was moving so slow gave it time to gather strength. When the wind picked up and a light rain started falling they were being chased across a mean looking sky by some of the darkest, ugliest storm clouds this mountain man had ever seen; and we have some dandy storms in the Rockies. Off in the distance to our south, and away from the approaching storm, I could see what looked like the line of a creek bed, the first one in a while, cutting a path across the prairie, and spread out along the creek, several stands of cottonwoods.

"Get the wagon to that stand of trees," I said to Mrs. Worthington. I had to speak up because the wind was getting strong. "We'll wait out the storm there." Lightning was flashing a half-mile to the north; we could hear the thunder rollin' across the plains.

Mrs. Worthington gave me a little wave. "Ok, looks like it could be quite a storm." She smiled at Andy and me. That woman surely had gumption, and I gotta admit that she took to the hardships of traveling a lot better than I thought she would.

Andy headed for the trees; I hung back trying to watch everything and everyone at once. Red was in the wagon with Mrs. Worthington and I could hear him howling at the storm. The closer to the trees we got the harder the wind blew and the harder the rain came.

If the wind got too strong, the last place we wanted to be was in amongst a bunch of cottonwoods, and I was starting to wonder about my decision. I could see that several of the cottonwoods were dead skeletons of their old selves.

We were within a hundred feet of the trees, with Andy a little ahead and Mrs. Worthington off to my right. Except for being wet to the bone we were doing fine, then suddenly all hell broke loose.

I'd just decided to warn Andy and Mrs. Worthington off, and avoid the trees, but I didn't get the chance; it hit so fast.

Now I've heard of tornados and I've heard of something they call a burst-storm or some damn thing, where a current of wind within the storm suddenly triples or more in strength. I don't rightly know what it was that hit us; but I know it was sent straight from Hell. One second it was just one hell of a thunderstorm, and the next second we were surrounded by the most god-awful wind and rain and lightning and thunder you can imagine, spawned by the devil himself.

I was trying to catch up to Andy to warn him to stay clear of the trees. I'd yelled at Mrs. Worthington as I rode past and wasn't sure if she'd heard me or not, but I figured I needed to get to Andy first. Just as I was getting close enough to yell at Andy a bolt of lightning struck behind me; between me and the wagon. The thunder hit before the flash disappeared, and was so loud it hurt. Skyhawk and I both flinched and turned away for a second. I turned back just in time to see the horses pulling the wagon shy away from the lightning strike and take off back towards the trail, over the open plains! I turned back the other way just in time to see Andy disappear into the stand of trees; exactly where I didn't want him going!

I paused a second deciding whether I should go after Andy, or chase the runaway wagon. I turned Skyhawk back toward the trees thinking to yell at Andy first. I'd gone only twenty feet or so when another bolt of lightning struck not ten feet away. Skyhawk reared up and twisted away from the strike both at the same time and I found myself flying through the air. I landed on my back, my head snapped back against the ground, and my world exploded into stars and lights; and oh Lord the pain. My sight cleared for a second, just in time to see the tree coming down on top of me, then my world went black and I heard, saw, and felt nothing.

The first sense to wake up was my sense of smell. I remember thinking, *what a nice smell, so clean and fresh, just like sitting under a cottonwood after a spring rain. Real nice and peaceful like.*

About then I remembered the storm! I remembered the wind, rain and lightning! I remembered seeing Andy disappearing into the trees and Mrs. Worthington stuck on a runaway wagon! I remembered getting thrown, hitting my head, and seeing the tree coming down on top of me. And that's about when I was reminded of the pain; oh Lord almighty the pain! With every beat of my heart, and folks, my heart was beatin' mighty fast, my head damn near exploded. I hadn't opened my eyes yet, and wasn't sure if I wanted to. Trying to move past the throbbing pain in my head so I could check what else was hurt wasn't easy.

I tried to wiggle my fingers; they wiggled. I tried to wiggle my toes and they worked too; so far so good! When I went to bend my knees only one would move. I didn't feel any pain especially, other than my head, but my left leg just wouldn't move. With no choice, I opened my eyes to check out the damage. My first view of the scene was clouded by a red haze due to the blood running from my head into my eyes. I wiped the blood away best I could with the back of my hand.

Luckily I was under the upper branches of the tree and not under the main trunk, which would've flattened me like a pile of horse shit after a buffalo stampede. I was able to shove a couple branches out of the way and got myself up on my elbows so I could see my leg. One of the larger branches coming off the main trunk had me pinned just above the knee. I figured this was the branch that'd clipped me on the head on its way down.

Looking back behind me, I found a broken limb about the size of my wrist and probably three feet long. I was just able to reach it. With some twisting and turning, and serious cussin' I worked it under the branch that had me trapped. Using both hands, and my right thigh, I was able to pry it up enough to pull my leg free.

"Oh hell yeah!" I shouted out loud. "Hell yeah!" I was thrilled to be free! I pulled myself clear using my elbows and sliding on my butt, then sat there feeling pretty damn good about myself. About then the pain hit my leg! As the blood started rushing back into my leg I nearly passed out, it hurt so damned bad. On the good side, I did forget the throbbing in my head for a while.

"Oh shit, oh damn, damn, damn!" I rubbed and punched my leg with both hands and wiggled my toes as fast as I could, like that was gonna help. I hauled myself further out away from the tree, dragging my leg. By the time I got out into the open the throbbing pain had let up a little and the prickliness started. You folks know that feeling, when whatever body part went to sleep wakes up, and it feels like a million stickpins poking you all at once? Well, this was like that, except I had a million hunting knives jabbing my leg.

The rain was still coming down pretty hard but the wind was light and the lightning had passed. I lay in the grass and mud and took stock of myself while I waited for my leg to recover. I decided I pretty much hurt all over, like I'd been beat with a club and rolled down a rocky hill, but everything seemed to work okay. I was pretty sure once my leg came back to life I'd be fine as a fly whisker.

I started to think about the Worthingtons, and what might've become of them. I could see Andy riding into the trees, and knew this tree probably wasn't the only one that'd blown over in the storm. I pictured Mrs. Worthington and the wagon, flying and bouncing off through the storm, headed back towards the trail. Was it my imagination, or did I see her look back over her shoulder at me just before my world turned upside down? I was even worried, a little, about Mr. Worthington. I hadn't seen what happened to him when the storm hit.

It took several minutes and a couple of tries, but I finally stood up and tried to walk; I was surprised to find I could. It hurt like hell, but nothing seemed to be broke!

I looked around. The stand of cottonwoods we had been headed for were still thirty feet away. The one that had fallen on me was a rogue growing out away from the others. It figures that I'd land under the one damn tree to get blown over; what the hell are the odds of that. Maybe it was a little nudge from God, reminding me who's in charge.

I saw something move off to my left. I turned and was truly relieved to see Skyhawk come around the fallen tree and look at me like *where the hell you been?* I went to him and gave his nose a good rubbing; one of his favorite things, then took the reins and started towards the stand of trees.

There wasn't but a few hours left till dark. I needed to find the Worthingtons, and I prayed that I'd find them all still breathing, and in one piece! I was mostly worried about Mrs. Worthington and that runaway wagon; anything could've happened...but I couldn't think of anything good!

As I entered the trees I stopped and listened. At first I didn't hear anything but the trees moaning and creaking and talkin' tree talk. Then, through the trees, I thought I heard someone crying. Maybe a little boy crying?

Under the stand of trees the wind and rain had stopped completely. The creek the trees were growing alongside of, cause of the storm was running strong. As I got closer to the rushing water I couldn't hear the crying any more, but I knew Andy couldn't be far. I led Skyhawk around a couple more trees, and there he was! Andy was sitting on the ground, leaning back on a fallen log, with his knees pulled up to his chest and his arms around his legs hugging them tight. He was crying like I'd never heard. He was sobbing so hard the deadfall he was leaning against was shaking.

"Andy." I was standing no more than fifteen feet away but hadn't used my voice much since getting knocked out, so it came out sort of sick frog sounding. I cleared my throat and tried again; speaking up to get over the noise of the water. "Hey Andy!"

Andy looked up and saw me standing there. I swear I've never seen anyone move so fast! His eyes got about the size of dinner plates, he let out a whoop and a holler, and the next thing I knew, I had a laughing and crying boy fastened onto my neck and squeezing like he was never letting go! I wanted to tell him everything was gonna be okay now, but I couldn't talk, mostly due to the fact Andy had my wind almost completely cut off.

"Mount...oh Mount...thank God! I thought I...I...I was alone...out here. I was...so scared! Thank...God you came!" He was still laughing and crying at the same time; and squeezing. I was starting to get dizzy from lack of air. I finally had to pry his arms loose a little so I could breathe.

"It's okay now Andy. Everything is gonna be just fine." I didn't know what else to say. Then I noticed blood on my hand that'd been on the back of his head. I pried him loose and stood him on the ground in front of me. "You're hurt. What did you hit your head on?" I asked.

"I'm not sure," he said. "I got thrown off when we got into the trees." He looked down at his hands and up at me. "What did you hit your head on?" He held up his hands. They too had blood on them.

"I'm not sure," I replied. It didn't take long, or too much doctoring to figure out neither of us was hurt bad, just a little goose egg, for the both of us, that would be sore for a few days.

"Mount?" Andy looked up at me with fear in his eyes and started to cry again. "Where are my folks?" I really didn't want to hear that question, because I didn't have an answer. "I really want my Mom." He started to cried harder.

"Well Andy, honestly, I don't rightly know where your folks are." I put an arm around his shoulders and he slid closer. "But I promise that we'll find them. I surely do promise you that."

"Do you think they're all right?" There was fear in his voice.

I wanted so bad to be able to say "ya, sure, they're gonna be fine," but I couldn't. Life just don't work that way. Sometimes bad things just happen for no apparent reason at all. Whether you believe it's God's work or just the luck of the draw, that's the way of it, and I couldn't lie to the boy.

"Well Andy, I reckon we'll find that out when we find them." I didn't want to give him false hope, but I didn't want to scare him either. "That was one hell of a storm and anything could've happened, but you and I made it through just fine didn't we? I see no reason to think your ma and pa didn't do just fine too. They're probably down the creek a ways wondering what's taking us so long to catch up."

That boy did a whole lot of growing up right then and there. He straightened up, took a deep breath, and even almost smiled. "Yes, you're probably right." He tried so hard to look brave; but we both knew I was lying.

"You know, I've been in a lot worse spots than this." I figured it might be a good time for a little story. "A lot worse! I remember the time…I was about your age…maybe a couple years older…and I'd been out adventuring, and I wandered a little too far away from home. I'd stopped at a creek to get a drink when suddenly I was attacked by Indians! They were Arapahos, and they hated white folk! It was a small hunting party. They hauled me off to their village down south in the flat land." Andy was staring at me with his eyes wide, his parents forgotten for the moment.

"And then what happened?" He was hanging on every word.

"Well, when we got to that village…them Indians took to beating on me and swatting me with willow branches just for the fun of it! Then they took me and tied me to a tree out away from the village a little ways." My voice even shook a bit with the memory. "They gathered a bunch of dried wood and stacked it all around that tree I was tied to!" I looked Andy right in the eyes. He was dang near ready to fall over leaning forward waiting for what came next!

"Then what happened Mount? How did you get away?" He asked breathlessly.

I looked away, off into the sky like I was looking back into the past, and lowered my voice just a little. "I didn't…they lit that pile of wood and burned me plumb up." I continued to stare off into the distance and waited. There was no sound for several seconds, then Andy actually howled with laughter. It took several minutes before he could look at me without busting out again.

"It's time we got busy and found your folks, don't you think boy?" I noticed it was starting to get dark.

He was still scared and worried, hell so was I, but he was doing better. "Yes Mount." Andy gave me a small, brave smile that nearly broke my heart. "We better get going."

Chapter Nine

Somehow my bedroll had stayed strapped onto Skyhawk. Guess maybe I should tie myself on with leather straps. We undid the bedroll, to make room for Andy, and he held it in his lap after we both mounted up. There was only a couple hours left till dark. We kept to the creek for a couple hundred yards till it met up with the trail we'd been following. From there on, the route and creek ran pretty much side by side for as far as we could see. It was a good thing the land had changed to a more clay and gumbo type of dirt; if all this rain had hit us even two or three days ago we would've been up to our asses in mud. I bet the trail would've been impassable.

We'd only ridden for maybe a half-hour when Andy spotted something movin' off to our right, coming from the north. As it got closer, it turned out to be a wagon being pulled by a team of mules. A quarter mile further up the trail and we stopped and waited for the wagon to meet us. When they pulled up we saw it was a pretty rough looking feller with a pretty rough looking woman beside him. They were riding on an awfully rough looking wagon; the two mules didn't look like they'd live to see sundown. I was sure glad to see the two water barrels on the side of the wagon though. With all the rain, the creek was running muddy as swamp water, and I was mighty thirsty.

"Howdy there folks," I greeted them.

"Well, hello there my good man," the feller answered back. Both him and her were smiling and seemed happy to see us. "And hello to you too there young man." He tipped his hat to Andy. "How are you gentlemen this fine day?"

"Well sir." I couldn't stop a little laugh. "We just came through the damndest storm I've ever seen," I explained. "We were both thrown from our horses, got our heads cracked, and I had a tree fall on me. We're down to one horse and have lost the rest of our party. We don't have any food and are thirsty as hell, but considering all that, I guess we ain't doing so bad." I eyed those water barrels. "We'd sure be much obliged if you'd let us have a drink from one of those water barrels."

"We were caught just on the edge of that storm, some pretty strong winds and a little rain was all we got. It did look like it was a lot darker and uglier down this way." The gentleman's smile turned into a chuckle as he started to climb down from the wagon. "And yes sir, you'd be more than welcome to have a drink from my barrels." He had a gleam in his eyes. "Maybe a little taste from both."

Andy and I dismounted and walked over to the wagon. The stranger and I shook hands. "Folks call me Mount," I said. "This here's Andy. It's a pleasure meeting you folks."

"Jake Bushly." He looked older, like he'd had a hard life, but I guessed him to be mid-forties. "That's my wife Mary." Mary smiled and gave us a little wave. "We're headed down south, probably Tennessee." Mr. Bushly pried the lid off the first barrel and with a dipper offered Andy some water. After Andy and I had drunk our fill Jake refitted the lid and started opening the second barrel.

"Oh no, Mr. Bushly thank you, but we've had plenty." I was a little confused as to why he'd open the other barrel. He pulled the lid off and my confusion melted away as the sweet smell of whiskey came up outta that barrel and wrapped itself around me like a warm scarf on a cold evening. Mr. Worthington had several bottles of whiskey in the wagon and I saw him taking a pull off one of them damn near every night. He had yet to ask if I'd like a taste. His whiskey didn't smell nearly as good as this did. This barrel had its own dipper. Mr. Bushly filled it half way and offered it to me. I smiled. "Well now, Mr. Bushly maybe just a sip if you truly don't mind."

"Mind? Hell no, I don't mind. And call me Jake." He got a small metal cup from inside the wagon, filled it and joined me in a taste. "Making whiskey is what I do, and I intend on making the best in the world living down in Tennessee. They have the best type of maple trees for the best charcoal to filter with. Someday, God willing, we'll have a son or two to share our business with, and we'll make the best whiskey that's ever been made." He refilled my dipper.

Now folks, I've been drinking whiskey since I was probably fifteen or so. Some good, some better...but never anything that came within a country mile of Mr. Jake Bushly's whiskey. I had to wonder how good it'd be if it was gonna get better down in Tennessee.

"Jake." I stopped and took another swallow, or two. "Jake, I swear this here is like sipping on pure magic. I've never had whiskey so smooth, yet so full of spirit." I raised the dipper up in a salute. "Best whiskey I've ever tasted!"

Jake looked like he'd just won the grand prize in the world whiskey competition. He beamed at me and motioned to the barrel for me to help myself. "Why, thank you, Mount. I take great pride in my whiskey, and I'm delighted you like it."

Now, under any other circumstance, I could've happily set up camp right there and then and spent the night swapping stories and sipping whiskey with the Bushlys, but there wasn't enough whiskey in the world to make me forget about Mrs. Worthington and what kind of fix she might be in. We thanked Jake for everything, filled my water skin with water from the first barrel, and bid them goodbye and good luck. I've often wondered what became of that feller, and his whiskey.

We followed the trail west. Here and there, where the trail had been protected from the rain by an overhanging tree or an embankment along the trail, I could see wagon tracks that I figured were from the Worthington's wagon. With dark coming on fast I didn't know if we should keep going and risk missing something in the dark, or wait till sunup and waste all that time. It wasn't like we needed time to prepare camp, as we didn't have a damn thing to set up. Build a fire and huddle around it, that was gonna be our camp. We kept looking until it was too dark to see any distance off the trail then stopped for the night.

"If my folks weren't hurt they would have found us by now Mount." Andy was near tears again. "If they weren't hurt...we...we would have met them coming back down the trail."

"Well now, not necessarily Andy. Maybe the wagon broke down and your pa's trying to fix it." He'd said exactly what I'd been thinking. They would've come back to find us if they could.

I told Andy to get a fire going, and I went in search of dinner. I'd spotted some beaver dams in the creek back down the trail a piece. Within half an hour I was back with enough for both of us. Andy had the fire going good by the time I got back and we'd just gotten the beavers skinned and had enough hot coals for cooking when we heard horses coming from the east.

Our fire was thirty feet or so off the trail. When we stepped away from the fire light there was enough moonlight to see a rider with a horse in tow. He was looking towards our fire.

"Sandra...Andrew?" It was Mr. Worthington. "Sandra...Andrew is that you over there?"

"It's me father!" Andy shouted and took off running. Mr. Worthington dismounted and stood waiting for his son. When Andy got there, instead of throwing himself on his pa like I expected him to do, he stopped and gave his father a polite hug. Even under these circumstances they couldn't get over the formalities that come with being rich. At least that's what I'm thinking it is. Never being rich, money wise, myself I'm only supposin'.

Turned out the only thing Mr. Worthington saw when the heart of that storm hit us was a lone horse taking off across country; he didn't know if there was anyone on it or not and didn't have any idea where anyone else was, so he decided to go after it. The horse was so spooked it ran for miles. Even that magnificent palomino of mine, that he was riding, was taking a long time to catch up. He finally cornered the horse when it ran itself into a coulee and was stopped by the sandstone shelves in the end. He'd started back immediately, but was forced to hole up for a while cause of the storm. He'd been south of the trail and had just met up with it again a little ways back. He hadn't seen any sign of Mrs. Worthington or the wagon.

We spent a very long night huddled around the fire. Andy slept some, wrapped in my blanket. Mr. Worthington and I mostly laid there and stared into the fire. My thoughts were with Mrs. Worthington and how she would survive the night if she was hurt and laying out there somewhere with no fire and no cover. I honestly didn't know if she could. I offered up a silent prayer for her.

At first light we were up and on the trail. It made sense that the horses would've stayed on the trail simply because it was the easiest route. We split up and I rode a couple hundred feet or so to the left of the trail, and Mr. Worthington rode to the right. Because of the rain there were no tracks.

We'd been riding for about an hour when Andy, who was on the trail and a little bit ahead, turned and shouted back to us.

"I see something, I see something." He was bouncing up and down on his horse. "It could be the wagon." He took off at a gallop. If it was his ma, I didn't know if he should be the first one there or not. Mr. Worthington and I had to make our way back to the trail and then follow. That palomino outdistanced Skyhawk easily and they were there ahead of me.

When I got there, it was indeed the Worthington wagon. You could see plain as day how those horses had tried to take a sharp turn and that wagon had swung around and off the trail, over some downfall, and was spread out in pieces for about twenty feet off the trail, with the Worthingtons' personal possessions spread out for another thirty feet past that.

The main body of the wagon had held mostly together and was on its side with the down side wheels torn off. Also the ribbing on top for the canvas was all shattered. The harness was busted and the leather ripped. There was no sign of the horses. I walked around the wagon to where I heard voices.

I couldn't believe my eyes. Mrs. Worthington was lying on the ground propped up on some clothes bundles from the wagon. She was wrapped up in the canvas, had a little fire burning beside her, and even had some jerky and cheese from the food supply. And I'd wasted time worrying?

Andy was in her arms giving her a proper hug; like a mother and son should hug under the circumstances. I thought Mrs. Worthington was doing just fine until I saw her left leg sticking out from under the canvas. Just below her knee the leg was cut and swelled to about the size of her thigh and was a deep dark purple color. Below that, just above her ankle, her leg was twisted and her foot was pointing in a direction a foot ain't supposed to point. Looking again at her face, I noticed now that Mrs. Worthington was white as a fresh blanket of snow, and there was a slight tremble in her hands, but those were the only signs of the pain she had to be in, and the fear she had to feel.

Again that lady had surprised the hell out of me. After being thrown from the wagon hard enough to break her leg bad, she had built a fire with pieces of the wagon, got herself covered up with the canvas, and had even gotten something to eat. I was damned impressed yet again. That leg was gonna have to be set, and I wasn't looking forward to that, but I knew that this lady would handle it.

I saw Andy suddenly stiffen in his mother's arms. He pulled back and looked at her with concern in his eyes.

"Where's Red mom?" He looked around like he may've just missed him. "Where's Ole Red? He was in the wagon wasn't he?"

Mrs. Worthington started to cry. She couldn't speak. She just pointed toward some juniper bushes behind her. There, a few feet inside the bushes lay Red's body. He'd been thrown and broken in the accident and would never, not catch a rabbit again. Hopefully in dog heaven he'd be a better hunter.

The wailing cry that escaped from Andy was impossible to describe; it was the sound of pure and total despair. By the time he got to the dog's body he was sobbing and threw himself on Red and hugged him like if he squeezed hard enough, it would maybe bring him back to life. It didn't. Mrs. Worthington was still crying. And I have to admit, even though Red and I hadn't spent a lot of time getting to know each other, I had a tear get away and meander down my cheek too. I couldn't think of a damn thing to say, which was good because I probably couldn't have talked anyway. Mr. Worthington was sitting there like he was in a trance or some damn thing. He was white as the clouds and his eyes had a real faraway look; like his mind had gone travelin'.

As bad as I felt for Andy, and as sorry as I was about Red, there were more important things to worry about right then.

"Mrs. Worthington, we need to see to that leg." Last thing I wanted was to have to do the doctorin' here but I was pretty sure it was me or nobody. "It's broke bad Mrs. Worthington and the sooner we get it set and splinted the better."

That got Mr. Worthington to snap out of his trance. I watched as his eyes focused. He looked down at his wife's leg and I swear he got even whiter. He made sort of a strangled choking sound, got up and ran around the wagon; we could hear him puking. Yep, I was gonna have to do the doctorin'.

I went over to where Andy still lay, holding Ole Red's body.

"Andy." I spoke softly. "Andy, your ma needs you now. We'll give Red a proper burial and say our goodbyes later, but right now I need to take care of your ma, and I need your help."

I went over to some willows and with my knife cut four strong branches. When I came back Andy was sitting by his ma holding her hand. They were both crying. Mr. Worthington was standing over by the end of the wagon, and you could tell he was having trouble watching even from there.

"Mr. Worthington," I called over to him. "I surely could use some of that whiskey of yours if you could find any bottles that ain't broke." We needed something a lot stronger than whiskey. "And bring me that piece of leather harness over there." I went to the wagon and cut the reins from the rigging, then back over to where Mrs. Worthington and Andy were waiting; both trying real hard to be brave. Mrs. Worthington even had a smile working around the edges as she looked up at me with tears in her eyes.

"This isn't going to hurt any…is it Mount?"

"Oh hell no, Mrs. Worthington!" Again, I had to admire this lady's spunk. Don't know that I could've laid there and made jokes if it'd been me with my foot pointing the wrong direction. I looked her square in the eyes. "I doubt I'll feel a thing…but thanks for askin'." I looked at Andy and he was smiling too; through his tears.

Mr. Worthington came from behind what was left of the wagon, and I was mighty glad to see him carrying two bottles that had taken the tumble and survived. He handed me the bottles, stood for a minute looking down at his wife. I think he was trying to gather the courage to stay and help, but in the end he lost his battle.

"I'm sorry." This was spoken very softly and quietly, and then he turned and walked back around to the other side of the wagon. If I would've had the time I would've maybe even felt a little sorry for him. I didn't have the time.

I took a bottle of whiskey, opened it up, and took three long pulls. When I was able to breathe again I gave Mrs. Worthington the bottle.

"Drink as much as you can," I said. She took the bottle and took a fair-sized swallow. She choked and coughed but kept it down. I took the bottle and took another swallow or two for myself.

"Andy, you scoot under your ma and hold her shoulders and head in your lap. Your gonna have to hold on tight." I handed Mrs. Worthington the bottle and had her take another drink. She choked and coughed but it stayed down. "Now, Mrs. Worthington here's what we're gonna do." I had her take another swallow. She choked and coughed a little less. "First, I'm gonna have to turn your leg so it's pointing the right direction." With a nod of my head Mrs. Worthington took another pull at the bottle. She barely coughed at all. "That's probably gonna be the worst part." I motioned and she took another drink. "Then I'm probably gonna have to tug a little on your lower leg until it goes back where it's suppose to be." Two more big swallows and I could see her eyes starting to lose their focus. "Then, I'll splint it with these willow branches and tie it off with the leather reins." Another drink…and another.

"Get ready Andy." I handed her the piece of leather harness. She held it in one hand and the bottle in the other. She took another drink. That was the one I'd been waiting for. Her dark brown eyes sort of rolled up till there was nothing but whites and her head rolled over onto her shoulder.

"Here we go Andy, hold on." Andy held on, and I took a hold of Mrs. Worthington's leg just below the break. I just had room for both hands. I slowly but firmly pulled down and turned it back around the right direction. Mrs. Worthington's whole body went stiff, she screamed and tried to pull away, but Andy held on tight. Her hand with the leather in it went to her mouth. She bit down on the leather and squeezed her eyes shut tight. Her screams still leaked out around the piece of harness.

"I'm almost done here Mrs. Worthington." I didn't know if she heard me or not. I pulled a little harder and then pushed the lower leg up to meet the upper half. A little twist that had her nearly chewing that leather in half, and I could feel her bones slip back into place. "That's it Mrs. Worthington, its back in place! Nothing to do now but tie on the splints." I looked up to see how she was taking it; she'd passed out. Andy was sitting there holding on to his mother's shoulders with all his might and had his eyes closed too.

"That's it Andy, we're done. Good job son." And I meant it. "You did real good Andy." I started to tie the splints in place on all four sides of Mrs. Worthington's leg with the reins from the wagon. Andy opened his eyes and looked down at his ma.

"She isn't...dead...is she Mount? Is she?" He looked at me with real fear in his eyes.

"Hell no, she ain't dead! Now don't you worry none." I tied the splints as tight as I dared while still loose enough to let the blood flow through her leg. "Ole Doc Mount ain't never lost a patient yet, and I ain't about to start now! When I started pulling and twisting on that leg your ma just decided she'd be better off somewhere else is all. She'll be back soon."

As if to prove me right, Mrs. Worthington moaned and her head rolled to the other side. Her eyes opened, blinked a couple times, and closed again. I think the pain was tolerable now. Her body was now dealing with the half bottle of whiskey she'd drank. She was still holdin' the bottle. I took it from her and had myself a couple of long pulls; my way of saying *good job doc*.

With her leg set and splinted, and Mrs. Worthington sleeping real peaceful like, there wasn't anything left for me to do. "Stay with your ma, Andy, I'm gonna see to the rest of this mess we got here."

I made a slow circle looking around. There were clothes and food and supplies laying everywhere. The clothes, except for being a little on the dirty side, were all okay. Most of the food was okay too being packed well in bags or barrels. We did lose the water barrel and a barrel of flour that'd split open and piled up against a log like a small snow drift. Some cheese had busted open and was covered with dirt and ants, but other than that, most everything was okay. Not that it mattered much. That wagon wasn't going any further, and we had a total of three horses. We weren't gonna be carrying a lot of supplies with us! Of course, we weren't going anywhere for a few days until Mrs. Worthington was ready for travelin'.

I came around the corner of the wagon and Mr. Worthington was sitting there. He stood up as soon as he saw me.

"I'm not a coward!" The look in his eyes dared me to disagree.

"Whoa there, Mr. Worthington, nobody here called you any such thing," I said.

"Not helping with Sandra...I mean. I'm not a coward, I just..." He had to stop and swallow. "I just...couldn't. I've never been in that circumstance before...and I just...couldn't." His eyes now pleaded with me to understand.

"Look, Mr. Worthington, I figure all folks are different. The fact that seeing your wife hurt bad like that affected you the way it did doesn't mean nothing." I wanted him to feel better, don't know why, but I also needed him to understand too. "You know...we ain't near halfway to Oregon, and I'd bet the entire Rocky Mountains that this ain't the last of our troubles along the way. Now, Mr. Worthington I respect the fact that you couldn't help with your wife, and this time we didn't need your help, she's gonna be just fine, but next time...who knows?" That was probably all I needed to say. "You've gotta be ready if your family needs you," I added. I watched his eyes; they hardened with determination, just like I was hoping they would.

"I will be ready and able when my family needs me Mr. Battner!" He fired back at me. "I will do whatever needs to be done to ensure the safety of my family!" He squared his shoulders and straightened his back; just what I wanted to see.

"I'm mighty glad to hear you say that Mr. Worthington." I slapped him on the back and continued around the wagon. "Your son needs someone to help him bury his dog; and I can't do that! The shovel's still strapped over there on the side of the wagon."

Mrs. Worthington was still sleeping. Andy was still sitting and holding her. I held her shoulders while he slid clear. I lay Mrs. Worthington down using a bag of clothes for a pillow and covered her with a couple of blankets from the wagon. Andy rubbed at his left leg a little then stood up. A strangled scream escaped him as he grabbed at his leg and fell back to the ground. His leg was about forty minutes into an hour nap, and he couldn't stand on it at all! Andy and I were able to share a little smile while he rubbed life back into his leg. Mr. Worthington stood over near the wagon lookin' sad.

"You and your pa need to take care of Ole Red," I said to Andy. "There are probably coyotes, maybe even some cougars around these parts...bury him deep."

Andy and his pa went over to Red's body. Mr. Worthington handed Andy the shovel then bent down and picked up the lifeless dog. Andy tried to hold back his tears but couldn't. Suddenly I got a pinch of sand in my eyes, or some damn thing, and they started burning and watering. I decided the other side of the wagon would be better for them.

Chapter Ten

I spent the next couple hours sorting through everything that was scattered within fifty feet of that wrecked wagon; separating the good from the ruined. Most of the supplies, clothes and food, were okay other than being a bit dirty. The pots and pans and such were all a little banged around, with a dent here and a scratch there, but most were useable. I made a pile of the useable stuff. The rest I built a large fire for, and buried what I couldn't burn. It didn't seem right to just leave all that junk laying on the ground.

Mrs. Worthington woke up a couple times just to nod off again. The third time she was able to eat a little something before going back to sleep. She was awful weak, and still in a lot of pain. Andy stayed by her side. Mr. Worthington helped me go through the belongings and set up camp.

It was early afternoon by the time we got everything situated. I decided to take Skyhawk and see if I could track the lost horses, and maybe bring back some meat; since we were gonna be there awhile.

Within a half-mile from camp I found the first of the three missing horses. It was dead. Looked like it'd stepped into a prairie dog hole while on the run and had broken its left front leg. There were signs that a critter of some sort had been at it. I'm guessin' a coyote. I made note of where he lay so if I couldn't find anything better I could come back; we had to eat something.

I was lucky. About a mile further on I found the other two horses. They were in a stand of trees beside the creek grazing on sweet grass like they didn't have a care in the world; which I guess they didn't. I used some rope I'd brought along and hobbled both horses so they wouldn't wander off, then went hunting.

There were deer tracks along the bank of the creek and a game trail leading into some tree and sage covered hills on the other side. I took my rifle and followed the game trail up onto the nearest high point for a look around. As I crested the top of the hill, staying hidden and being real quiet, damned if they weren't right there waiting on me.

Not fifty yards away were about twenty head of mule deer, awful small by Rocky Mountain standards, but I reckon still mighty good eating. I lay and watched them for a little, enjoying how that spring's fawns were running, jumping, and chasing each other around in circles. Their little legs weren't very sturdy yet, and a couple times they damn near toppled over as they ran around. I nearly laughed out loud a couple times. Then I picked out a nice, big three-year-old buck, and shot him. I would've rather had a doe because they're better eating, but the fawns were still at the teat.

The rest of the deer were gone in a second. I walked up to the one I'd killed and felt the sadness I always feel after killing any critter. He looked a lot prettier standing and eating grass than lying on the ground bleedin'. I said a prayer of thanks and asked the Lord to watch over his spirit, then I slit his throat to let him bleed out. Ten minutes later, gutted and cleaned, it was just meat.

I had a little trouble getting the horse to take the carcass. I had to tie the horse up short to a tree and blindfold it before it'd let me pack that deer onto its back. Once it got used to the smell of blood it settled right down, and I led the two horses back to camp.

When I got back Mrs. Worthington was awake. She was propped up on a pile of clothes bags and covered with blankets from the wagon. Andy sat on the ground beside her. She smiled when I rode up. I hitched the horses to some willows and walked over.

"Hello Doctor Battner," she called out, in an awfully weak voice. She wasn't what I'd call rosy cheeked yet, but there was some color. "The doctors in St. Louis could set my leg, but I doubt that they would then go out and get my supper." Now that I was closer I could see the hurting in her eyes. The smile and light talk were a damn good sign, but they were also covering up some serious pain.

"I don't think I'd want to be within a country mile of one of them St. Louis doctors when he was packing a loaded rifle," I answered. "He probably would've shot one of the horses and rode the damn deer back to camp." She tried to laugh and cried out in pain. "Let me have a look at that leg."

Where the break had been, just above her ankle, her leg was nearly black and pretty swollen, but I figured that was to be expected. Above that, just below her knee I'd noticed a pretty bad gash in her calf. I'd rinsed it out before, a little, but had been mostly concerned with getting the bone set. That cut had to get cleaned out to avoid infection. I had Andy fetch a pail of water from the creek.

"This just might hurt a bit Mrs. Worthington," I said; like she didn't know that! "Do you want a couple swallows of whiskey before I start?"

"No thank you Mount, I surely don't." She shuddered just thinking about it. "I doubt if I'll ever drink whiskey again. I still have this piece of leather to bite on if I need. You go ahead."

I took the whiskey bottle and had a couple pulls. I used a drinking cup and poured hot water over the wound to rinse it out the best I could. Mrs. Worthington bit down on the leather and did fine.

"Well now that wasn't so bad" she said.

Then I took the whiskey bottle and poured it over the wound. She changed her mind in a hurry! Even around the leather she bit down on, her scream spooked the horses. I handed her the whiskey bottle and she took a long swallow. After her coughing fit ended she took another smaller drink.

"Sorry about that Mrs. Worthington, but we needed to get rid of any infection there might be." I rinsed the wound twice more with water and worked a bandage, made from a nearly clean piece of cloth, under the splints and wrapped the wound. With Andy's help we moved her away from the wet ground and made her comfortable beside the fire. I started to walk away to take care of the deer.

"Mount," she called; even after what I'd just put her through, her voice was stronger. I stopped and turned. There were tears in her eyes. "I don't know how to say thank you for all you've done."

I smiled down at her. "You just did, Mrs. Worthington. You just did. The only other thing you need to do for me is heal up real good, so I look like one of those big city doctors." I started to walk away.

"Mount." I stopped and turned. "Please...call me Sandra." Even through the pain she was feeling, the smile she smiled up at me lit up the day in a way the sun just couldn't. Damned if I didn't get another pinch of dirt or something in my eye, and had to walk away.

I called her Sandy once, the next day. I was informed that sandy was a type of soil; "Sandra" was a ladies name. I sorta liked the sound of Sandy and Andy, but I was a group of one. Mr. Worthington, of course, didn't like it, and wanted to say something real bad the first time he heard me use "Sandra." you could see it in his whole body, but to his credit he walked away.

We stayed put for six or seven days before Sandra felt able to try and mount up. We adjusted the stirrup on the right side for her good leg, and using Mr. Worthington and me for support she managed to get the broke leg up and over to stick damn near straight out on the other side. Looked pretty funny; but she could ride. We put her on the palomino, and that horse was so smart it seemed to sense that the rider was hurt, and it was gentle as a carousel pony. Once Sandra had practiced getting up and down a few times and had ridden around a little, we were ready to get back on trail.

We were up early next morning, and while Andy fixed up a breakfast of flapjacks and venison steaks, Mr. Worthington and I argued about what we needed and what we could do without; since we could only pack so much on the one spare horse we had. I thought we should take mostly food, clothes, and blankets and such, being that we were going to be in the mountains at some point, and summer or not, it gets cold. Mr. Worthington wanted food, then his personal business paraphernalia, which was a bunch of useless shit, and took up valuable room. The only thing we agreed had to come, were the two full bottles of whiskey, Andy finding one more that hadn't broke.

As often happens when two men can't decide an issue the deciding was made by the nearest female. As we argued, Sandra told us what to take and what to leave, and for the most part that's just what we did. Mr. Worthington insisted on a bunch of papers, but left a couple satchels full behind. By mid-morning we were packed and ready to go.

The going was slow. Sandra was in a lot of pain and we had to stop pretty regular for her to stretch out a bit and rest up. The second day out I had us set up camp early, and I went hunting; not only for food, but for medicine too. I'd learned a thing or two from my Indian friends about plants used for healing. It took some doing in these parts, being on the edge of the great plains like we were, but when I came back to camp, not only did I have supper, three nice fat jackrabbits, but also some white willow bark, some turmeric leaves, and a few flowers my Indian friends called leopard bane.

I shredded and pounded the white willow bark into sort of a paste and smeared it on a fresh bandage. Don't know if it did as much good as the whiskey but it sure hurt a hell of a lot less; and didn't waste good drinking whiskey. I'd made sure one bottle of whiskey went into my pack so I could have a taste now and again in the evenings. With the leaves and leopard bane I made a strong and nasty smelling tea. Sandra drank it down saying it couldn't be worse than the whiskey, but from the look on her face I'm not so sure. Damn howdy did it work though! Within half an hour of drinking that tea Sandra was sound asleep, and slept till well after sunup the next morning. She said it was the first time since the accident that she was mostly free of pain.

We got a big lift a couple days later. We were well into the Great Plains now, and hadn't seen a thing but prairie grass and sagebrush for two days. The horses didn't do well on prairie grass and needed something different or they'd get sick. Early in the afternoon we spotted some very thin, spread out patches of trees in a real sketchy line off in the distance to our right, running southwest and looking like it'd meet up with the trail a couple miles or so down the way. As we got closer I was more and more sure it was what I'd been hoping for. Soon there was no doubt. We'd met up with the Platte River, the first real landmark of our trip!

Don't know why three people would go gettin' all crazy over a silly river; but we did! Andy, Sandra, and I commenced to whooping and hollering, like we'd just struck gold or something. Mr. Worthington, as usual, was somber, and basically a pompous jackass.

After a couple days along the Platte we were tired of the plains and ready for a change. Even with a stand of trees every few miles and enough good foliage for the horses to stay alive, the scenery was still drab and dull.

It got hot as hell! So hot, the sky was white with just a little fringe of blue around the edges. The horizon was lost in a wavering line of heat. That heat took a toll on us and the horses.

It was also a learning experience for the Worthingtons. The first day along the Platte we saw our first buffalo herd. It was a small one, as far as buffalo herds go, with only a few hundred head. Andy was especially excited and stood just watching them for a long time. I managed to knock down a small yearling and the Worthingtons got to try buffalo meat. They preferred the deer.

Due to the lack of trees, the Worthingtons got to experience their first cook fire made from dried buffalo chips. They preferred wood.

On the third day after meeting up with the Platte we rode up to Fort Kearny. Again, there was some whooping and hollering. We'd been on the trail, out from the Fur Company, for around a month. Sandra had a broke leg, we'd lost our wagon, one dog, one horse, most of our supplies, and weren't even near the halfway point yet, but by the way we acted you'd have thought we had the Pacific Ocean in sight!

Fort Kearny wasn't a fort. At least, not a fort the way I pictured one, with solid log walls and big heavy gates with guard towers. Fort Kearny was simply a cluster of buildings huddled around one another alongside the trail; most of them made of sod.

I sure hoped there wouldn't be any Indian attacks while we were there. It looked like a couple of mad squaws with a mean dog could probably overrun the place. It was a military fort, but there was very little military activity going on that I could see. Nearly all of the men were just lying around, and most weren't even in uniform. Those that were looked just as bad as those that weren't. You'd a thought with the river so close by they would've stayed a little cleaner.

Fort Kearny did however have the three things we needed the worst. It had a pretty well-stocked supply store. It had a stable, with a corral out back full of horses; hopefully some of which would be for sale. And it had a real doctor; well sort of. The first thing we did when we got to Kearny was ask where the doctor's office was.

"Well now, Doc Fletcher's office is the door right next to ours," the store clerk told us. "But Doc Fletcher himself would most likely be over to the public hall. It's only two thirty in the afternoon so he may not be too drunk yet, if you hurry. As long as you don't need any serious doctoring, he should be okay."

Leaving Sandra still sitting on her horse in front of the doc's office with Andy, Mr. Worthington and I went down to the public hall a couple hundred feet from the store. It was two rooms we could see. There was a small room with a wood stove and food supplies in it. Then there was a large meeting and greeting room. There were tables along the side wall where they musta sat and had meals. Along one end wall was a bar, with a hallway behind it and five small round tables out front of it. Men sat at three different tables. We walked up to the bar and Mr. Worthington ordered up a whiskey. I cleared my throat and looked down at him. He ordered up another, then turned and faced the fellers at the tables.

"I'm looking for Doctor Fletcher." Everybody was looking, but nobody moved. "I said we need Doctor Fletcher," he repeated. "My wife is hurt and we need the doctor." Everybody continued to stare, like a roomful of deaf mutes.

We'd been in Fort Kearny for maybe twenty minutes and I was already sick and tired of people. I was also worried about Mrs. Worthington. I stepped up to the bar, reached across, grabbed the barkeep by his string tie and the front of his shirt and drug him halfway across the bar. I heard a couple chairs scrape on the floor as men sat up to take notice. As I held the barman on the bar I kept my eyes on the men at the tables. No one got up.

"The man asked about the doctor." I spoke as polite as a minister. "You think any of you gentlemen could help us out?" I looked down at the fella lying across the bar and gave him a little shake.

"Down there." He nodded the best he could toward the hallway behind the bar. "He's with Sally...second door on the right."

Mr. Worthington headed around the bar toward the hall. I thanked the barkeep, set him back down behind the bar, and followed Mr. Worthington. He got to the door and knocked loudly.

"Doctor Fletcher! Doctor Fletcher, you're needed at your office!" he yelled at the closed door. We listened and heard grunting and bed springs squeaking. Mr. Worthington gave me a disgusted look and knocked again. "Doctor Fletcher you in there? Do you hear me?"

"I'm...busy...now..." He was not exactly in a position to talk. Well, guess I didn't rightly know what position he was in. "I'll...be...there...in...a...bit." He gasped through the door.

"You'll be here now, you son of a bitch!" Mr. Worthington beat on the door till it shook and rattled on its hinges. "If you're not out here in thirty seconds I'm coming in there and dragging you out!" Some more door banging. "My wife is hurt and you're damn well going to look to her right now! Do you hear me?"

The good Doc Fletcher let loose with some of the most colorful cussing and carrying on that I'd ever heard. The bed stopped squeaking and we could hear him wrestling with his clothes. When the door flew open and Doc Fletcher stepped out he was ready to fight. He was a big man, over six feet, and although thirty pounds or so overweight he looked damn strong. He had his pants on with the suspenders hanging down, only an undershirt on top. He smelled of whiskey and looked mad as a wounded grizzly. He was toe to toe with Mr. Worthington and two or three inches taller.

"Look, I don't know who you think you…" His eyes moved up from Mr. Worthington and saw me standing behind him. My size, and the anger that had to show on my face, caused him to pause. I was fully prepared to move Mr. Worthington out of the way and teach the good doctor some proper respect, but I didn't get the chance. I saw Mr. Worthington's right arm draw back and I had just time to think *no, he's not gonna*, when he did! He hit Doc Fletcher square on the chin and knocked him up against the wall beside the door where he stuck for a couple seconds with this bewildered expression on his face. Then he slid down the wall gentle as you please to end up sitting on the floor wonderin' what the hell just happened.

"Now, I'm only going to say this one more time doctor." Mr. Worthington still maintained his composure. "My wife has a broken leg. She is in a considerable amount of pain, and you are going to tend to her right now. Isn't that right Doctor Fletcher?"

The doctor looked up from the floor at Mr. Worthington, then shifted his gaze to me. We were both glaring down at him.

"Yeah." He tried to get up. "Yeah, I guess that's what I'm gonna do."

Mr. Worthington turned around and walked away. I stepped up and offered the doctor my hand and helped him up. I smiled and introduced myself to show there were no hard feelings.

Once we got Doc Fletcher back to his office, and got Sandra dismounted and inside, he turned out to be a pretty fair doctor, charming and witty, but still professional; it took him no time at all to win Sandra and Andy over. The good doctor had them giggling and carrying on like school kids. He checked out Sandra's leg and was happy with what we'd done and the way everything seemed to be healing, the break had been set well, and seemed to be mending well. There might be a little bump there but nothing more. The gash on her calf, above the break, had some infection, but the white willow paste I'd put under the bandage had done the job, and the infection was minor.

We were able to move into a small three-room cabin out behind the main store. Mr. and Mrs. Worthington's room even had a bed in it; Andy and I slept on the floor in our room. We ate over to the public hall and carried Sandra's food back to her for the first two days; then she insisted on walking over herself.

We stayed at Fort Kearny for about two weeks. That made not quite six weeks since her leg had been broken and Sandra was walking around with just a slight limp. Where the cut had been she was gonna have a nasty scar, but other than that it was healing real nice.

Mr. Worthington had arranged to buy another horse so we would have two pack horses. We both had a chance to sit down with Captain Hawkins, who was in charge at Fort Kearny, and talk about the trail ahead and what to expect. It was nearly five hundred miles to Fort Laramie, which was our next goal. According to the captain the trail would be easy, being mostly plains, pretty much like we'd been passing through, with some rolling hills as we got closer to Fort Laramie. There'd be mountains in sight by then too, and I was really looking forward to that because I'd been missing the mountains somethin' awful.

Captain Hawkins was worried about the Indians though. Seems there were several raiding parties of Sioux that had been raising hell in the area, and he recommended we stay put until the next batch of settlers passed by and we could join up with them. He had no idea when that might be, and Mr. Worthington wasn't about to wait.

We stocked up on what supplies we thought we'd need, and could pack on two horses, plus a bedroll pack behind each rider. We'd be following the Platte River most of the way to Fort Laramie, so water shouldn't be a problem. We knew enough not to drink too much water right out of the river, so we'd be drinking only as much as we needed, to avoid getting sick. We each carried a water skin filled with good water, and with care that would last us several days.

Mr. Worthington bought saddles for Andy and Sandra so that the stirrups fit and each was as comfortable as possible. We also had some medical supplies from Doc Fletcher; a couple different herbs, for pain and such, along with some bandages and salve.

Captain Hawkins and the men at Fort Kearny threw us a little party the night before we left. We had beef steak, which was something new to me, sweet corn, and potatoes with gravy. After dinner one of the soldiers brought out a harmonica and another had something he called a guitar. I'd never seen one of those before; it sounded mighty fine. Some of the other soldiers took to dancing. Sandra tried, but after only one tune her leg was hurting. Before bed we each had a real bath, with hot water and soap; the last ones we'd have for a while.

Next morning shortly after sunup we were packed, mounted, and ready to go. I had one of the pack horses behind me and Andy had the other. Damn near everyone at the fort turned out to see us off. We rode away to shouts of "good luck" and "God bless." We'd need both!

Chapter Eleven

When we left Fort Kearny we found ourselves in a fine and dandy mood. Well, who knows about Mr. Worthington? At least he wasn't scowlin' or yelling at anybody. Mr. Worthington rode out front, sometimes up to half a mile ahead. Sandra and Andy rode side by side, when the trail allowed, and I trailed behind. I figured we were movin' past spring and into summer by now, but the weather was holding fine. It got plenty warm during the day, but not "summertime, roast ya like a pig" hot. It cooled down so that you needed a blanket at night; and our campfire felt mighty good a few nights. We had a week or so of the plains left, then would start seeing rolling hills with some tree-lined creeks coming down to empty into the Platte. Most importantly there would be better forage for the horses.

Sandra's leg had healed up real nice. There was just a little bump where the break was, and she didn't even walk with much of a limp. The scar on her calf was a jagged white line, but I thought it added character to her "porcelain doll" skin. Her leg still pained her some, but not too bad. Doc Fletcher told her she'd be able to use it to tell when the weather was fixin' to change.

We'd stocked up on all the supplies we could carry, so were as comfortable as we could be. Sandra and Andy even took to singing. Some of the songs, I remembered Ma singing when I was little. Some, I remembered from Rendezvous. Sandra asked me to sing along. I said "no.".

"Oh come on Mount, the words are easy, we can teach you," she continued.

"It ain't that, Sandra." And I wasn't being modest folks, just honest. "The fact of the matter is, I just flat can't sing! I've tried before and it ain't pretty."

"Oh now Mount, you can't be that bad." She persisted. "Some people are better than others, most certainly, but anybody can sing if they try. Come on Mount, give it a try."

"Yeah Mount!" Andy had to join in. "Let's hear you…give it a try."

Some folks just have to learn the hard way!

"Don't say I didn't warn you," I said. I took a deep breath, sat up straight in the saddle, and started singing a tune called "The Settler's Lament," nice and strong. I sang as good as I know how. I got to about the third line when Sandra and Andy looked at each other, covered their ears, started yelling for mercy, and kicked their horses into a run. When I caught up to them down the trail a piece, they were singing "Shenandoah," one of my favorites. They didn't ask me to sing along! Hell, they didn't even try to hide it when they'd glance back at me and start to giggling at each other.

Around the fourth day out the weather took a turn. Just past noon the clouds started moving in. Not black mean looking thunderstorm clouds, but gray serious looking rain clouds. Clouds that looked like they'd hang around for a while. By mid-afternoon it started rainin'. That afternoon it felt good. After four days of sun, the light, steady rain was nice. The packs on the horses, even our individual bedroll packs, were wrapped in large pieces of oilcloth which was pretty much waterproof, so we weren't worried about our supplies.

By that evening we'd had enough rain! We were ready for it to go away. It didn't! I found enough dry wood sheltered under some trees that we were able to have a small fire, but supper was a solemn affair. Shortly after we were done eating the trees above us became saturated, the rain came through, put our fire out, and soaked us to the bone.

It didn't stop rainin' for nearly five full days! Day and night it rained. Sometimes harder, sometimes just barely a sprinkle; but it never stopped. During the day we rode in single file, heads down, and shoulders slumped. No one was singing now; hell, we didn't even talk!

The nights were the worst. There was nothing dry enough to burn. We'd have a cold supper of side pork and beans, then each wrap up the best we could under whatever protection we could find. We'd gotten to the hilly country, and that helped some. Sometimes we'd find a stand of cottonwoods to hide under, sometimes a willow patch. Once we even burrowed our way under the branches of a huge ole pine tree. I think that was the only time in five days we were completely out of the rain for a while. We couldn't move, and it was uncomfortable as hell, but we were dry.

The Platte had already been running pretty high due to the spring runoff, and now with all the rain it was threatening to spill over; in some places it already had. The trail had gotten sloppy and treacherous for the horses; it was mighty slow going. Tempers were short, which of course meant Mr. Worthington was constantly riled up about somthin'. All in all it was a pretty miserable stretch!

Early afternoon of the fifth day of rain, we were still riding single file, still with heads down, Mr. Worthington still mumbling under his breath about some damn thing or another, the rain still coming down, although it'd let up some.

"Look! Look!" Andy yelled and pointed off to the northeast. Above us the sky was still a dark gray. Off a few miles or so it turned a couple shades lighter. And way off in the distance, almost like a vision, was a patch of blue sky. Honest to God blue sky!

Within half an hour the rain had stopped completely and an hour after that we were riding under blue skies and sunshine. Everyone's spirits soared. I think I even caught Mr. Worthington looking up into the sky with a touch of a smile.

When we came across a reasonably big stand of cottonwoods with some fairly dry downfall under them I decided we'd set up camp early. It took some doing, but using my fire steel and some dry tree moss, I finally got a good fire blazing. While the Worthingtons set up the rest of camp, I went huntin'. I'd had about all the cold beans and dried side pork I could handle. It was time for some red meat! Problem was I didn't find any!

I knew we weren't in prime hunting country yet. We'd left the buffalo behind on the prairie and hadn't gotten to prime deer or elk country yet, but I figured I should be able to find a deer; or even an antelope would do. There didn't seem to be any game of any sort around; I couldn't even find any fresh sign. Kind of gave me the spooks for some reason. I was able to get a couple of rabbits and four grouse that didn't hear me coming.

It wasn't what I wanted, but it was meat, and it was hot. Nobody turned it down.

The trail dried up in a day or so, and the traveling was a whole bunch easier after that. Summer came back like it meant to grab ahold and hang on. It got hotter than a pine cone in a forest fire during the day, and stayed pretty damned warm all night long. After five days of being soaked to the bone and cold, the sun felt good; for a while. Two days after the rain quit we were jumping into the river to cool off. The crazy shit folks do sometimes is plumb amazing!

There still wasn't any real game to be seen, and that was starting to bother me more and more; eating at me like a tick burrowed in someplace I couldn't reach. We had plenty to eat; lots of greens, fish and small critters like rabbits, squirrels, beaver and the like…but there was no big game; and there should've been.

Now there were only two reasons that I could come up with. One was that there was a damn mean killer bear or maybe mountain lion roaming the territory. The other is that there'd been a lot of hunting going on; in these parts that meant Indian hunting parties. Since we'd been warned about hostile Indians at Fort Kearny, I wasn't real excited about either explanation. Hopefully there was some other reason I hadn't thought of.

It happened about a week after the rain stopped. I've heard it said that Indians won't attack at night. Their Gods don't approve, or some damn thing. Now, I don't know about all Indians…but

I'm here to tell you folks, that for the Sioux, that's a whole wagonload of horseshit!

We'd had a good day; as it hadn't been too hot. Andy and Mr. Worthington had caught several fish; and we had fish and flapjacks for supper. After supper, a couple long swallows from the whiskey bottle, a couple stories around the campfire, and nodding off to sleep under a blanket of a couple million glittering stars.

Ain't sure what woke me up. I didn't come wide awake and alert like I would've if I'd heard something. I just sort of came around slowly, opened my eyes part way, and saw the leftovers of our campfire just a few feet in front of me. I even had a second or two to think about how pretty it was; the still glowing embers, pulsing with heat like some exotic dance.

Suddenly the stillness of the night exploded with the most god-awful inhuman screams! As my eyes flew wide open I saw a moccasined foot on the other side of the fire. It kicked out, and all those glowing embers I'd just been admiring, erupted and came flying into my face! As I twisted around to protect myself from the flying fire balls I heard more of the insane Indian screeching, and it was mixed with cries of horror and pain coming from the Worthingtons!

I rolled twice to my right to get clear of the fire and started to get to my feet while grabbing for the knife at my side. I didn't make either! I can't say how many of them screamin' bastards there were that jumped on me, but I know for certain I had two or three on each arm and leg, and there had to be two sitting on my gut and chest, and another two doing nothing but beating my head back and forth between them. Their screaming and laughing was the last thing I remembered.

In my whole damned life I'd never gotten knocked out; not once! Now it'd happened twice within the last month; and I can't say I particularly cared for it either time. I will say waking up under a tree with my leg trapped and my head bleedin' was the better of the two.

Bee stings. That was the first thing I was aware of. First on my shoulder, then my chest, then my stomach, then my chest again, they wouldn't stop. I got stung over and over. As awareness slowly returned, I realized there was music playing, along with the bee stings. Well, sort of music. I heard drums beating and this awful wailing sound. As my eyes focused and became adjusted to the dim light, I saw that the wailing was comin' from an old Indian medicine man standing not twenty feet away by a roaring fire. My deerskin shirt was still on, but had been torn open in front and just hung from my shoulders.

The bee stings that kept at me turned out to be sharpened sticks in the hands of some Indian children playing a rousing game of "Poke the Mountain Man." There were five of the little heathens, four boys and a girl, and they danced around in front of where I was bound to a tree. Every few seconds one of them would spring forward and jab me with the sharpened stick he held, then he'd jump back, and they'd all laugh and carry on like it was great fun. The few adults that paid any attention at all seemed to enjoy the show too. Everybody was having fun but me!

I was in a small movable Indian village; a temporary encampment that could be set up and tore down quickly and easily. Certain tribes would set up several camps like this one in different places around a territory and then send hunting parties out from each one; preparing for the coming winter.

From where I was tied I could see the whole camp site. Unless they were in one of the tepees, the Worthingtons weren't here. I wasn't too surprised. It was common practice for Indians to separate their prisoners and take them to different camps. I had no idea where the Worthingtons could be, and that was assuming they were all still alive!

I needed to bust loose and get the hell out of there soon if I was gonna be of any help to anyone! I looked behind a couple tepees to my left and could see where the horses were tethered. My heart leapt with joy when I saw Mr. Worthington's palomino, still saddled up, in with the Indian ponies. Since we'd been in camp when attacked, the Indians had no way of knowing whose horse belonged to who. They must've assumed that the big horse went with the big man. Now all I needed to do was get loose and onto that horse. That's all!

As it turned out, that mean little Indian girl with the sharpened stick was my salvation. After a spell the kids got tired of poking me with just a stick and commenced to heating up the ends in the fire first. The smell of burning hair and flesh must've made the game just that much more fun. I couldn't stop a flinch or two but they sure as hell didn't get any thrills from hearing my screams, because there weren't any. One of those damn sticks would've had to gone plumb through me before I'd a given those little sons a bitches the satisfaction of a scream.

About the third time the girl came at me with her burning stick she hit me hard in the chest and a small, stone sized ember broke off and fell into my hands which were tied at my waist in front of me. I didn't realize what was happening until my hand started burning. Out of instinct, I damn near shook my hand and dropped the ember, but luckily realized what I had in time. Without anyone noticing, I took that ember and wedged it between two wraps of the rope that was holding me. I got a little help from the good Lord at that point, when the adults called the kids away to eat.

There were probably seventy-five Indians in the camp. At the moment they were either gathered around the main fire, or by their own tepee having their evening meals. No one noticed when I lowered my head as far as I could and started blowing lightly on that ember. When I blew it glowed and heated up, and when I quit it dimmed. Over and over I blew until I started to get light headed. Finally I was rewarded by a small column of smoke from the rope. A few more light blows and the rope was burning! I had to be careful to cover the small flame with my hand so no one would spot it. It only took seconds after it started for it to burn through far enough for me to bust the rope. Since no one seemed to be watching, and I couldn't count on getting a better chance, I snapped the rope, sunk down low, and crept as quickly and quietly as I could toward the horses. I was behind the nearest tepee when someone noticed I was gone.

Whoever noticed I wasn't tied to the tree anymore commenced yelling. About two heartbeats after that every Indian in the camp was yelling! They stood, looked around in circles, and yelled. I made it all the way to the palomino before they spotted me. I couldn't understand what they were saying, but I could tell when I'd been spotted by the change in pitch and excitement of their hollering. I tore the hobble from his front legs, jumped into the saddle, and kicked that horse harder than I'd ever kicked anything!

As we were leaving the camp I saw two arrows fly past, and just before I got out of range damned if one of them didn't stick me. An arrow lodged into the back of my left arm, high up near my shoulder. I cried out in pain and urged that palomino on even faster!

I don't know if any of those Indians gave chase or not. Once that big quarter horse got up to speed there wasn't a horse anywhere in the west that could've kept up, let alone caught up! That horse was even more magnificent than I'd imagined he'd be! He ran with the speed of the wind and smooth as if we were walking through a meadow. Even runnin' for my life, with an arrow sticking out of my arm, I couldn't help but admire what an incredible animal he was. After a half-hour or so I slowed the palomino and checked behind me. If they'd tried to catch me they'd given up long ago. We slowed to a trot and started looking for a place to hole up for the rest of the night so I could doctor myself up, and come up with a plan of some sort.

When I made my break I'd run south, so now I worked my way back north until I got back to the river. Then I found a big patch of willows and used that palomino's big chest to burrow into the middle where there was a small clearing. I felt fairly safe. My left shoulder was starting to ache real bad and had stiffened up...but that arrow was the second thing I had to take care of...right after taking that horse down to the river, fifty feet away, for a much needed and well deserved drink. I literally owed my life to that palomino.

After both of us had drunk our fill I went back into the willows. I couldn't have been in the Indian camp for very long when I woke because they hadn't even gotten around to taking the bedroll off Mr. Worthington's horse yet; so I still had whatever had been in his pack. I used a large drinking mug he had to carry some water back into my hiding spot.

As for the arrow, I was about as lucky as a feller can be that's got an arrow sticking out of him. After going through the deer hide, it hadn't hit nothing but muscle, and wasn't in very far. A quick jerk and a small yelp, I had it out! Also in the pack, thank you Lord, was a nearly full bottle of whiskey.

I put a little on the hole in my arm, and a little on each of the many burn marks I had all over my upper body; which started them burning all over again. Then I put several long pulls into my stomach for medicinal purposes. About the time I was done doing all the doctorin' I could do, and was comfortable enough to lay down and get some rest, the sun started coming up.

I knew I had to get started finding the Worthingtons, God only knew what kind of danger they were in right now! But I also knew I wasn't gonna be any good to anybody if I wasn't able to think or fight. I lay down and managed about two hours of very uneasy, but much needed rest.

After I woke up, I cut a leather strip from the bottom of my shirt and made three laces so I could tie the front back together. I repacked the bedroll, got the horse and myself a drink, and headed back the way I'd come. My plan was to make my way back to where we'd been ambushed and see if I could follow another set of tracks other than the group that I'd been with. Then I hoped by the time I found the Worthingtons I'd have a plan. This was, of course, all assuming I could find them alive and able to be rescued!

As I headed back along the river to find the ambush site, I couldn't help but ponder on the mess I was in. I'd lost the Worthingtons, could barely use my left arm, had burns and bruises all over my body, had no food, and no real idea what the hell I was gonna do! On the bright side, if I lived through this, I probably wouldn't be asked to guide anymore.

Chapter Twelve

Finding the spot where the Indians had attacked us was easy. It was further back along the trail than I thought it was gonna be, but I found it easy enough. Reading the tracks, coming and going, was another matter. The best I could decipher it, a large group came at us from the northeast. They must've crossed the river a ways back, and followed our trail right to us. Leaving the campsite I could only see one group of tracks, lots of horses, headin' west, upriver. I followed.

A half-mile or so upriver I found the spot that I figured to be where the group that took me had broken away from the main party. I could recognize the shoe prints of that big palomino among the Indian ponies. The rest went on a piece, then crossed over the river. The Platte isn't a very deep river, moving through the mostly flat country it does, but it was still running deeper than usual with spring runoff and the recent rains. We hadn't had to ford the river yet, and I wasn't sure about how that palomino was gonna act. I didn't need to worry. I walked him down to the river edge, and with just a nudge of my knees he entered the river and went straight across no problem. I picked up the Indian trail again and continued to follow. Not long after leaving the river the trail turned north, into the hills.

As I moved up a draw between two hills, the trail I was following split again. One set of tracks heading north up the draw, the other swingin' around east over the hill to my right. I got down and studied the hoof marks. There were so many it was hard to make any sense of them, and I saw prints of horses wearing shoes among both sets. It looked to me like maybe they'd split up their prisoners again. I thought there were more shod tracks going straight, so that's the set I followed.

Within a mile I spotted a thin wisp of smoke rising up over the hilltops to my left. There wasn't a lot of cover, the hills still being mostly covered with sagebrush, so I stayed down in the valley, between the hills, and moved slow and careful.

I crossed over the top of the hill several hundred feet above the camp, then worked my way back down so I could get a look. The Indian camp was set up along a creek that ran from higher ground down to empty into the Platte. The camp was a smaller group than what had captured me; looking to be not more than thirty or so. This bunch had fewer women and children with it. There were tepees set up in two rows. The first was set twenty feet or so back from the creek, the next twenty feet back from the first line. There was a large fire ring at the far end of the two rows. Over near the creek, where the trees grew, tied to two different trees, were Mr. and Mrs. Worthington. Mr. Worthington was either unconscious or asleep, as his head hung down onto his chest, a little trickle of blood coming from his nose. Sandra was awake, and even from this distance I could see the terror in her face. Her eyes were wide open and her head moved from side to side trying to watch everything and everyone at the same time; my heart ached to see her like that.

So, I'd found them! Now all I had to do was get them free without getting caught or killed! No problem!

I needed a plan.

The creek was lined with trees and brush. The Worthingtons were tied to a pair of birch trees. Since the trees along the creek were the only cover anywhere, that's where my rescue plan had to start. If I could get behind the Worthingtons without being seen I'd have a chance.

I backtracked, crossed over to the other ravine, and dropped down below the Indian camp. I made my way into the trees along the creek about a quarter-mile below the camp and I left my horse tied to a tree with plenty of slack so he could reach the grass to feed and the water to drink. I worked my way on foot up towards the camp till I could see the fire ring, now on the near side, and a couple tepees through the trees, then I settled down in some thick brush to wait till dark.

I woke with a start, and had no idea where I was! I lay there and stared at a single blade of grass that was slowly waving back and forth in front of me, for a full five seconds before it all came back. About the time I remembered where I was, I realized I was hearing someone talking and laughing. I slowly rolled onto my back and rose up onto my elbows. It was evening and the sun had dropped behind the hilltops.

About fifty feet up the creek from my hiding spot were three Indian squaws walking down the creek and headin' my way. As they walked and talked they bent and checked the undergrowth and in amongst the trees. I figured they must've been looking for mushrooms or something. I knew for a fact they were gonna find a mountain man if they kept coming down the creek. They were too close for me to back out and move without being seen. They were within thirty feet and I did my best to fold my six and a half foot body around a tall wide-leafed weed that grew in amongst the brush patch I was hiding in. I'm pretty sure some parts were still sticking out.

They were within twenty feet and I was nearly in a full panic. *Do I jump up and run?* They moved even closer. *Do I let them stumble onto me?* They were a dozen feet away, and I was a heartbeat away from jumping up and runnin' for my life, when one of the squaws let out a delighted yelp and ran off to her left pointing to some juniper growing up away from the creek. The other two joined her, they dropped down to their knees, and started gathering up some morels.

When they were done, two of them headed back towards camp. The third said something to the others, turned, and headed straight for the bushes where I was laying. How I kept from jumping up and runnin' as she got closer I don't know. I'll credit it to instinct, although the truth be known I was probably just too damn scared to move. That Indian girl walked up to within five feet of my boots. I lay there and prayed she wouldn't look behind her. She didn't. She stood for a few seconds, turned and headed back to camp. I realized then that I hadn't been breathin'! I took in a lungful of air, and moved a couple hundred feet further down the creek to wait for full dark.

As daylight followed the sun over the hills to the west and was replaced by a deep violet sky, I tried to come up with a plan. Getting the Worthingtons loose wasn't gonna be an easy trick, made a whole lot harder by the fact that I didn't have a clue in hell what it was I was gonna do. I'd gone through Mr. Worthington's bed roll on the palomino and found a lot of stuff that didn't help a damned bit. There was a small hunting knife in a sheath that I could certainly use, but other than that there wasn't much; a drinking cup, half a bottle of whiskey, the load fixings for Mr. Worthington's rifle, which I didn't have, a piece of rope, and some odds and ends. I took the knife, the rope, and the bag of gunpowder and balls, just in case I should somehow get my hands on a flintlock.

As I cautiously made my way back up the creek, the evening darkened and the stars began to fill the sky. I worked my way up the creek to where I could see the Indians' campfire burning, then I moved over to the other side of the creek, opposite the camp, and started moving up, real slow and careful like.

When I got closer I got down on my hands and knees and crawled through the underbrush growing at the foot of the trees. I was nearly even with the campfire when my left hand came down on something that damn near made me yell out loud. It was sticky, slimy, and nasty; and the smell! If you've ever smelled a rotting carcass I don't need to describe it to you, and if you haven't, I can't describe it to you.

When I stuck my hand in it I damn near screamed. Then the smell hit me, and I damn near puked. It turned out to be a large dead owl. I tossed it into the brush, cleaned off my hand the best I could, and continued on.

The Worthingtons were located between the fire and where the tepees began. I belly crawled until I was right across the creek from the trees they were tied to. I still didn't have a plan!

The Indians had built up the fire to a real blaze and had begun to dance around in a circle and chant. As they danced they would look over toward the prisoners. I don't know a lot about Indian doings, but I was fairly sure they weren't getting ready to turn the Worthingtons loose. Over by one of the tepees closest to the fire I saw the medicine man. He was chanting, praying, smearing stuff all over his face, and sticking feathers in his hair. I had a flicker of an idea. After the medicine man got all gussied up, he started dancing and chanting his way over toward the prisoners. I got the feeling I was runnin' out of time. The half-assed idea I'd had was crazy, but it was the only half-assed idea I could come up with. I backed away and headed back down the creek.

With a three-quarter moon and the stars shining, it wasn't a pitch black night, but it was mighty dark in amongst those trees. It took me a while to find where I'd thrown that owl carcass. When I found it, I made my way back up so I was across from the Worthingtons. The medicine man was directly in front of them doing his medicine man dance and sayin' all sorts of stuff that I'm pretty sure wasn't wishing the Worthingtons well. Most of the Indians in camp had gathered around to take part in the fun. I backed up so there was more cover between me and them and I went to work.

First I took out the gunpowder skin and then the small piece of flint rock I'd always kept in my pocket. I'd nearly forgotten it was there since we had a couple fire steels we'd been using daily. I poured the gunpowder out onto a pile of dried leaves and some moss I pulled off a tree. I found a dead pine branch with lots of needles on it. When I had everything ready I checked the scene one more time.

I was behind the Worthingtons so I couldn't see their faces, but just from watching how they fought and struggled against the ropes holding them, I could imagine how scared they were. The medicine man was right up close now, throwin' dirt or some damn thing on them while he continued his chant. The rest of the Indians were dancing and jumping around, getting all worked up into a frenzy. Something bad was gonna happen, and real soon! It was time to save the Worthingtons; or die trying!

I hurried back to my pile. I used the blade from the knife and scraped across the flint rock to send sparks onto the gunpowder, moss, and leaves. When the powder took off and the leaves caught fire I thought I'd be noticed too soon, but the noise coming from across the creek didn't change. I sheathed the knife and put it in my pocket, then I grabbed up that dead owl in my right hand, picked up the pine branch in my left hand, offered up a quick prayer to cover my stupidity, and laid that branch down onto the fire.

The branch caught with a rush, and commenced to burning. I held the owl up, face forward, about head high. I held the burning pine branch behind and over the owl. I'd nearly forgotten about my hurt shoulder until I lifted that burning branch up, my shoulder screamed in protest, but I had no choice, and forced my arm up even higher. I then took to howling and carryin' on like I figured a God on the warpath would sound like. Carrying my burning owl's head, and screamin' like a madman I went running full speed through the trees, across the creek, and right into the middle of that medicine man's party.

What I was hoping would happen, was that they'd think I was an angry God come to punish them, and they'd get shook up enough that I'd have time to cut the Worthingtons loose and we could make a run for it in the chaos.

What I expected to happen was that they'd see it was nothing but some damn fool with a burning stick and a dead bird and fill me full of arrows.

I certainly didn't expect what *did* happen! When I came rushing across that creek holding the owl and burning pine branch, that medicine man's eyes got about the size of a half-dollar, his chanting turned into a sort of choking sound, and he fell over backwards in a dead faint right on the spot! Folks, I gotta tell ya, it was plumb comical how the rest of them Indians started screaming and took off runnin' for the hills like the devil himself was on their heels. There weren't that many of them, and there were lots of hills, but they were still running over each other trying to get away. In about three shakes of a dog's tail there were only four people left in camp; the Worthingtons, me, and the medicine man still out cold on the ground.

I cut the Worthingtons loose and pointed up the creek to the right.

"The horses are up the creek behind the tepees! Run for the horses!" I yelled.

That's when I discovered a major flaw in my scheme. They both dropped to the ground like gunny sacks full of rocks and lay there. They'd been tied to those trees so long they'd lost the use of their legs; which makes running for your life more of a challenge. Those Indians weren't gonna stay fooled for long! The Worthingtons were both flopping around like fish out of water trying to get feeling back, but it wasn't gonna happen soon enough. I ran for the horses.

The horses were all tethered to some willows on the other side of the tepees. Sure enough, three of our horses were with them. I ripped the tethers loose, grabbed all three reins, and ran back to where the Worthingtons waited. As I ran I saw a couple of Indians on the top of the nearest hill watching. Mr. Worthington had made it to a sitting position and was rubbing his legs. Sandra was still lying on the ground with her hands trying to work life back into hers. She was rocking back and forth in pain as the blood returned.

By the time I got back to them I heard the Indians starting to yell at each other. They'd be comin' soon! With no time to be polite, I picked Sandra up and laid her across one horse. Mr. Worthington was trying to get up on his own. I grabbed him under the arms and damn near threw him up onto its back. The Indians had started screaming and some of the bucks were running back towards camp. I jumped onto the last mount, grabbed the rein from Sandra's and headed down the creek.

We had to go fast, but with Sandra just draped over the saddle, I had to be real careful not to bounce her off. Luckily, by the time we got to where the palomino waited, her arms and legs was coming around a little, and she was able to sit up and take her own reins. I took the time to jump from the horse I was on to the palomino, and down the creek we raced. We could hear the Indians taking up the chase behind us.

The first little ways we were in the trees, and couldn't pick up a lot of speed. Then the hills pulled back a bit and the land beside the creek flattened out. That palomino sensed we were runnin' for our lives again and took off like the wind. I looked back over my shoulder and saw I was leaving the Worthingtons behind. I reined in a bit and waited for them to catch up.

"Go ahead...you lead!" I yelled at Mr. Worthington as he drew up to me. I figured to keep them in front of me so I wouldn't outrun them. Mr. Worthington flew by; Sandra close behind. As I started to follow, the Indians broke from the trees, saw us, and took to howling and urging their horses faster. I knew I could easily outrun them, but I wasn't so sure about the Worthingtons.

I knew when we got nearer to the river the land was gonna flatten out even more. Except for the palomino I rode, I didn't know if our quarter horses could outrun the smaller Indian mustangs. If we stayed ahead long enough I was pretty sure their smaller horses would tire before ours. I glanced behind. They were closer! This wasn't gonna be a long chase. We still had a considerable lead, but they were definitely gaining ground.

Then, up ahead, I saw what could be our chance. A hundred yards ahead or so the hills drew down nearer the creek, and over the hilltop I could see the black silhouette of trees against the black night sky moving up the draw to our right. I nudged that palomino and he sped up and easily passed Sandra, then Mr. Worthington, who was leading the spare horse.

"Follow me! We're going up the draw to the right!" I shouted as I took the lead. I wasn't sure if he'd heard me or not. We couldn't let the Indians see us slow down, so I kept up top speed going around the end of the hill, then had to rein in hard to slow that big horse down enough to make the sharp turn up into the draw. As we headed up into the tree-covered ravine between the hills I was awful glad to see it looked like it had heavy cover. There was a little side creek running down to empty into the bigger creek below; which accounted for all the growth. We got three or four hundred feet up the draw, that palomino breaking trail through the underbrush with his chest when I noticed the waterfall ahead of us. The moonlight was reflecting off the falling water and for most of a second I admired the beauty, then I realized the low sandstone cliffs that the waterfall was coming off of were the end of the line. I'd led us up into a dead end! The draw continued for a couple hundred feet more, then ended abruptly at the falls.

I let the Worthingtons ride ahead of me. I turned to watch the Indians, hopefully, ride past. In the dark it was hard to see well. The Indian in the lead came into view and reined up hard. He yelled something back over his shoulder and continued on down the main creek. The other Indians began to follow. I almost made the mistake of taking an easy breath when the last two braves in line turned and started coming up our way. They must have known it was a dead end because they moved slow, looking and checking the underbrush real careful like. They knew that if we were up there we weren't going anywhere!

I signaled to the Worthingtons to keep moving up the stream, and whispered to hide the best they could. Then I dismounted and led my horse down into the water. There was a downed tree lying kitty-corner across the creek. The grass and weeds had grown especially thick along its trunk. Putting that big horse right up against the bank beside the tree, he was as hidden as he could be. I hunkered down under his neck and waited. I couldn't see them, but as they got closer I could hear those two Indians making their way up the draw. Soon they were even with my spot. They stopped. I could hear at least one of them working his way down to the creek. He would have to step into the water to see us standing up against the bank in the dark. When I heard his moccasin touch the water I was gonna attack. It never did.

I guess he didn't figure it was worth getting his feet wet.

I heard him turn and go back, and then they both continued up the draw. I left the palomino there, and followed on foot.

I stayed close enough to keep them in sight. They were moving slow enough that it was no trouble. I didn't know what the Worthingtons would do, so I needed to be as close as possible without getting spotted. The two braves had gone about a hundred more feet or so when one of them let out a howl and they both hurried forward. They'd found the Worthingtons! I took off up the draw at a run.

I busted through some brush and there were the Indian ponies. I hadn't heard any more yelling or sounds of fighting. I hurried forward and made my way around an outcropping of sandstone, and there they were. Standing in front of two downfallen trees, at the end of the ravine, stood Mr. and Mrs. Worthington. Twenty feet in front of them, with their backs to me, stood the Indians. They had bows and arrows, but didn't seem anxious to use them. I guess they wanted their prisoners alive. As I watched, Mr. Worthington stepped forward.

"Come on you damn savages!" he yelled at them. "You may win, but I swear you'll pay dearly for our lives!" He squared up, bent forward a little, and looked for all the world like one of those wrestlers I've seen at Rendezvous. You know, when they're circlin' one another, eying each other before they actually take to wrestling? Those two Indian bucks looked at each other and seemed to come to an agreement. They both reached for an arrow.

All the while the Indians and Mr. Worthington were having their little standoff, I'd been slowly moving up behind them. I didn't know if the Worthingtons had seen me or not; they hadn't made any sign. All that mattered was that the Indians didn't know I was there.

As both braves reached over their backs for an arrow I realized there was no way in hell I was gonna get to them in time to stop their shots. I picked up a short, stout log lying there, and threw it with all my might. It hit the Indian farthest away from me on the

100

arm as he was reaching back for his arrow, then clipped the back of his head. I was running as I threw, and by the time the one nearest to me had turned around I was nearly on him. I didn't even remember pulling out the knife, but suddenly it was there in my hand. The Indian was bringing his bow up, but by then I was too close. Before he could draw back I was there. I knocked the bow away with my left arm and slashed with my right. An ugly red line appeared from just below his left ear across his neck and down onto his right chest. I kept moving. The one I'd hit with the log hadn't been hurt, only shook up for a second. He'd recovered and was aiming his bow.

Dammit, I was gonna be late again!

As he let his arrow fly I dove as hard as I could at his feet. I hit the ground, rolled once, and made contact. With a very satisfying yelp of surprise that Indian buck crumbled under my weight and went down. I rolled over once more and came up on top of him. I hit him hard in the side of the head with my right fist, followed by my left fist to the other side of his head, followed by my right fist, followed by my left fist, followed by my right fist...until my arms got tired and I had to quit. As I sat on his chest trying to catch my breath, that young Indian brave took his last breath. His eyes went blank and started clouding over.

I crawled off him and collapsed. I felt like I'd been running uphill for days. It was all I could do to sit up and see where the Worthingtons were. They were standing over the other Indian. His throat was cut and he'd bled out; I could see the dark pool on the ground. His sightless eyes were staring up into the sky. I'd never seriously hurt another person my whole life; but in those couple minutes I'd killed two men. As that reality struck home I turned away from the Worthingtons and puked. Then I walked down the creek to where I'd left the palomino. I knew we didn't have much time, but I needed to be alone.

By the time the Worthingtons made their way down to where I waited, I'd made a sort of peace with myself. Taking a man's life, with just reason or not, is a hard thing to do. I guess it's a damn good thing that it is. I knew I'd had no choice in the matter, but it was still tough for me to stomach. Two young men would never grow up...because of me. Their mothers would never get to see them again...because of me. Hell, they may've had wives and children. I knew deep down inside that I'd done what I had to do, but that didn't make it any easier.

We made our way down out of the draw and headed back up the main creek to the next valley that forked off to the east. We followed it up and away from the Indian camp as fast as those horses could go. We ran all out for a long time, following first one valley leading to the next valley, then the next. We had to be several miles away when I finally stopped. I had no idea where the hell we were; and didn't care as long as those Indians couldn't find us.

I found a little spring bubbling up out of the ground in a narrow, steep-sided ravine. There were some trees for cover, and plenty of sweet green grass for the horses. I dismounted and quickly hobbled the palomino and the other horse I'd been leading. Mr. Worthington had dismounted and was working on rigging a hobble for his horse. Sandra still sat her horse. I went to help her get down, but when I saw the look in her eyes I froze. A truer, more pure look of agony and despair I've never seen; or will ever see.

"My baby...Mount...those savages have my baby!" She started to cry. She turned and looked to where Mr. Worthington stood watching. "Andrew, they have our baby boy! We have to get him! We have to help him!" She collapsed. Luckily I was standing right there. I caught her as she slid off the horse, carried her over near the spring, and laid her down in the soft grass. She looked up at me, her eyes pleading. "Save my son Mount. Please...you must save my son!"

Chapter Thirteen

Never, in my whole damned life, had I ever felt so helpless. Mr. and Mrs. Worthington sat by the spring. Mr. Worthington even went so far as to put his hand on Sandra's shoulder. It was the first time I'd ever seen him show any sort of tenderness to either Sandra or Andy. I'd walked a little ways back down the draw, so I could be alone to think, and to keep an eye out. Then was one hell of a time to start being careful, huh? What a guide I'd turned out to be! I'd known we were in hostile Indian Territory since leaving Fort Kearny, and didn't even think about posting a lookout at night. There was no excuse for my stupidity!

As I sat on the hillside, I tried to come up with a plan to find and rescue Andy; without letting my mind wander to the horrible things that could be happening to him. Or maybe not...I'd heard of tribes that actually would adopt captured white children into the tribe, turning them into Indians; or at least tryin'. There was a band of Flathead Indians that lived somewhere in the mountains back home that'd stopped and visited with Ma and Pa a few times that had a white brave among 'em. He'd seemed as much Indian as any of the others. I assume he'd been raised by them since a baby. Not that it mattered whether Andy was being tortured or treated like an Indian Chief; we needed to find him and get him back!

Where do we start? I had no idea where the group that had Andy could be. It might be possible to backtrack and find him like I had the Worthingtons, but the tracks were older and the hills were crawling with Indian braves looking to take our scalps...or even worse for Sandra. The bedrolls had all been taken from the horses, so between the three of us we had what'd been left on the palomino; a large tin mug, a knife, some rope, half a bottle of whiskey, one blanket, and a piece of oilcloth wrapped around it all, not exactly living high on the hog.

I sat on that hillside all night long thinking. Somewhere along the way I came up with what was gonna have to pass as a plan. I worked it out the best I could, then lay back and dozed for a couple hours till the sun started coming up. When it was light enough to see, I went looking for breakfast.

It didn't take but fifteen minutes or so. The spring went underground a couple hundred feet down the little draw, but the water must've been close to the surface cause there was plenty growing. Ma and Pa had both been knowledgeable in the ways of edible plants and such, something you damn well better know to survive mountain living.

I came back to where the Worthingtons were waiting with a hat full of breakfast. Mr. Worthington sat up on the hillside and Sandra sat down near the spring wrapped in the blanket. As I approached she looked up. The empty, haunted look in her eyes scared the hell out of me. She was in far more pain now than with any damned ole broke leg.

I sat down next to Sandra and put my hat full of foodstuff on my lap. It had to be moving into the latter part of June by now, but the burdock, thistle, curly-dock root, and lamb's quarters were all still fairly young and tender. If we would've had something to cook in, and a few spices, I could've made a right tasty soup. I peeled a young burdock stem and handed it to Sandra.

"Here, chew on this," I said. I put it into her hand. Her hand went to her mouth and she started chewing like she was lost in some sort of trance; as though her mind couldn't handle what it'd been thinkin', so it'd simply shut down. Mr. Worthington moved down to join us, and sat on the other side of Sandra. Using the knife, I cleaned up a burdock root, broke it in half, and handed him a piece.

"What's this?" he asked, wrinkling up his nose.

"That'd be breakfast," I answered. "The best I can do. All we got is a knife with a four-inch blade; meat's liable to be pretty scarce for a while.

Mr. Worthington took a bite, made a disgusted face, and spit the burdock root out. "That's horrible!" he exclaimed, throwing the piece of root he held on the ground. I handed him a lamb's quarters stem.

"Peel that and try it. It's the best we got, so eat or go hungry." I took a bite of burdock root and started chewing. I hoped he didn't see the small shudder that I just couldn't stop; the bitter burdock root wasn't quite elk steak. Mr. Worthington seemed to do better with the lamb's quarter.

The three of us ate fairly well actually; once we got started, we realized just how famished we really were. Mr. Worthington and I anyway; I don't think Sandra realized much of nothing. She'd closed herself off somehow…to protect herself from the pain I guess…but she'd blocked out the whole world. She ate whatever I handed her, staring down into the spring. I polished off my meal with a couple of grasshoppers; Mr. Worthington didn't care for any. When we'd finished, and each had a long drink of spring water, it was time to talk.

"Now folks, we're in quite a fix here, and that ain't fooling," I started. "I blame myself for everything that's happened…and for that, I'm truly sorry." Mr. Worthington was looking square at me and it was obvious he blamed me too. Sandra still stared down into the flowing water. "Now I know that finding Andy and getting him back is the most important thing." At that Sandra's head turned, and those pain-filled eyes locked on mine. I swallowed hard, and went on. "But Andy isn't the only concern we need to think about." It was a bad choice of words.

"Yes he is!" Sandra fairly shouted. "My son is the only important thing!" Her eyes showed pure anger now. "We have to get him back!" Her voice broke; then she did. "We have to get my baby back." She drew her knees up to her chest, wrapped her arms around her legs, and started rocking back and forth crying. "We have to get my baby; we have to get my baby!"

I turned to Mr. Worthington; he was watching his wife with his own pained look in his eyes. I was beginning to think maybe he just might have emotions just like anybody else; he just didn't know how to let them out. He looked up at me and his eyes got hard again and very serious.

"What are you suggesting we do then?" he asked.

"Well, the way I see it, we got us a whole bushel basket of problems." I was still planning as I talked. "Yes...we need to find Andy and get him back. But, we need to stay free and alive to do that. These hills are filled with Indians lookin' for us. Also, we don't have any weapons, we don't have any food, or much of anything else." Sandra's crying had slowed and she sat listening.

"The way I figure it, we should be about two weeks out from Fort Laramie," I began.

"No!" I really wished Sandra wouldn't shout out like that with them Indians roaming the hills lookin' to take our scalps. "No! We are not leaving without Andy! I won't abandon my son!" She started to cry again, but her eyes never left mine.

"Now Sandra, that ain't at all what I'm suggesting." I needed to get them both to understand the fix we were in. "But the three of us just go hightailing it around the hills until we stumble on the right camp. That'd do nothing but get us all tied to a tree somewhere again...or worse. I ain't saying we don't look for Andy, but we need to be smart and think it through." They were both looking at me with questions in their eyes.

"What I think we need to do is make our way back down to the Platte River and the Oregon Trail. I need to give the two of you a couple lessons in what plants you can eat and, more importantly, which ones you can't. I also have an idea or two to get some meat." I didn't give them a chance to interrupt. "Then my idea is to have the two of you follow the trail upriver to Fort Laramie, being real careful, traveling under cover when possible, and hiding good when you stop to rest. As long as the two of you can find food enough to keep going on your own, I plan to find Andy and bring him back."

"I don't like it," Mr. Worthington said. "I don't think we should split up. We are safer staying together."

"Well sir, if we was gonna hightail it for Fort Laramie as quick as we could, I'd agree," I replied. "But the three of us together searching the hills for Andy just ain't a good idea. First off, one man and one horse have a much better chance of going about unnoticed. Second, with your permission, I'd like to take the palomino so I know I can outrun those Indians if I have to. I don't know that the other horses can do that. And third, if I was to get caught, which I'm not planning on, I'd be obliged if the two of you would get to Fort Laramie and inform the army. Might be, they could rescue Andy and me."

"I still don't like it." It seemed Mr. Worthington had his mind set. "I don't think separating is a good idea. We have more of a chance if there is trouble with the three of us together."

I looked into his eyes. Behind the stubborn, and behind the anger, kinda leaking out around the sides, was fear. Mr. Worthington was afraid of their being on their own. I think Sandra had read his eyes too.

"Andrew." Her voice was firm. She'd gotten herself under some sort of control, and although her hands were twisting nonstop around each other as she spoke, and the fear and pain were still there in her eyes, her brain had kicked in and started to function again. "Andrew, Mount is right. If you think it through, Mount's idea makes sense." She even worked up a sorry looking bit of a smile "You and I will be just fine. We can move slow, stay hidden, and forage for food along the way. We'll be all right." She sounded like she really meant it. Then she looked at me, and the fear and pain grew in her eyes. "You will find him, won't you Mount?" Her eyes and voice pleaded with me. "You will find my baby and bring him back to me won't you?"

"Well now Sandra, that's my plan." I tried to smile. How do I give them a feeling of hope that I didn't all together feel myself? Finding Andy and getting him back was not gonna be easy. "Shoot, I'll probably have him and join up with you two in just a day or so." I smiled what I hoped was a confident smile. Mr. Worthington looked from Sandra to me and back again then shook his head and walked to the horses. He mounted the chestnut mare and left the palomino for me.

It took us most of the day to work our way back down to the Platte. We'd gone farther north than I'd thought, and I made sure we traveled slow and careful. I scouted out around every turn and over every hilltop as we went.

When the gully we were following opened up and the land flattened out to the river below, I found a fairly well-hidden spot, and had the Worthingtons wait while I scouted. I made my way down to the river, eagle-eyeing all four directions for any movement. I'd hoped beyond hope that there would be a group of settlers passing by on the trail, or better yet, a regiment of cavalry would've been nice, but no such luck. When I got to the river I felt safer as there was growth of some sort almost always along the river bank. If there weren't trees there were at least tall grasses, weeds, and brush, along with a lot of willow and such. Of course, what was cover for me could also be cover for the Indians, so I went with care.

Within a couple miles the small rolling hills that'd been to the north flattened out and the plains returned. I wasn't sure if that was good news or bad. I made my way back to where the Worthingtons were waiting. It was near dark when I got there.

"A couple miles upriver these hills flatten out," I explained. "It's plains as far as I can see after that. Now that means a couple things. I figure the Indians will stay in the hills near their camps. That helps us in two ways. It reduces my search area, and I don't think you two will have to worry as much once you're clear of the hills. The bad thing for you is that it limits where you can hide. I want you to still travel real careful, staying hidden when you can, all the way to Fort Laramie; no matter how safe you might feel." Mr. Worthington had seemed to accept the fact that this was the way it was gonna be. He didn't have anything to say, but he nodded that he understood.

Now we needed some real food. With the little light that was left I did some scouting. When I got back, shortly after dark, I explained my plan to a very doubtful looking couple. I think Mr. Worthington actually snorted his disbelief.

None of us had slept much the night before. We were still worried and scared, but at least now we had a plan of sorts, and we all slept much better. Sandra lay in some tall grass beside the spring, wrapped in the one and only blanket. Mr. Worthington lay a few feet away with the oilcloth cover over him. I moved up the draw a little and kept watch for several hours, then lay back and fell asleep.

I got the Worthingtons up nearly an hour before sunup. I could tell from their looks that they still didn't give my idea much of a chance, but they came along willingly enough.

The spot I'd picked was a half-mile or so down the main river valley, where a good-sized creek emptied into the Platte. Up the creek, into the draw a couple hundred feet, there was a place where a smaller side-creek met up with the bigger one. The smaller one was dry already. Where the two creeks met there was a pool, and all around the pool there were deer tracks.

I picked the game trail that looked most used, and up the trail twenty feet from the pond was the spot I was lookin' for. The game trail ran down beside the smaller creek to the pool between two large cottonwoods. I took the rope we had and tied one end to the tree nearest the deer's route, about two feet up on the main trunk. The other end Mr. Worthington held while he sat in some tall grass and brush behind the other tree. I put Sandra up the game trail a couple hundred feet, on the downwind side of the trail and hidden in the grass behind some deadfall. I went back to the trees and climbed up onto a branch about eight feet or so above the ground. We waited.

As daylight slowly grew from just a hint and promise in the east to full-fledged day, I watched the night world slip away and the day world come to life. The deer, being comfortable in both worlds, weren't in any hurry to get to bed, and sure enough it wasn't long till a small band came down the trail heading for a drink before turnin' in. Sandra waited for them to pass like she'd been told, then started making just enough noise, by knocking a couple sticks together, to spook the deer a little, but not send them into full flight. It worked perfectly. They sped up to a trot and came down the trail toward the pool. As they came I picked out a smaller sized doe; she was the third one in line.

Just as the lead deer got to the trees, Mr. Worthington pulled the rope up tight. The deer were moving fast enough that the first two went clear down to the ground. The one I had my eye on stumbled over the others and dropped to her knees. At that second I plunged out of the tree and landed square on her back, driving her down to the ground. I wrapped my legs around her belly, reached around her neck with my left arm, pulled back as hard as I could, and started stabbing and sawing at her throat with the knife.

She decided not to die without a fight. That damned deer took to twisting and rolling around like a wild bronc. She never did quite make it all the way up onto her feet, but it was still one hell of a ride. At one point, when we rolled over, my right leg came loose from around her belly and I felt a hoof slice across my leg. Then she rolled backwards somehow and I started to slip off. I held on tighter and kept sawing with that little knife! A couple more turns and twists and I lost my grip. I slipped off over her front shoulder headed directly for under her front hooves. Hooves I already knew were like razors. I was in trouble.

As I hit the ground I tried to roll away. I felt the deer thrash against my back, then nothing for a second, then she came crashing down on top of me. I covered my head the best I could, and waited for the slashing hooves to start tearing me to pieces. They never came. I lay covered up for several seconds before I realized the deer wasn't moving. Carefully, I uncovered my face and looked. She lay over top of me with her head near my chest. Her throat lay open, and both of us were covered in blood. Most of it hers; some of it mine.

I had a bad gash on my lower leg from her hoof, a bloodied nose, and a horrible gut ache from landing astraddle that deer's back and mashing my private parts.

Like I've said before, I've killed hundreds of animals for food, and I felt a little bad for each and every one of them; for a short while anyway. Not this time!

When I got untangled from that deer and stood up, I felt like I'd taken on the whole damned Sioux Nation and kicked their asses. I nearly let out a hoop and a holler, but remembered in time that the hills were filled with Sioux braves looking for us. I settled for doing a little jig around my kill, then set to work.

If you've never gutted and skinned a deer with a dull four inch blade, I don't recommend it.

After the deer was cleaned out, and I got scrubbed up, we moved back up the draw a ways to where there was heavy cover. I found some very dry deadfall, started a small belly fire, and showed Sandra how to feed the dry branches on real slow like as to make as little smoke as possible. While she built up a good bed of coals, Mr. Worthington helped me butcher the deer. We cut the meat in strips. I cut some live willows and fashioned a hanger over the coals. We spent nearly all day slow cooking that deer. By evening we had enough jerked venison to last a couple weeks with care. All three of us, all day long, were nearly sick with worry and concern for Andy, and I was chompin' at the bit to get looking for him, but we also knew the need for food.

We were all too anxious to sleep, so early next morning we were ready to go. I kept the knife, the rope, the piece of oilcloth that covered the bedroll, and some of the jerky. The Worthingtons took what was left; which wasn't much.

On the way out of the draw I pointed out those plants that were edible, and the ones that weren't. I taught them that if they weren't sure to just take a small bite and wait half an hour or so; if you're not cramping up or puking it's probably okay to take two bites. I gave them a chunk of my flint rock and had Mr.

Worthington make a fire so I knew he could do it. They were as ready as I could make them under the circumstances.

We got to the river, and back to the Oregon Trail, without any excitement. We made our way upriver, staying near the water under cover, rather than traveling on the trail itself. When we got to where the hills flattened and the plains took over, it was time to split up.

"Now you folks be careful. Travel hidden whenever you can, and hide good when you stop to rest." I put on my most confident smile, and tried to muster some certainty into my voice. "I'll go get Andy and meet up with you in a couple days at the most."

Mr. Worthington swallowed hard, simply nodded, turned, and rode slowly away. I knew he was scared clear to the bone and fighting within himself for the resolve to do what needed done. I'm not sure why, Mr. Worthington hadn't shown me much backbone, but I had the feeling that when it came down to it, he'd do just fine.

Sandra was fighting within herself for control too. She was trying awful hard not to break down.

"You get him Mount. You get my son and bring him back to me." Anger suddenly took over from the pain in her voice. "Get him, and then you kill those savages that stole him from us. You hear me Mount...you kill them!" I'd never heard such pure hate in my life.

Sandra turned and followed Mr. Worthington. As I watched them go I really, truly hoped I would see them again someday. I looked into the heavens and offered up a little prayer, "Lord, when I see them again let me have their son with me; please Lord, let it be so."

Chapter Fourteen

I watched the Worthingtons till they were gone up river. For a long time I could see them, now and then, in the open breaks between cover. I trusted I was the only one watching, and I sure as hell hoped I'd made the right decision to send them on alone.

Being at the end of the hills like I was, it only made sense to start searching from there. That incredible palomino and I had already gotten to know each other; and I swear nearly all I had to do was think a thing and that horse did it. I thought I needed to get into the hills fast before I was spotted, and with hardly a nudge of my knees, that palomino took off like the wind. Once I got up into the hills and felt fairly safe I slowed. I knew the Indians would set up camp along a water source, so my plan was to go from draw to draw sorta ziggy and zaggy and any that had a running creek I'd check out.

The rest of that day I spent checking the western section of the hills, from where they flattened out and the prairie took over eastward. It had to be the end of June or early July. Plenty of wild flowers were still in bloom and the larger creeks were still running fairly strong, with plenty of green undergrowth along their banks, but already the grass-covered hills were starting to turn a dried out shade of faded yellow; spotted here and there with a grayish, greenish spot of sagebrush.

It was a mighty warm day; the heat lay over me like a thick wool blanket. Sometime, mid-afternoon, I stumbled on a pretty little spring coming up outta some sandstone shelves. There was water, cover, and several edible plants growing near the spring. I decided to rest there during the hottest part of the day and search more after it cooled off a touch. I ate a meal consisting of dandelion and thistle leaves, a couple grasshoppers, a piece of jerky, and a long cool drink of spring water, then I lay back in the shade to think.

I thought for about four hours, and when I woke up it was getting on towards evening. I lay in that groggy half asleep condition, remembering just where I was and what I was doing. I saw movement off to my left, woke up completely, and slowly turned. With relief, I realized it was the palomino. I'd given him a loose hobble so he could feed and drink. As I was admiring what a fine-looking horse he was, the sun dropped to just the proper angle, and hit his golden coat just right, and that horse lit up like he'd burst into a magical golden flame. The sight was so beautiful it took my breath away, and in that second I had a name for what I'd already took to thinking of as my horse.

I got up off the ground and walked to where he stood. "Goldfire." I looked into his eyes and stroked his neck. "That's your name now, Goldfire." As I stroked his neck the sun continued to shine on him and make him glow. "Yep, Goldfire fits you just fine." He lowered his head and rubbed up and down on my arm.

I spent two and a half days searching up and down the draws, valleys, gullies, arroyos, and ravines in them damn hills. For such little rolling hills the damn things seemed to go on forever. Of course, I was taking it pretty slow; traveling real careful to make sure I didn't wind up in another fix. In the two and a half days I'd come across two of the small moveable Indian camps. I'd studied each until I was sure Andy wasn't among 'em. I also saw three hunting parties with six or seven braves in each group. Were they hunting for game or for me? They'd probably take either. Just past midday of the third day my luck changed.

As I rode up yet another draw, I noticed a thin column of smoke rising up outta the next valley over. I left Goldfire and walked up onto the hill. I crawled to the edge where I could see down into the bottom of a fairly large ravine, with a strong creek running down the bottom. There, set up on the near side of the creek, was the largest Indian camp I'd seen yet; this one being more permanent looking than the others. There must'a been nearly a hundred tepees set up, a huge main fire ring near the center, which hadn't been lit yet, but was still smoking a bit; just enough to let me know they were there.

There must have been a couple hundred or more, men, women, and children stirring around like an ant pile busy at work. At the far end of the camp they had a makeshift corral built with poles stuck in the ground and rawhide strips tied from one to the other. Even from where I was I could see Skyhawk milling around amongst the Indian ponies. Since I'd found Skyhawk, I had to figure I'd found Andy too. Now what the hell to do?

Fifty feet or so up the hill from where I lay there were several juniper bushes growing together. I backed off, circled around, and came up behind them. I got down and snake crawled in under the bushes. When I'd made my way clear through till I could see out the other side and down into the valley I was hidden about as good as a man can get. I lay there studying the camp trying to spot Andy, and trying to figure a way in and out for when I did find him. I lay there for an hour or so and was just getting ready to back out when I heard riders coming in from the northeast, down a connecting gully. Five braves rode into sight, two of them had deer lying over their horses, one of them had Andy sitting behind him. I watched as they stopped up near the horse corral. The brave in front of Andy slid off, grabbed Andy's wrist and jerked him off the horse. He nearly fell, but as the brave turned and walked away, Andy was yanked upright and took a couple of running steps to catch up. That's when I noticed they were tied together. There was a length of rawhide, four or five feet worth, tied from Andy's left wrist to the right wrist of the Indian. Other than being tied to a young Indian brave's wrist, Andy looked to be okay. He wasn't injured any that I could see, and even from the top of the hill I was plumb proud to see him pullin' at the end of that tether. He hadn't given up yet. Now all I had to do was go down there and get him.

I lay under that damned juniper all afternoon watching; the hot sun beating down on me like a physical weight. I could move around a little, but my muscles were screaming. I wasn't sure if the Indian brave Andy was tethered to was his captor, protector, or owner. It looked like they'd been tied for a while because they worked well together. They watered the horse they'd ridden, let it loose in the corral, and went into camp to join a squaw by one of the tepees. There was a small fire in front of the tepee and some venison strips cooking. The brave and Andy ate, spent some time wandering around camp, then walked up past the makeshift corral and started gathering grass to feed the horses. All that time, no one in camp seemed to pay any attention at all to Andy; like he wasn't even there.

My muscles, and my bladder, wouldn't let me stay hidden any longer. I backed out, slipped down the hillside out of sight, stretched, peed, and went back to where Goldfire waited.

I moved over one more hill into the next draw, and found a fairly well-hidden spot to spend the night. I had the beginnings of a plan, but it had more holes in it than my worn-out britches.

Next morning I was under the juniper bush before sunup. Shortly after dawn, I saw the brave, with Andy in tow, along with five other men, mount their horses and head out. I was happy to see it, as my plan counted on today being a repeat of yesterday. If I was right they wouldn't be back in camp for hours.

I went back and got Goldfire. Very slowly and very cautiously we made our way over the creek, around a hill, and settled in a stand of cottonwoods and heavy brush that was across the creek and a little upstream from the horse corral. I put Goldfire on a loose tether several hundred feet further up the creek so there wouldn't be any chance of the Indian horses sensing he was there and causin' a ruckus. I settled down to wait.

Mid-afternoon, just like I'd figured, the hunting party came riding into camp. Today they had a deer, an antelope, and several rabbits. Again, just like yesterday, a group of squaws came and took over the game. Andy and his brave watered their horse, put it in the corral, and went to the tepee where today there was what looked like an iron kettle hanging over the fire on a tripod of large green branches. I wondered if they'd traded for the kettle...or killed for it. After eating a little bit, the brave lay down on a deerskin beside the tepee and seemed to go to sleep. Andy sat beside him cross-legged staring at the ground. I noticed that while taking care of the horses and the little time he'd spent in camp, Andy seemed different today. The feeling I got was that the fight seemed to be seeping out of him. He followed behind the brave with his hands folded and his eyes cast on the ground or just staring around expressionless. He was giving up.

Andy's Indian didn't nap long. Within half an hour he was up and they came back to the corral. They spent some time in amongst the horses checking them out, then sure enough, came up above the corral, just like yesterday, to gather fresh feed and dump it into the corral. I worked my way to the creek's edge and kneeled behind some bushes. There was a patch of what looked like clover directly on the other side of the creek. That was where I hoped they'd come to pick. They didn't. They were thirty feet down the creek pulling up tall grass. As I watched I noticed that while the brave bent and picked the grass, Andy mostly stood and looked around, working only when the brave forced him.

A little bend in the creek helped block my position from most of the camp, but I could still be seen if I wasn't careful. I watched until Andy was looking my general direction, then, holding my breath, I half stood and waved my arms in a flying motion to draw his attention. I saw his eyes sweep over me and keep on going; he hadn't seen me. A minute later Andy was looking my way again, and again I stood and waved, and again he didn't notice. The brave scolded him for not working, and he got busy picking for a bit. They were slowly working their way closer. They were within twenty feet or so when their arms were full and they carried their loads back down to the corral. Damn.

When they turned and headed back to continue picking, the brave started toward a patch of grass further from the creek. As they walked Andy's gaze strayed my way yet again. I stood clear up, waved both hands, and then quickly dropped back down. Andy saw! The Indian brave noticed when Andy tensed and he became instantly alert. He stared around, looking right at me a couple times. Andy did a good job of calming himself and stood staring at the ground. The Indian brave didn't see any threat and went back to picking grass. When the brave looked away, Andy looked immediately back to my bushes. I stuck my head up just enough so he could see me, and pointed to the green patch across the creek. Andy understood, he tugged at the rawhide to get the brave's attention and pointed out the sweet clover. They headed my way.

As they got to the patch of clover, Andy very casually circled around the patch and started picking. The Indian brave followed, putting his back to me as he bent over and started pulling. From where I was hidden I could see less than half of the Indian camp. I knew when I stepped out I'd be in plain sight to most of it; but there wasn't any other choice. No one I could see seemed to be paying a damn bit of attention. I took a deep breath and went to get Andy.

I stayed in a crouch and moved real slow until I got right up behind the Indian brave. He sensed something, and started to straighten up. I clobbered him on the back of the head, down low near his neck. He went out like a candle in a wind storm. As he fell I wrapped my arm around his waist and carried him backwards across the creek; Andy followed. Behind the bushes again, I dropped the brave and turned to listen if anyone in camp had noticed.

Suddenly, I was flat on my back with a laughing, crying, nearly hysterical boy on top of me. Andy knew he couldn't make much noise, but how he managed not to I don't know. He was hugging me, kissing me, jumpin' around and clapping his hands; and all nearly silent. I couldn't help but laugh too.

"I knew you'd come Mount!" He tried to keep his excitement in check. "I knew you'd come get me!" I'd worked my way to a sitting position and he threw his arms around my neck and hugged and cried. I got a little something in my eyes, and couldn't talk for a bit.

"Of course I was gonna come get you," I whispered after I got my voice back. "I still need someone to tend the fire and take care of the horses don't I? You don't expect me to do that stuff myself do you?" We both laughed as quietly as we could. Suddenly Andy's smile went away and he started to choke up again.

"Mom and Dad?" There was fear in his voice. "Are my Mom and Dad..." He couldn't finish.

"Your folks are just fine Andy." I hoped I was telling the truth. "They're on their way to Fort Laramie right now. Your ma is sure gonna be glad to see you."

A small groan escaped from the unconscious Indian laying at our feet, and that brought the danger of our situation back to me.

"My horse is up the creek aways." I whispered to Andy as I untied the rawhide from his wrist. "Let's go."

"What about Skyhawk?" There was desperation in his voice. "We can't leave Skyhawk." He saw the look in my eyes. "No Mount, we can't leave him!"

"Now Andy, there are a couple hundred Indians over..." That was as far as I got. Andy leapt back away from me and ran across the creek. When he got in full view of the camp he slowed to a walk, and just as casual as can be, meandered down to the corral, under the rawhide rope, and just as slick as you please took Skyhawk's reins, led him to the creek side of the corral, slipped under the rawhide, and crossed the creek. No one in the camp seemed to notice. I didn't know whether to hug him or paddle his ass, so I did both; the hug a little more heartfelt than the spankin'.

I threw the young Indian brave over my shoulder and we made our way up the creek to where Goldfire waited. I had to figure those Indians would notice the two of them being gone soon. By the time we got to Goldfire the Indian was waking up. I gagged him with a piece of deerskin from my britches and one end of the rawhide, tied his hands together with the other end, threw him across Goldfire in front of me, and we rode up the creek as fast as Skyhawk could go.

I led the way, being careful not to run away from Skyhawk. We'd gone maybe three miles or so when I reined up long enough to untie the Indian's hands and shove him off the horse. I heard Sandra's words. "Kill those savages that stole him from us Mount, kill them." I looked down on that Indian brave and hell; he was barely more than a kid himself. I couldn't no more kill him than I could've killed Andy. It'd probably take him forty-five minutes or so to walk back to camp; I let him go.

We were headed north. After we were out of sight of the Indian brave, at the next draw, we turned left and went up and over a hill, then northwest up another longer valley, left again at the next one. We were now making our way south towards the river; I hoped. We went as fast as Skyhawk could go, and eventually found ourselves at the edge of the hills, with the plains stretched out to the end of sight. A couple miles off to the south I could make out the line of trees that had to be the Platte River. Beside the Platte River was the Oregon Trail and Mr. and Mrs. Worthington somewhere on their way to Fort Laramie.

We still had three or four hours till dark, and I'd had my fill of those damned Indian infested hills, so we kept riding. We rode west from the hills out onto the prairie at a steady fast trot. I knew Skyhawk could keep that pace up for hours. After a mile or so, we started angling south, headed for the river. Shortly before sundown we made it to the river and the trail and I immediately began looking for a good, safe place to spend the night. Not far upriver I found it. There was a large stand of cottonwoods and willows, and right on the riverbank grew some tall grass. We picked a spot where the grass and willows met. We were well hidden, although I didn't expect the Indians to mess with us out this far away from the hills.

We hobbled the horses where they had grass and water, then prepared to spend the night; not that there was a lot of preparing to do, since we didn't have a damn thing. A fire would've been nice, just to cheer us up a bit, but I didn't feel comfortable starting one just yet.

After we'd each had a couple pieces of jerky, we settled down in the grass and got comfortable. Andy had the oil cloth cover if he needed it although it was a mighty warm night. I told Andy the story of my escape, and his folks' rescue.

He told me of the awful days tied to that Indian brave. During the nights he was bound hand and foot in a hot, smelly tepee. It must've been a living nightmare for the boy. After the story telling we both lay back, drifted off to sleep, and slept the sleep of the totally exhausted.

It was well after sunup when I woke. I looked over, and Andy wasn't lying where he should've been. I had a moment of pure panic as I scrambled to my feet, but there he was, coming back from doing his morning business.

"Good morning Mount." Damned if he didn't sound downright cheerful. "I'm starving. What's for breakfast?"

So much for his cheerful mood. I reached down and snatched up a large grasshopper. "Well, you can start with this." I held it out to him with a straight face. He looked at the grasshopper, then at me, then at the hopper again, then at me again. I believe he was actually considering it; which was more then I'd expected.

"Oh, yuck Mount." His face crinkled all up like only a kid's can do. "You don't really mean eat a grasshopper do you?"

"Well you sure can't have this one," I said. "He's too fat and juicy to give away." And I popped that hopper into my mouth and started crunching. I thought Andy was gonna faint right away.

I had a couple more hoppers, some dandelion and nettles leaves, and a young pokeweed root to top it off; a drink from the river, and I was ready to go. Andy decided to go with jerky. He did have a couple of the leaves, but wouldn't try any insects. I didn't know how long the jerky would last, but I knew it wouldn't get us to Fort Laramie; we'd be talking about eating bugs again in a few days.

Chapter Fifteen

I figured the Worthingtons had nearly a six-day head start on us. Not that it mattered much if we caught up to them before Fort Laramie or met them there, but now that I had Andy, I felt an urgency to get him back to his folks. I knew Sandra was sick with worry six days ago. I'd bet pine cones to beaver pelts that her worrying hadn't lessened any. Hell, Mr. Worthington might even be missin' his boy a little.

For the first two days, although I felt the need to hurry, I also felt the need to not get captured by Indians again, so we kept to the cover along the river. Because of that we crept along snail slow.

Late afternoon of the second day I decided we needed a change in plans; as sluggish as we were moving, the snow'd be flying before we reached Fort Laramie. I figured we could make much better time on the trail than picking our way along the river. I still wasn't comfortable traveling out in the open, so I decided we'd start traveling at night. Once I'd made the decision, I looked for the next good place to hole up for a while. I told Andy my plan, and said we needed to have something to eat, then sleep till dark. The jerky was nearly gone, and I didn't think I'd be wrestling any deer down out here in the prairie. We'd seen some buffalo off in the distance, but I didn't have any way to bring one of them down either. It was time to talk with Andy about eatin' bugs again.

"Ya hungry?" I asked, while I pulled up some curly dock for the taproot and peeled some thistle stalks.

"Yes, I'm starved...but not for that." He wrinkled up his nose and his voice turned sorta whiney. "I want some real food Mount."

"You're surrounded by real food boy!" I wasn't angry, but Andy had to understand. "You're just too damned squeamish to eat any of it."

"If you're talking about eating grasshoppers...I just don't think I can." There was more reluctance, maybe just plain ole fear, in his voice than stubborn attitude.

"I'm talking hoppers, caterpillars, grubs, crickets, and plenty more of God's creations. They're most all edible, some taste better than others, but none will make you sick, and all will keep you alive." We still had a long way to go, and I'd be damned if I was gonna risk my scalp to rescue this kid, only to have him starve to death on the trail. "Now, being back next to the water opens up some possibilities. We don't have anything to fish with but I bet we can catch us some frogs; maybe trap a beaver or snake."

"I'm not eating any snake or frog!" I think it was said before Andy even knew he'd spoken, but once it was out Andy puffed up, put his hands on his hips, and obviously meant to back up it up. I decided that maybe it was time to stop being so damned nice. I didn't really want to, but I needed to shake the boy up a little. When I stepped up next to him I was nearly a foot and a half taller.

"Now you listen, and you listen good, you little shit!" I glared down on him the way I figured God would do to me when the time came; for scarin' the hell out of a little boy. "I didn't rescue you from those Indians just so you could starve on the trail. You'll eat, and you'll eat what we got!" That may've been the longest speech, in anger, I'd ever made. Now I softened my tone. "You wanna see your ma and pa again right? You ain't gonna make it there eating a few leaves and stems."

His eyes were about to overflow, and his bottom lip was quivering faster than a riled up rattler's tail.

"Andy, I wouldn't ask you to eat anything I wouldn't eat myself." I had to get back on his good side now. "Shoot, I've eaten frog and snake plenty of times. They both taste just like your mama's fried chicken...well you know...mostly."

"We had a cook who made the fried chicken." He was still pouting, and couldn't wait to point out my mistake.

"My point being...," I replied patiently, "...is that there's plenty to eat along the trail; you just have to be willing to eat it. It's just in your head that you're not gonna like it; and if you want to catch up with your folks, you gotta eat." I'd backed off so I wasn't towering over him anymore. I looked him square in the eyes and challenged him. "Are you gonna eat and stay alive, or are you gonna stay stubborn and just waste away?"

Andy looked away. He looked at the ground, then up into the sky, seeming to study the clouds lazily rolling past. He looked both left and right, and both up and down again. He looked everywhere except back at me. He finally came to his decision. He took a deep breath, and met my eyes.

"Can't we at least cook them somehow?" There was only a touch of whine in his voice.

"You damn betcha we can cook them Andy!" I felt happier than the situation really called for. "If I had a proper pot, and a few add-ins, I could make us a dandy soup, but bugs roasted on a stick ain't bad either; you'll see." Andy's nose started to wrinkle, but then I saw his resolve set in. He set his face, squared up his shoulders, and even tried on a crooked little smile.

I got a small fire going, and while Andy tended it, I prepared to cook us some breakfast. I found two small willow branches and sharpened one end. They were small enough that we could spear a hopper or other fairly large bug, and roast it over the fire. I also cut a larger branch that had a crotch in it, then used the fat, wet leaves of an elephant plant wrapped around each leg of the branch as sort of a pan. That was for cooking the smaller bugs; ants, grubs, and the like.

We started with hoppers. I snatched up two medium-sized ones. I stabbed one with my stick and handed the other to Andy. He took it, it spit some brown juice on his finger, and he dropped the hopper with a little shriek; Andy, not the hopper.

I looked away ignoring him the best I could, and held my hopper over the fire. Andy watched, fascinated as only a kid can be. The hopper crinkled up, turned brown, and the legs and antenna burned off; those being the parts that tickled your throat if you ate them raw. When it was done I popped it in my mouth real quick like.

"You wanna eat them while they're still hot," I explained, while chewing.

I could see the determination grow in Andy's eyes. He grabbed a fairly large hopper, stuck it on his stick, and held it in the fire, all in one motion. He stared straight ahead. His eyes were set, his mouth shut so tight with resolve that it was just a slit under his nose. He was looking directly at that hopper, but I don't think he saw it. I was afraid to speak because I didn't want to break his spell; but the hopper was done. Hell...everyone knows you don't wanna cook all the juice out.

In nearly a whisper I said. "Now Andy."

I guess he'd been waiting for me to give the word. He pulled the stick from the fire, plucked that hopper off, and popped it into his mouth without a pause. His eyes were shut tight while he chewed and swallowed. His eyes opened and he looked at the end of his stick as if to confirm he'd really done it. Then he looked over at me and a grin broke free and spread from ear to ear and his eyes lit up like the rising sun.

"It was good!" He sounded amazed. "It was really good." He was already looking for another one. There were plenty.

We spent the next half-hour or so roasting up different insects. I went downriver a bit and brought back an old rotten cottonwood log. When I busted it open there were bugs enough for several meals. Once Andy got over his squeamishness, he dove in with the enthusiasm of a teenage boy. He ate several hoppers, a couple different caterpillars, and even a spider. We roasted several ants at a time in my elephant leaf pan. Andy declared grasshoppers to be his favorite, followed by ants. He said the roasted ants reminded him of something called popcorn. Near as I can figure it, if Andy knew what he was talkin' about, it seems if you get a kernel of this special corn hot enough it sorta turns inside out and is soft and fluffy. Sounds kinda peculiar if you ask me. Andy thought the caterpillars and spiders were bitter. Mixed with some leaves and stalks of nearby plants, we had a right fine meal.

After we'd eaten, and slaked our thirst from a creek that emptied into the Platte, we settled down and slept hard till after dark. I woke up to a half-moon, and a sky so full of stars I wondered how they didn't run into each other up there. The moon lit the world with a ghostly pale glow. I woke Andy and it didn't take long before we were mounted, and riding up the trail at a good pace. We kept it up clear till dawn.

That became our routine for the next few days. We slept as much as we could during the day. We were having a real hot spell, and that's hard to hide from. Wherever the sun couldn't get to was where we crawled in to sleep.

I built a beaver trap by weaving small willow branches together and using twisted plant stems to tie the corners and as hinges for the door. It could be triggered manually with a piece of rope, or with a prop stick in the door. It worked. The only drawback was that it took a beaver around five seconds to claw and chew his way out, so you had to be right there when he got trapped or he'd get away. We actually caught several beaver this way. We also had plenty of frogs' legs. The first time I cooked some up while Andy was gathering fire wood. When he sat at the fire I handed him some frog meat. Without thinking about it he popped it in his mouth and chewed.

"What is this Mount?" It was obvious he liked it. "This isn't beaver is it?"

"Frog," I said around my mouthful.

He'd picked up one on the bone and was studying it. "What did you say it was Mount?"

I pointed to several legless frog carcasses at my feet, and still with my mouth full mumbled. "Frog."

A few days ago, the old Andy, would've nearly gagged and went to chewin' on a cattail root or some damn thing. The new Andy studied the frog leg, smelled it, and stuck it in his mouth bone and all. As he pulled out the cleaned off bone and began to chew he smiled over at me.

"Not bad, tastes just like our cook's fried chicken." We shared a laugh, and several more frog legs.

Five or six days after getting back on the trail we came to the spot where the North and South forks came together to form the Platte River. The Oregon Trail didn't follow either. We forded the river and headed west between the two. We made dang good time traveling at night. It was cooler, so the horses could keep a steady pace for longer without needing rest. A few days after leaving the hills behind I felt safe enough that we rode on into the morning until it got too hot, then we'd find a place to hole up, eat, and try to sleep through the hottest part of the day. Toward evening, after it started to cool off, but still with a couple hours of daylight left, we'd start riding again. The only problem I could see would be if we rode right on past the Worthingtons' camp during the night, but I was betting they'd be waiting at Fort Laramie.

Then one morning it happened. We were riding side by side and I was telling Andy about the time I tried to ride a seven point bull elk across the Yellowstone, fell off into a strong undertow and drown. As I talked the first hint of the rising sun began behind us. As it rose, the world around us was slowly revealed. I don't even remember where in the story I was when my voice just trailed off as my mind realized what it was my eyes were seeing. It was a mountain! It was way off in the distance, sorta hazy, but hot damn, God Almighty it was a mountain!

"Look there, Andy!" You'd a thought I'd just discovered the damn mountain, I was so excited. Andy looked where I pointed, but wasn't sure what he was seeing. I guess I'd never thought about the fact that he'd never seen a real mountain.

"What is that?" Andy was catching my excitement. He looked at me with wide eyes. "Is that the Rocky Mountains? Are we gonna see your cabin, Mount?"

Being close to bubbling over already, I damn near fell off Goldfire laughing. It took a full minute before I was able to talk.

"Well Andy that'd be a little piece of the Rockies." How do you explain a whole mountain range to someone who's never seen a mountain? "The Rocky Mountains stretch for hundreds of miles and are made up of thousands of those that you can see stacked atop and alongside each other." I didn't know if I was educating Andy or confusing him. "They run north and south, and my cabin is probably three or four hundred miles north of here." I thought back to what we'd been told before leaving Fort Kearny.

"If I remember right, Andy," I said, "that peak there would be called Pole Mountain, and not far past it we'll be finding Fort Laramie...and I hope your ma and pa."

Andy's eyes grew even wider, he let out a hoop and a holler, and took off at a gallop like he was gonna ride there in just a few minutes. I let them run for a while, to use up some of his excitement, staying close behind, then caught up and hauled Andy in, slowing him back to a walk.

"Now Andy, you need to just hunker back a bit." Skyhawk had slowed to a walk, but Andy was still at a full gallop; bouncing up and down in the saddle. "That mountain is still a full day and then some away." I knew neither of us was gonna be able to sleep the day away. "We'll ride till it gets too hot, then hole up for a few hours like usual; only we'll start riding earlier this afternoon. That ok with you?"

I could tell he wanted to take off at a gallop again and not stop till he got there, but he knew better.

"Yes, okay Mount." He had to really try to calm himself down. "But I don't think I'm gonna sleep a lot."

We rode in silence after that. My eyes were on that distant mountain, but I realized my mind had drifted to thoughts of Sandra. I didn't recollect starting to think about her, she was just suddenly there. I was picturing her, with her dark brown eyes and glossy black hair shining in the sun; the way her face lit up the whole day when she smiled. The way she looked stepping into that river to bathe back on the Missouri. The way she...what the hell was I doing? A man didn't have thoughts like that about another man's wife. It just wasn't proper; even if the man was a pompous ass like Mr. Worthington.

After that I tried to concentrate on the mountains, and my cabin up north...and if I was ever gonna get back to it. I had to concentrate hard.

As we rode, and as the day brightened, we could make out more mountains on the horizon. They trailed south until they disappeared off in the distance, and to the north there appeared to be a smaller range.

We rode till around noon; the mountains didn't seem any closer. When I looked over and saw Andy nodding off, I figured it was time to rest. We found a shady spot in some cottonwoods along a creek and neither of us bothered to eat anything; we just stretched out among some foliage, and it didn't take but a flicker and both of us were snoozing.

We both slept better than I figured we would. When I woke it was late afternoon, and hotter than hell in a heat wave. Soon as I started moving around Andy woke. We were both anxious to get on the trail so we didn't bother with a fire. We had a little something to eat; Andy hadn't taken to eating bugs raw yet so he had some taproot and leaves. We took care of our personal business, dunked our heads in the creek to cool off; then hit the trail. Andy wanted to hurry, but I knew we still had a long way to go, and insisted we stay at our normal pace for the sake of the horses. We took a break while the heat was with us for cool-off dunks in the couple of creeks we came across; then we rode on into the night.

The sky was overcast and the night was darker than the inside of a buffalo's gut. We could barely make out the trail we were riding on. As excited as we were to get there, the night seemed to drag on forever. Finally, as dawn approached and light crept back into the world, the mountains we were riding toward were slowly revealed, and it seemed like they were right there! Pole Mountain was off to our left, and towered up into the sky. What a beautiful sight! Andy stopped and just stared for quite a while, having never been so close to a mountain. Pole Mountain stood kind of alone; with the rest of the mountain range rising up a little south and trailing off into the distance. The mountains running north were farther away and looked to be smaller.

With the sun came the heat again, but there was no question about stopping today. We would ride until we got to Fort Laramie, or fall out of the saddle from heat stroke, whichever came first. With a couple stops to cool off in the creeks, Fort Laramie came first.

"What's that Mount?" Andy suddenly yelled pointing straight ahead. "Is that it? Is that Fort Laramie?"

Sure enough, off in the distance, through the waves of heat rising up off the ground, damned if it didn't look like buildings. They waved and danced in the heat like a vision in a dream.

"Reckon so," I said. Again, Andy wanted to gallop all the way there. I wanted to too, but knew we were still aways away. The horses had held up well in the heat of the last few days and I meant to keep them in good shape. It was hard for both of us, but we kept to a fast walk. As we got closer, Fort Laramie merged from that wavy, dream-like vision, to solidify into real buildings. Andy couldn't hold back any longer, and we galloped the last couple miles or so. We got to Fort Laramie around midday.

Again, like Fort Kearny, Fort Laramie wasn't a fort. Unlike Fort Kearny, Fort Laramie wasn't a military base. It'd been built by a feller named William Sublette as a trading post in the mid 1830s. The American Fur Company had bought it from Mr. Sublette in the late '30s. It was five wooden buildings strung out between the trail and what they called Lodge Pole Creek. Behind the buildings there was a large adobe structure about half built. There were a handful of men working there, but other than that no one was to be seen. One of the main buildings was bigger than the rest, and looked to be a trader's store. We tied the horses to a post out front and went in. We walked smack dab into the middle of a story bein' told by a gentleman that was nearly as wide as he was tall.

"...then we come around the bend and low and behold there was one of the biggest mule deer bucks I've ever laid eyes on. You ain't never seen such a sight. We were just getting ready to...."

The room was a big one. There was traveling supplies, clothes, and food goods for sale on shelves to our right. Directly in front of us was the pay counter, and around the counter stood six or seven men. The one doin' the talking was a squat feller with very little hair and a bad case of Donelap Disease. For those of you that don't know, that's when your stomach done laps over your belt buckle. Andy and I walked up to the group.

"...the damned thing rolled over and came to a stop about a foot away from dropping off the bank," the short, round gentleman was saying.

"Excuse me." I tried to interrupt.

He continued. "Then ole Hal and me pounced on him and got his throat cut before he could..."

"Excuse me please." This time I was a little louder. Everybody stopped and looked at us. No one spoke. Since he was the one talking I addressed the guy telling the story. "I was wondering if you...."

"What the hell's wrong with you mister?" This interruption came from a tall slender feller standing behind the counter.

"Excuse me?" I was confused. Other then interrupting a huntin' story I didn't figure I'd done anything wrong.

"I said, what the hell's wrong with you?" There was a mischievous little smile on his face. "Ole Del here talks pretty much nonstop from the time he gets up till he goes to bed. Some say he even talks in his sleep, although how they'd know is beyond me. And he does it without ever being prompted." His smile grew, as did the smiles on the other men's faces. "Now here you come, and start asking him questions? The one thing we don't need around here is someone encouraging Del to talk."

Everyone in the group busted out laughing. Even Del smiled and started to say something, but I figured if I wanted to get my question out I'd better push the issue.

This time I spoke to the feller behind the counter. "Well I can just as easy ask you then, don't rightly matter to me. I'm wondering if you've seen...."

This time I was interrupted by the door behind me exploding open and a screaming, crying, blue blur ran across the room and threw herself on Andy. Sandra was hugging and kissing her son, and crying up a storm all at the same time. She would hug him tight, then hold him at arm's length so she could look at him, then pull him back against her. Andy too was laughing and crying at the same time.

"My baby, my baby!" Were the only words she could get out for a while. "My baby's back." She just kept crying and hugging.

Mr. Worthington came in and walked over to Andy and Sandra. When Sandra noticed him she backed away and Mr. Worthington stepped up and actually put his arm around Andy's shoulders. "Good to have you back son. How are you?"

I didn't hear Andy's response. I glanced over at Sandra and our eyes locked. In her eyes I saw joy, relief, and gratitude. I also saw something else reflected in those dark pools. Damned if I don't think Sandra was more than just a little happy to see me too. That look in her eyes said more than just thank you. She stepped over in front of me, stood on tip toes, put her right hand on my shoulder and pulled me down so she could kiss my cheek. I instantly felt my blood rise and my face turned red.

"Thank you Mount." She was ready to cry again. "We can never repay you for what you've done." She started to cry. "You brought my baby back to me. Oh, thank you Mount, thank you." She put her arms around me, laid her head against my chest and cried. When I looked up, everyone was staring at us, and I didn't like the look in Mr. Worthington's eyes at all.

Chapter Sixteen

We stayed at Fort Laramie for nearly two weeks. The Worthingtons had been there only two days when Andy and I pulled in. We all needed a good rest in the relative safety of the fort. The four of us stayed in one of the buildings beside the trader's store. It had two rooms, Mr. and Mrs. Worthington stayed in one and Andy and I stayed in the other. We slept on small, hard cots, and they felt like sleeping on a damned cloud after so many nights on the ground; even with my feet hanging over and having to rest on a chair.

We were hoping a group of settlers would come through headed our way and we could ride along. Unfortunately, the Oregon Trail was just brand new and travelers were still few and far between. It could've been months till the next group, and Mr. Worthington wasn't gonna wait anywhere near that long.

I ain't real sure how it works, but the fact that Mr. Worthington was rich back in St. Louis meant he was rich there in Fort Laramie too, even though he didn't have any cash money. I don't understand it, but I'm damn glad it's so.

When Sandra first offered, I'd refused, feeling uncomfortable taking what I figured was a handout, but she and Andy both raised a ruckus and made such a fuss about me not getting paid more than a horse for my services, that finally I agreed. I got new britches and a shirt that I was needing awful bad. They could've been a little bigger, and they were heavy wool, so not nearly as comfortable as my deerskins, but at least they were in one piece and I wasn't peeking out all over. When I came out with my new duds on Sandra and Andy were waiting.

"Wow, look at you, Mount." Andy laughed and pointed. "Those are some mighty fancy clothes. You're looking awfully debonair."

Now, I didn't know what that debon...whatever meant, but I did know that I musta looked nothing but ridiculous with my legs stickin' outta my new britches, and the shirt stretched to near ripping across my chest; the sleeves halfway to my elbows.

I decided Andy was making fun. I stepped over and snatched him up over my head and looked for a watering trough or maybe a fresh pile of horse droppings. Andy was laughing hard and trying to squirm free. I looked over at Sandra. She was smiling that real tender kinda smile that I'd seen the day we rode in. It made me feel warm and happy; and guilty as hell.

"You look just fine, Mount." She continued to smile up at me, her eyes slowly changed till they held only friendship. "Don't let Andy tease you."

"If it wasn't such a damned long walk down to the horse's watering trough, I'd cool the little troublemaker off some." I shook Andy a little and he laughed harder. "Maybe I can throw him that far." I brought him down waist high and made like I was gonna pitch him through the air; he screamed like a little girl. Sandra and I shared a good laugh.

The store proprietor's wife, Marylou, was kind enough to move the buttons on my shirt so it fit better. Then she added about six inches to the pants legs; the wool wasn't quite the same, but I sure didn't give a damn. I'd be working on new deerskins first chance I got.

We were able to buy a pack horse and stocked up on food and other supplies. The store had some knives, and we each got one, but they didn't have any firearms. Mr. Worthington talked a couple fellas out of their own personal guns...for a mighty handsome price I'd bet. We also, at my suggestion, bought a warm blanket for each of us; the last four in the place. We were headed into the mountains, and summer or not, it'd be getting cold at night.

We had a good couple weeks at Fort Laramie. It was mighty nice eating real food, although Andy caused quite a stir the first time he roasted a big ole grasshopper and ate it in front of the folks. We were sitting around a fire one evening with some of the locals, and casual as you please Andy picked up a little stick, a big hopper, joined the two and stuck them in the fire. I saw Sandra and some of the others watching him but not saying anything, probably thinking he was just being a boy; which I guess he was. But they sure as hell weren't expecting him to pop that hopper into his mouth after cooking it, and when he did four different people, one being Sandra, let out squeals at the same time, two groaned and turned away, and two others damn near puked into the fire. Andy looked over at me with an evil gleam in his eyes that only a teenage boy could muster and a grin from ear to ear while he chewed. I laughed till tears ran down my cheeks.

Speaking of my cheeks…while we were at Fort Laramie I had a real bath with actual hot water, and a shave with a straight-edge razor. It was the cleanest I'd been since I'd left my cabin nearly five months ago.

Two of the evenings we were there, after it'd cooled off a bit, we played a game they called rounders. There were two teams, and four small square chunks of sod they called bases that were laid out in a big diamond shape with thirty feet or so between them. A feller stood by three of the bases and a couple others were rovers behind them. Another person, standing in the middle of the diamond, threw a horsehide ball over the base they called the home base. A feller from the other team stood at the home base and tried to hit the ball with a long round stick. When he hit it, he ran to each of the bases in order, trying to make it around back to the home base. The men from the other team ran and got the ball and tried to hit the feller running around the bases. If the ball hit him, he was done; if he made it back to home base his team got a point. After three men got hit by the ball the two teams traded places. Kinda confusing I know. It was fun, except too much running. I don't know that it'll ever catch on.

We also spent considerable time in the trader's store. Damn near any time of the day, there'd be ole Del Haney talkin' up a storm. Del was the short, round feller we'd run into when Andy and I first got to the fort, and they weren't kidding about his love for chattering. That man barely took time to breathe. I swear he could talk a fresh cut tree stump rotten.

It seemed that just that previous March the United States of America had gotten a new president, a gentleman by the name of Mr. William Harrison. Then damned if within a month he didn't up and die, and was replaced by a Mr. John Tyler. This alone could've kept ole Del talking till President Tyler died. I didn't know much about presidents and such, and it didn't take long for me to have my fill of listening.

I spent some time riding with Andy around in the mountains and enjoyed watching him take pleasure in them. He was hungry to learn all he could, and I was happy to teach him.

The first day we went riding I mounted Goldfire and was moving before I realized what I'd done. I looked around and saw Mr. Worthington standing outside the store watching. I turned and started back to trade horses when he spun around and went in. I sat for a few seconds pondering what to do. Andy rode Skyhawk up beside me and nodded his encouragement. "He's your horse now Mount."

I turned again and rode Goldfire off into the mountains. From that day on he was my horse, and a word was never said. Mr. Worthington traded the horse he'd come in on for a bigger, stronger saddle horse for himself. With Andy on Skyhawk and Sandra riding the same coal black mare she'd been riding, we were all set with good horseflesh. The pack horse was a sturdy Morgan, and would pack anything we wanted as far as we needed.

A good share of the time we were at Fort Laramie, Mr. Worthington was with Mr. Rollins, the proprietor of the trader's store. Mr. Rollins was in the employ of the American Fur Company, and I think Mr. Worthington was already working on business dealings for when he got to Oregon. I joined them one day figuring I needed to ask about the lay of the land we were gonna be passing through. Mr. Worthington, Mr. Rollins, and a few others were sitting around a table.

"So they were telling us at Fort Kearny that South Pass is the way through the mountains," I started. "Is the trail to the pass and through the mountains plain enough to follow? What about the pass itself, how steep and narrow? Is there likely to still be snow this time of year?"

The locals all looked at each other and took to laughing. I don't think he knew what the hell they were laughing at, but Mr. Worthington laughed too. I didn't see where I'd said anything that damned funny.

Turned out what was funny was that South Pass ain't really a pass at all, but a twenty mile swath of plains through the mountains. Of course I had no way of knowing that. Everybody quieted down pretty quick, except this one feller, he kept laughing and his laugh kept getting louder and somehow, mean sounding.

His name was Randy, and he was big as a damned house; one of the few men I'd met that looked me in the eye from straight across, and he was probably forty pounds heavier than me. We'd crossed paths a few times since I'd gotten to the fort and I had the feeling that Randy just flat didn't like me much; can't say as I'd developed much of a fondness for him either. When he spoke there was no doubt how he felt.

"Well now, if you ain't one hell of a guide, cowboy." He sorta snarled it. "Ain't ya supposed to know the land if you're guiding folks through, huh cowboy?" He looked around at the rest. They looked a little uncomfortable and no one encouraged him, but they didn't stop him either. "Hell, I think you'd need an Indian scout to find your own ass cowboy." He thought that was awful funny; no one else laughed. "Hell, seems to me you're stealing these folks' money."

Like I've said before, I tend to be slow to anger and fairly quick to let it go; it's just the way I was brought up, but this Randy feller was crowding his luck. I looked at Mr. Worthington; he wouldn't look at me. It appeared he'd been struck deaf and dumb as well as blind. I took a deep breath, and looked Randy in the eye.

"Well Randy, let me set you straight on a couple things." I kept my voice even and calm. "First off, I ain't a guide...never claimed to be one. Mr. Worthington there talked me into leading them and insisted we take a route I've never been on. That leads me to point number two, how the hell am I suppose to know the lay of the land when I've never been through here before? Mr. Worthington knew that too." Mr. Worthington was still deaf and blind to us; sitting and staring out the window like there was something mighty interesting just outside. Randy on the other hand, was getting more riled up. "Thirdly...," I continued, "...I'd never seen a cow till this spring outside of St. Louis. Now I don't reckon being a cowboy would be such a bad thing, but I ain't one of those either." I didn't figure adding that I was getting paid with a horse would gain me anything.

Randy stood and stepped up to me. I can honestly say there was pure hate in that man's eyes. I guess to some folks anger and hate just come easy.

"As far as I'm concerned, you ain't nothin' but a yellow-bellied coward." He spit on me as he growled. "I figure the Indians will probably kill all four of you the next time they get..."

I swear, I don't even remember deciding to hit him. I just did. I hit him with a punch that went from my side directly to his chin, a blow that would've knocked most men out cold and would've surely knocked the rest on their butt. It barely made Randy stop talking. It was like hitting a buffalo. He stopped talking and started laughing that real mean sorta laugh. "That the best you got cowboy?"

I just had time to think *oh damn* before he hit me. I saw it coming so I was moving backwards when it got there; it still felt like gettin' clubbed by a tree. I stumbled back a few steps and my legs got real unreliable like, so I decided to sit for a spell. Sitting felt real good, and I'd just started to shake some sense back into my head when I saw the boot coming. I got my left arm up, so the kick caught me in the ribs and armpit, rather than the head. I locked my arm around his leg and held on while I tried to suck some air back into my lungs, and clear my head. Randy tried to pull away instead of just pummeling me, which gave me a few extra seconds to gather myself; while being drug across the floor. Finally my lungs kicked in and I was able to take a huge, shuddering breath. As my lungs filled with air, the rest of me filled with rage. A fury I'd never felt before. Even killing those two Indians, I was mostly scared, and desperate to save Sandra. As the anger grew...as the rage filled me, my breath and strength returned and my head cleared. I rolled onto my back, Randy had turned to face me, and I found myself lying between his legs. I grabbed an ankle with each hand, put my knees up against his thighs, and pushed for all I was worth. Randy toppled over backwards like a damned ole dead cottonwood. Before he stopped bouncing I was on my feet, and since I was still between his legs, that's where I kicked him; a heel stomp straight to the private parts, with all I had. I heard a real satisfying groan; he rolled onto his side and curled up. I'd gotten through to him.

I'd been in enough fights during Rendezvous to recognize an opening when I saw one, and with a big feller like Randy you didn't take any chances. I kicked him in the back, which was about all I could get at. When he rolled onto his back I kicked him in the ribs, and was rewarded with a nice cracking sound followed by a whooshing as the wind left his lungs. I straddled him, came down on his chest with all my weight, and started boxing his head left and right, back and forth, again and again. I heard someone yell, but they sounded like a real long ways away, then two men were grabbing my arms and trying to pull me off; even as I started to fight them off, I slowly came back to my senses.

"Let me alone!" I shouted. "Let me alone, I'm done." And just like that the anger was gone.

They let go of me and I crawled off Randy and just sat on the floor trying to catch my breath. I started shaking all over, and suddenly felt sick to my stomach. I looked over at Randy laying there beside me and felt even sicker. He was unconscious and had blood coming from his nose, mouth, and ears but what really scared me was that he hadn't started breathing yet since I'd kicked the wind out of him. Mr. Rollins hurried over to him.

"If he's dead, I'll see that you hang you bastard!" He glared at me as he knelt beside Randy.

From where I was sitting I could see the big vein in Randy's neck and the one in his temple pulsing, so I knew his heart was still beating, but it wouldn't stay that way if he didn't breath soon. He was already turning blue. Not knowing what to do, but knowing that someone needed to do something, I stood up and grabbed Randy by the arms and started pulling him up.

"What the hell you doin?" Mr. Rollins yelled, and tried to pull me away.

"I don't know!" I yelled back. "But I figure somebody's gotta do something!" I was behind Randy, and I lifted him from under his armpits up off the floor and shook him. I ain't sure if what I did helped or not, but damned if his whole body didn't jerk as his lungs tried to work, then suddenly he inhaled a huge breath. His lungs shuddered for the next couple breaths, then took off like a bellows.

I dropped him back to the floor and sat back down myself, enjoying a huge sigh of relief. My face hurt where he'd hit me, and I suddenly realized that my ribs were screaming in pain. I figured the son of a bitch probably deserved a beating, even though I already felt bad about it, but I never wanted to kill anyone...again...ever; and the thought of hanging didn't appeal me any either.

Randy was still unconscious, but his heart was beating and his lungs were working; beyond that I really didn't much give a damn. Mr. Rollins was still looking at me like the enemy, and Mr. Worthington still wouldn't look at me at all. When I looked his way something really interesting suddenly appeared on the floor by his feet. The door opened.

"...when that rope wrapped around his..." It was Del Haney and a couple of the local men that had been working on the adobe building. Del was telling a story as usual. "...he went down like a...what the hell!" He looked from Mr. Rollins to Randy, still stretched out on the floor, to me sitting on the floor beside him; my left eye had already nearly swelled shut. Del looked back at Mr. Rollins and started to say something and stopped. He looked around again, started to say something again and stopped. I can honestly say, even though it didn't last long, in the nearly two weeks we were in Fort Laramie that was the only time I saw Del without something to say. It was nice while it lasted.

"Carl, what's going on here?" He was still looking at Mr. Rollins. "Just what the hell's going on?"

Mr. Rollins looked at me and the fire in his eyes had burned out. He looked down at Randy, then back to Del.

"Well...seems Randy's quick tongue and ornery disposition finally went off in the direction of the wrong man." He looked at me. "Sorry Mount, I know you did what you had to do. Randy acts like that to most strangers. Thing is, most strangers come up to about his chest and don't often try to fight. Those that try don't last long." I think he could tell I felt bad about what had happened. "If you hadn't hit him when you did he would have kept at you until you did; and if you wouldn't have laid him out he would have hurt you bad. He's done it before."

I looked at Randy, then at Mr. Rollins. "I could've walked away," I said.

Randy groaned and his eyes went from closed to squeezed tight. His right hand went to his left side where I was pretty sure he had a couple broke ribs. His left hand went to his...well you know where his left hand went. He groaned again.

"Hell, I remember back in '39 when I was captured by a Blackfeet war party down south." It was Del, of course. "I made a deal with the War Chief that if I could whip three of his top braves I could keep my hair. Well let me tell ya them warriors was mean ones, and I had to..."

I got up off the floor, took one last look at Mr. Worthington, who suddenly became extremely interested in Del's story, and left. I wasn't in the mood to hear stories, and didn't want to be there when Randy opened his eyes. I walked down to the creek and found a spot I thought was fairly well hidden so I could be alone.

Randy was a mean, nasty bastard, but I couldn't shake the feeling that he was also right. Who the hell did I think I was, being responsible for three other lives? Leading them across country I didn't know; country that was full of ways to die. I had no right thinking I could protect a teenage boy and a woman all the way across the land. Everybody would be better off if I just went on home, and the Worthingtons waited here for a group of settlers, or maybe a real guide to take them the rest of the way. Of course I'd have to give Goldfire back, and that made me feel sad. When I thought of not seeing Sandra or Andy any more I felt sick to my stomach; or maybe that was just the mushrooms I'd had at breakfast.

I heard someone coming down the path behind me. I hunkered down and hoped they'd stay on the path and walk on by. I saw a shadow coming around the willows and knew they weren't staying on the path; and I knew who it was.

"Mount?" Sandra stepped into view. I had to look away. "Are you ok? I heard about what happened. It wasn't your fault; it sounds like that cad got just what he deserved." She stepped closer and saw my eye. "Oh you're hurt!" She stepped up and got down on her knees beside me. She reached out and touched my swollen cheek. I jerked away. "I'm sorry Mount. That eye is cut and needs to be cleaned out."

"I think you folks should wait here for the next group of settlers, and go on with them," I suddenly said. I still couldn't trust myself to look at her. "I'll give Mr. Worthington back his horse, and head home. I want Andy to keep Skyhawk. I'll take one of the other horses."

"Thaddeus Battner, how dare you!" Her reaction, and the "Thaddeus Battner" caught me off guard, and I turned to face her.

Our faces were six inches apart. Her beauty struck me like a physical blow and I struggled to control my emotions. Sandra didn't even try to control hers, and for the second time that day I got spit on while getting yelled at. "How dare you even consider leaving us stranded here in the middle of nowhere! You signed up for a job, and I expect you to fulfill your obligation." She paused and took a couple deep breaths. Her burst of anger faded like the sun in the evening. "Mount...we need you; we need you to help us get to Oregon...Andy and I need you."

"But I ain't the man for the job, Sandra." As long as I looked anywhere other than her eyes, I was okay. "I ain't a guide...I've never been over the Oregon Trail...and I obviously don't know a damn thing about Indians. It could get you all killed sticking with me." I ground a snail shell under my toe.

"That's nonsense Mount. Look at me." I was gazing out over the foothills, there was a red-tailed hawk circling in the sky. Right then I would've traded places in a second. "I said look at me...please." I did; and was lost. Staring into those deep, dark brown eyes, at that perfect, fragile doll face, I could believe anything. If that wasn't bad enough, she put her hand on my arm and squeezed. "Mount...we trust you. You may not know the land, but you know how to keep us alive crossing it. You know what to eat, what not to. You know how to hunt with or without a gun. You've saved our lives several times since St. Louis." As if I wasn't befuddled enough, she smiled. "And most importantly...most importantly, you're our friend. Andy and I wouldn't know what to do without you. You have taught us so much." Those brown eyes filled with tears. "You have helped turn Andy into a fine young man, Mount. It started with teaching him to ride I think, but when the two of you got here to Fort Laramie it was complete. You've helped Andy become a man. Something his father didn't have time to do." Suddenly the tears were gone and that "more than just friends" look was in her eyes again. "And me too, you've helped me grow too. Your...friendship is very important to me." As she said this her voice dropped to a whisper.

Somehow my left hand had moved over onto her hand that rested on my arm. She leaned forward a little, her lips not six inches from mine. I leaned forward.

"Hey Mom, hey Mount, you guys down here?" It was Andy yelling at the top of his lungs. "Ma, Mount, hey where are you?"

Sandra and I both sat up straight like we'd been stung in the ass by a hornet. There was an embarrassing moment while our hands pulled away from each other. I looked at the ground; Sandra looked towards where Andy was coming from. We were both red faced.

"Over here, Andy," Sandra called. "We're over here."

Andy came around the willows at full speed, saw us, and pulled up. He was all excited and out of breath. He looked at me and when he saw my eye he gasped.

"It must be true huh Mount?" He was much too happy. "You really beat up that Randy feller? He's the biggest man I've ever seen, even bigger than you ,Mount. Did you really whoop him? I saw them helping him to his tent, and I heard Mr. Haney talking about it. You really whooped him, huh Mount?" His eyes were huge and he was grinning ear to ear.

"And my hurting another man makes you happy does it?" I frowned up at him. "How the hell is my hurting someone a good thing?" I said this a little louder than I meant to. Andy's eyes got even bigger, but his grin disappeared fast.

"I...I'm sor...I'm sorry Mount," he stammered. "I just thought that..."

"Andy, come over here and sit," I interrupted him. He came and sat. "Andy, the only time a man should lay a violent hand on another man is if he's protecting himself, a loved one, or his belongings; and he should never get pleasure from it." I stopped for a second to decide if I should tell him. "Getting your ma and pa away from the Indians I had to kill two of them." His eyes widened. I saw a shiver run through Sandra as she remembered. "Now I'm not sorry I did it because it had to be done, but I surely do regret it, and it's been wearing on my mind ever since. Now that Randy feller, he has a big mouth and no respect for other folks, but that ain't no reason he should get hurt. And I could've hurt him real bad, or even killed him, then what, huh? I'd a hung cause Randy has a loose mouth. I should've just walked away."

"Yes, okay, I understand what you're saying, I guess." Andy looked solemn. "But to hear Mr. Haney tell it, it didn't sound like you had much of a choice."

"First off, Mr. Haney wasn't even there till after. I had a choice. With the Indians in the hills I didn't, but with Randy I could've walked away. I should've walked away." I looked at Andy then at Sandra. I reached up and touched my bruised cheek. "Besides, if I would've walked away my damned eye wouldn't be swelled nearly shut, and my ribs wouldn't hurt like I'd been kicked by a mule." I rubbed my side and we all shared a laugh; laughing hurt like hell.

"We should get back." Sandra said.

As we neared the buildings returning from the river I noticed Mr. Worthington standing out front of the trader's store staring at us. As we got closer he turned and went inside. The door slammed shut hard. Sandra and I shared a guilty look.

Chapter Seventeen

It was two days after my fight with Randy that we headed out. I'd seen Randy a couple times, and made a point of keeping my distance. He didn't seem too eager to start anything else either. My bruised cheek and eye were an ugly purplish black color, kinda like a real angry sky packing one hell of a spring thunderstorm. My eye at least had started to open a little. My ribs still hurt like hell when I laughed, sneezed, coughed, or even took a deep breath, but I was pretty sure they were just bruised, not broken. Randy had two black eyes and his lower lip was split clear down to his chin. Marylou, the proprietor's wife, had stitched it up the best she could. He also had some bruised or broken ribs, and walked real slow, sorta leaning to the left. When I saw him hurting like that, and saw the hatred in his eyes, I felt lower than a grub worm.

We got all the horses packed up first thing in the morning. Mr. Worthington was real quiet like. Instead of taking over and telling everybody what to do and how to do it like usual, he just went about his business of loading, and spent some more time jawing with Mr. Rollins. After we got packed up, we had a real nice breakfast, and said goodbye to the local folks. I went up and offered my hand to Randy. He didn't accept it, and just turned and walked away, but I felt better for trying. By mid-morning we were back on the Oregon Trail heading west.

The trail itself hadn't changed much; it still ran along fairly flat, plain and easy to follow in most places, nearly disappearing in others. The scenery sure had taken a turn for the better though. Pine covered foothills leading up to the mountains not far off to the south, and more mountains off in the distance to the north. Being near the end of July, a lot of the low-land flowers had been used up, but there were still enough to color the burnt grass and gray sagebrush with patches of bright yellow buttercups or heartleaf and spots of blue larkspur, with white columbine and aster. There was also a lot of Indian paintbrush in different colors, though mostly red. We weren't traveling alongside a river anymore, and I missed that, but there were streams running by pretty regular. I was glad to be back on the trail.

We did things a little different now. At Fort Laramie they'd said the local Indians had been real calm and sociable, even stopping by the fort now and again to trade. But that sure didn't mean we couldn't have more trouble if we ran into the wrong bunch. We still traveled during the day, but at night I took care in finding a well-hidden spot that could be defended if need be; up a narrow draw, or up against a creek bed or sandstone cliff. We also posted a lookout. Mr. Worthington and I would do two or three hours apiece and Andy or Sandra would do a couple hours every other night. During the day Mr. Worthington again took to riding ahead of the rest of us, only now he kept his eyes and ears open, ready to ride back with a warning if need be. I rode a ways back behind Sandra and Andy most of the time; just in case.

Mr. Worthington remained real quiet. Even when we were in camp he tended to stay by himself and didn't talk a lot. When he did talk, he showed no sign that anything was bothering him, but I did catch him staring at me a couple of times from over yonder with a strange look. Sandra and I exchanged meaningful glances now and then, but that was all. I got my courage up and tried to talk to her about it one evening when we were alone but she wouldn't. I believe she was just as confused as I was.

And damn, was I confused. With lookout duty at night and riding alone most of the day, I had plenty of time to think. The more I thought the more confused I was. There was no denying that Sandra and I had a strong attraction for each other. I'd never met a woman like her before. She was easily the most beautiful woman I'd ever seen, and seemed just as beautiful on the inside. She was cultured and sophisticated, yet she had a fiery, fighting spirit. She wouldn't have made it as far as she had without it. What she saw in this big, ugly ole mountain man, you'd have to ask her.

On the other hand, she was legally wed, and that ain't something you mess with; a man ain't nothing if he ain't honorable, and having relations with a married woman ain't honorable. I don't know that Mr. Worthington loved Sandra and Andy or not, you sure couldn't tell by the way he acted. He never showed any affection to either of them, with words or actions. Even after escaping from the Indians the most I saw was a hand on the shoulder. Makes you wonder how they ever got close enough to have Andy. But whether I thought he was a good husband and father or not didn't matter a damn bit, fact was, he was husband and father and that's all that mattered. As much as I seemed to be becoming smitten with Sandra, I couldn't let it happen.

It was the third or fourth night out from Fort Laramie, and I'd been on lookout for a half-hour or so when a shadow emerged from the darkness behind me. Without a word Mr. Worthington sat down beside me and just sat staring up at the stars. It was an absolutely clear night and the mountain sky was really showing off. He sat there for a long time before he spoke. He turned to me; his eyes were hard, not showing much.

"I need to know Mr. Battner, what exactly are your intentions concerning my wife?" His voice was steady and calm, like he was talking business with Mr. Rollins from the fort. "You and she seem to be getting awfully close. Am I wrong, Mr. Battner?"

My only clue to his feelings were the two "Mr. Battners," and the tone of his voice as he said it; like it left a bad taste in his mouth. It was my turn to stare up at the stars for a while. How do I answer him? He turned away and stared at the sky too, and that helped.

"Well now Mr. Worthington, that ain't necessarily an easy question to answer," I finally started. "If you're asking if anything romantic like has happened between the two of us, the answer's no. I'm an honorable man Mr. Worthington, and fooling with a married woman just ain't right." I thought I noticed his shoulders relax a little, and I continued. "On the other hand, I think Sandra, and Andy too, are awfully special. I've grown very fond of both of them." I couldn't stop now. "And if you don't mind my saying Mr. Worthington, they don't seem to get a whole lot of attention from you, unless it's bad attention for something you think they've done wrong." I was getting wound up now. "In the three months we've been traveling together I ain't seen any sort of affection pass from you to either one of them." I stopped to take a breath, wondering if I'd gone too far.

He turned, and had that same non-emotional look. Damn he was a hard, unfeeling bastard.

"As a matter of fact, I do mind your saying. Just because I don't waste my time with pointless showing of affection, or senseless roughhousing and childish shenanigans, doesn't mean I don't care for my family, Mr. Battner," he said. "Sandra and Andrew need a strong, successful man to provide for them, not a playmate. They've had, and again will have, the finest luxuries available." He stood and looked down at me. "I want you to leave my wife alone Mr. Battner. I trust we won't need to have this discussion again."

I knew there was no sense trying to tell the damn fool that what he wasn't giving Sandra and Andy was just what they were needing the most; and I wasn't about to back down as Sandra's friend.

"Well now Mr. Worthington, like I said, you don't need to worry about anything improper happening between Sandra and me." I stood and looked down on him. "But if you're asking me to stop being her friend, to stop talking and laughing and trying to enjoy this god-awful trip the best we can, well sir that just ain't gonna happen. Enjoying Sandra and Andy's company has been about the only pleasurable part of this adventure."

He stared hard at me, looking like he wanted to say something else real bad, but he didn't.

"I suppose you could send me packing," I continued. "We could ride back to Fort Laramie, and you folks could wait there for a guide, and I could go home. I'm gonna insist on keeping Goldfire though. I believe I've earned that right."

He walked away and disappeared into the night. It was almost like he hadn't been there at all. When I went to get him to relieve me three hours later he was sound asleep. I lay down, but didn't sleep the rest of the night.

I don't know if it was the ornery in me or what, but after that night, when I played with Andy, I played just a little harder. When I joked around with him and Sandra I laughed just a little louder; even though my ribs still hurt like hell doin' both. Sandra and I both were real careful to avoid being alone together, or any other situations that could lead to trouble. We did share some meaningful looks across the campfire that said a lot.

When we left Fort Laramie the trail headed northwest. The day after Mr. Worthington and I had our late night talk, we hit the North Fork of the Platte. It'd circled around and passed us, headed south. We knew from the folks at Fort Laramie that we would travel up the North Platte for a couple days to where a tributary called the Sweetwater joined up. There we'd turn due west and head up the Sweetwater, which would take us to South Pass; our way through the Rocky Mountains. The next known outpost would be Fort Hall and the next major landmark was something they called Independence Rock. I'd seen big rocks before; I couldn't figure what all the fuss was about.

The trip up the Platte to the juncture with the Sweetwater was nice and easy with nothing worthy of telling here happening. Food was plentiful, with fish, beaver, squirrel, rabbit, and other small game. It sure was nice having pots and some spices again so we could do some real cooking. There were deer and antelope around too, but I didn't see the sense in taking the time to butcher and jerk that much meat when we didn't really need it. I'd been taught by my pa and the Indians that if you couldn't use it all, you didn't kill it. Some chunks of squirrel or rabbit meat in a pot with some wild roots, wild onions, greens, a little salt and such, and we had ourselves a damn fine meal.

By the time we got to the joining up with the Sweetwater I was feeling pretty danged good again. My eye was open and working fine. I only had a small scab on my cheek bone where I was still healing. My ribs were damn tender, but hurting less all the time.

We got to the Sweetwater mid-morning. We had to cross the North Platte, and it was moving faster than normal because of the lay of the land. The crossing wasn't a problem, but I knew we had to be getting closer to mountainous country, and the other crossings from here on wouldn't be so easy. We crossed and turned west, headed up river.

By mid-afternoon we could see it, and even from that distance, I could see what all the fuss was about. It was a monstrous granite rock sticking up out of the ground in the middle of no damn place. There were mountains off in the distance, but where we were along the river it was flat, and there was this gigantic damned rock like God had set it down there just to make folks wonder. As we got closer, off the north end of the rock, I saw a column of smoke. Someone was camping there, but were they friendly or not? I wasn't about to take any chances with the Worthingtons' safety. I lead them off the trail down into some tall grass and willows beside the river. I had them dismount, get comfortable. I went to see who was waiting for us at Independence Rock.

I went back to the trail and rode up to the rock like I didn't have a care in the world. The muzzleloader hanging by my leg was primed, tamped and ready. Although I was watching real careful for anything or anyone, I couldn't help but be impressed with that rock. That damned thing had to've been fifteen hundred feet long by five hundred feet wide and over a hundred feet tall. Near the end of it, away from the water, was a campfire. It'd been stoked up recently and was just catching good, but nobody was in sight. I dismounted Goldfire and with my muzzleloader at the ready, started to circle the campsite, looking for a sign. There was a mess of prints, both boot and horse.

I was down on one knee checking signs when I sensed someone behind me. He'd stepped from behind the rock. I turned my head just enough to see an Indian brave standing not twenty feet away. I reacted instantly. Clutching that gun to my chest I rolled once to my right, my sore ribs complaining like hell, and came up on one knee ready to fire. As I aimed and began to squeeze down on the trigger, two things happened damn near on top of each other. The first was that I realized the Indian hadn't moved. He stood right where he was, with his hands by his sides, and I just had time to notice the blank, vacant look in his eyes. The second thing that happened was a rock bounced off the side of my head. I cried out in pain and covered my head with my arm. After a couple seconds, when no other rocks came flyin', I snuck a look over my shoulder. What I saw was a large reddish-brown bear wearing deerskins, a coonskin hat holding another rock in its paw.

"If yer a thinkin' man you'll lay that shooting rod on the ground," the bear said to me, with a voice that sounded just like you'd imagine a bear's voice to sound. "If you don't, the next one'll go in yer eye." He shook the rock threateningly.

Now, I've always thought it a good idea to listen when a rock throwin' bear tells you to do something, so I did just what he said and laid my gun down. I glanced over at the Indian and he still hadn't moved. I looked back to the bear and he was coming closer, and was smiling. When he got up next to me he dropped the rock and offered his hand. I stood up and shook it. He had the grip of a bear.

"Name's Rusty." He was a mountain man, and I placed him somewhere between forty and ninety years old; it was hard to tell. He had reddish-brown hair growing down from his head and beard, up from his chest, out his sleeves and covering the backs of his hands. You had to look close to see his eyes and the tip of his nose; which was red too. When he smiled or talked you could see his mouth. He motioned over to the motionless Indian. "I been calling him Injin."

"Mount," I said as I took my hand back. I nodded toward the Indian. "He gave me quite a start sneaking up like that. I just had a bad time with some Indians a while back." Don't know why I felt like I had to explain.

"He didn't sneak, he just happened around the corner. You ain't gotta worry none about Injin." Rusty made this rock rolling over other rocks sound that I think was laughter. "He's barely got the wits to feed his self. He wouldn't cause no trouble even if he had a mind to; and he don't."

"You two traveling together?" I asked. They made strange traveling partners.

"I'm headed north into the high country," Rusty replied. "I found Injin three days ago, south of here. I reckon his people put him out to die cause of the way he is. I found him sitting beside a stone cold fire ring nearly starved to death. There's surely something wrong with him, but I couldn't just let him sit there and die, so I brought him along." He looked me up and down like he was seeing me for the first time. "Maybe you should take him. Big strapping feller like you. You maybe needing a traveling companion?"

Now it was my turn to laugh. "No thanks Rusty, you'll have to keep your Indian. I've got me a whole damn family to watch out for." He looked around confused. "They're back down the trail a piece waiting on me," I explained. "If you don't mind us joining you I'll go get them."

"A whole danged family?" What I could see of Rusty's eyes through the hair, beard, and the bushiest eyebrows I've ever seen, lit up and sparkled like a clear night sky. "We'll have us a party. Injin's the most company I've had in nearly a month; and he ain't much. Listens good though." He leaned forward a bit. "You folks got any whiskey?"

"Nope, no whiskey." You could see the disappointment sorta sag his whole body. "But we got plenty of other supplies. We can have us a hell of a feed, and then stories by the campfire."

The thought of a good meal and company soon overrode the disappointment of no whiskey, and Rusty was damn near dancing around the fire with excitement.

"Go get 'em, go on then," he said to me. "Hurry yourself up. I'll fetch some more dry driftwood. We're gonna need us a raging fire tonight. Go, go, go!" He looked like an excited ninety-year-old youngun. I went.

When I got to the Worthingtons, Sandra and Andy were both sleeping and Mr. Worthington was sitting and staring across the river. When he saw me he got up and walked to the horses without a word. Sandra and Andy woke up when he started moving around.

"Well Mount, who's camped at Independence Rock?" Sandra asked as she got up and brushed herself off. I was watching but not listening.

"What?" I looked into her eyes, and was nearly lost again.

"Who's camped at the rock?" she asked again, pretending not to notice the way I looked at her, and not knowing what she did to me. This time I heard her, but didn't take time to think through my answer.

"An old mountain man and an Indian," I answered. Panic struck both Sandra and Andy immediately. Andy actually sat back down and hugged his knees to his chest. Sandra's face lost all color, her eyes grew big and frightened, and she began to shake her head back and forth.

"No, no, no...Mount, no Indians," she stammered. "Not Indians." Mr. Worthington stood by his horse staring.

"It's okay." I smiled hoping it'd help calm them down. "It ain't a real Indian. This one's not right in the head. He just sits and stares. He ain't gonna cause any trouble, but don't make the old man mad because he throws one hell of a rock." I rubbed the sore little knot on the side of my head. I explained again how the Indian was and everybody seemed okay; although Sandra and Andy were still obviously nervous as a fawn in a forest fire.

When we got to the camp, just as promised, Rusty had a damned bonfire going, and a big pile of wood waiting its turn. It wasn't even dark yet and we were ready to have a fire all night long if we wanted. Rusty wasn't anywhere to be seen. The Indian was sitting back away from the heat of the fire staring into it. He didn't even look up when we rode in. We stopped a couple hundred feet from the fire by a nice little grassy spot. We tethered the horses and walked to the fire. I was watching Sandra and Andy close. As we got closer I could see both of them getting fidgety. When we got to within fifteen feet or so the Indian turned his head and looked at us; Sandra and Andy froze in their tracks.

"Mount, I don't know if I can do this," Sandra said in a loud whisper. She reached out and pulled Andy to her. "I don't know if I can go over there Mount." Andy didn't say anything, but his eyes said he agreed with his ma. They were scared. I turned and faced both of them.

"Now Sandra, Andy, there's something you just got to understand." I wasn't paying any attention to Mr. Worthington. I saw him off to the side of us staring toward the fire. "You're in Indian country, and will be as long as you're out west. Most Indians are friendly enough. Ain't but a few like the ones that gave us trouble back along…"

A low growl had started deep down in Mr. Worthington's chest. I heard it, but wasn't sure what it was until it suddenly erupted into a ragged war cry and he took off. I spun around and went after him, but wasn't fast enough. That Indian was just bright enough to realize that the man running at him had murder on his mind. Injin started to stand but only got halfway up when Mr. Worthington got to him. Mr. Worthington hit him two or three times before Injin fell to the ground, and then kicked him a couple times before I got there.

I sorta bulldogged Mr. Worthington to the ground. I rolled on top of him, sat on his chest, and pinned his arms to the side. He tried to struggle free, but I just tightened my grip.

"What the hell's wrong with you?" I yelled into his face. "Didn't you hear a word I said? That Indian is harmless. Hell, he's less than harmless, he's helpless." Mr. Worthington had quit fighting but I didn't loosen my grip, I may've even tightened it a little.

"He's a savage!" He spat out the words. "He's a damned savage, like all of his kind."

"Well now, Mr. Worthington, if that's how you feel we'd best turn around and hightail it back to St. Louis right now, cause if you plan on doing business in Oregon you'll be doing business with Indians, and that's a fact." He at least looked like he was listening; not that he had much choice. "There ain't enough white folks out here for business to work without the Indian trade. Besides, this damned Indian ain't no more than a ten-year-old child anyway." His body had gone totally relaxed; he didn't resist me at all. I let up a little. "Now if I was to let you up you ain't to go after that Indian again, or I'm libel to put you down real hard next time. Okay?"

"Yeah, okay." He still had hate burning in his eyes, but I think it was mostly for me now. At least he'd lost the wild, crazy look. I think talking to his business side got to him, or at least gave him something to think about.

I stood up, turned around, and was surprised again. Sandra and Andy were both on the ground with that Indian, tending to him. He had a bloody nose and lip and his eyes, instead of being blank, were filled with confusion. They had him sitting up, Sandra on one side, Andy on the other. Andy was supporting him while Sandra wiped the blood off his face. When we walked up Injin cowered away and covered his head with an arm. Sandra glared up at her husband.

"What the hell's going' on here?" It was Rusty. He'd just come around the corner of the giant rock. He had three rabbits dangling from one hand and six or seven fish hanging from a line in the other hand. When he saw Injin on the ground bleeding he dropped the rabbits and picked up a rock. "I said, what the hell's going on here?" He stared directly at Mr. Worthington like he knew where the trouble was.

"Everything's okay Rusty," I said. "Mr. Worthington here got a little bit rambunctious. I told you we'd had some Indian trouble back along the trail." I looked down at Mr. Worthington. "And he's sorry too, ain't you Mr. Worthington?"

He glared at me for only a second then looked at Injin still on the ground with Sandra and Andy helping him, then he looked at Rusty.

"Yeah," Mr. Worthington mumbled. He glared at Injin, walked around to the other side of the fire and sat down.

Rusty picked up his rabbits, put them in the same hand as the fish, then picked up a couple good throwin' rocks.

"That feller best stay over yonder," he said to me as he walked to the fire. He lay down his food cache then went to where Sandra was just finishing cleaning up Injin's face. "Thank you ma'am." He nodded to Sandra. From where I stood I could tell that Rusty was taken by her beauty, and felt a twinge of jealousy. When he looked at Injin again I could see the concern and caring in his eyes even though his words didn't show it. "Hell, Injin's so dense he probably forgot he got hit already." Rusty glared over towards Mr. Worthington as if to let him know that Rusty wouldn't be forgetting.

After getting off to kinda a rough start we ended up having a real nice night. We had a big pot of rabbit stew and pan-fried fish. By the time we were done eating and cleaning up, it was getting dark. We stoked up the fire and spent a good piece of the night swapping stories. Rusty and I did the swapping while Sandra and Andy sat wide eyed and leaning forward listening. They both did a good job laughing and oohing and ahhing at the right places. Mr. Worthington stayed on the other side of the fire and pretended not to be listening. Injin sat and stared into the fire; don't know if he listened or not. It was a warm enough night that we were able to each fall asleep right where we sat. Andy went first, just kinda settled back on his blanket and dozed off, Injin was next, then Sandra. Rusty and I spent most of the night watching the fire and telling lies to each other.

Next morning after some stew for breakfast, Rusty and Injin packed up their few belongings, said their goodbyes, and headed north. They had two riding horses and a pack mule hobbled on the upriver side of Independence Rock. Mr. Worthington kept his distance till they were gone. Another twenty minutes or so and we were back on the trail headed west.

It took nearly three more weeks to reach Fort Hall, the next outpost along the Oregon Trail. The country after Fort Laramie flattened out and turned into desert. Mr. Worthington continued to ride out front, and in camp stayed quiet and moody. Sandra and I continued to pretend we weren't drawn to each other. We would talk and laugh and joke around, then suddenly our eyes would lock and we'd both forget to talk or laugh or anything else for a second, then we'd both suddenly look at the ground, turn, and walk away. Andy and I became great friends, laughing and wrestling and exploring, when the land called for it.

South Pass turned out to be just what they'd said. I have to admit I had a hard time swallowing the tale of a twenty to thirty mile piece of flatland going through the mountains, but there it was. The mountains moved in a little both north and south, and the land did climb some, but nothing like any of the mountain passes I'd ever been through, where damned if you didn't actually have to climb up and over the mountains; if you could. The trail did climb up onto the north side of the mountain as we cleared the pass. It wasn't real hard traveling, but we did find out that Sandra suffered from a fear of heights.

I was riding along not paying a whole lot of attention to anything but the view from the mountainside. I didn't notice Sandra had stopped until Goldfire had to stop or run into her horse. She was sitting there looking down into the valley, which dropped off several hundred feet to our left. Her eyes were open wide and her mouth was hanging open too.

"Sandra...Sandra you ok?" I asked. Andy had noticed and was stopped thirty feet ahead of us. She didn't react so I raised my voice. "Sandra...Hey Sandra!"

She didn't move anything except her mouth. "I'm scared Mount. I've never been up high like this before, and I don't like it. I don't like it a bit."

I'd never heard of such a thing and didn't have any idea what to do. Going back wasn't a choice. We had to keep headed west; and it was gonna be dark soon so we had to get going soon.

"Mother, look at me." I'd forgotten about Andy. "Hey, Ma look here." She slowly lifted her head and looked forward. "Good Ma, good."

"Ok now Sandra." I knew what Andy was trying to do. "See that little white cloud up there, the one that looks kinda like a bird with its wings spread? Do you see the one?"

Sandra's head nodded slowly. "Yeah, I see it."

"We need you to keep watching that cloud Ma." Andy took over again. "You just keep your eyes on that cloud until we get down off this mountain side."

"I don't know if I can." She sounded like she was the teenager. "I don't know."

"We know you can Sandra," I said. "We know you can do anything you have to do. Now you just watch that cloud and we'll take it nice and slow, and we'll be off this mountain before you know it."

It took a couple hours before we were down off the mountain and into the valley bottom. I don't think Sandra ever took her eyes from the sky. The cloud she'd started watching was long gone but her eyes were still locked on something in the darkening sky, till we were down.

We'd followed the Sweetwater River into the pass, then it turned north and moved off into the mountains to its source. The trail continued headed west. The next day, after we made our way back to the valley floor, we came across another river. We'd been told to watch for the Green River, but I don't think that was it. It was running southwest and the trail only followed it for a little before crossing and moving on. While we rode along the river bank I noticed Andy and Sandra having quite a discussion up in front of me. They kept looking and pointing and talking back and forth. Finally Andy turned and waved me to come up.

"Mount," Sandra started when I rode up. "Since we've left St. Louis we've traveled along one river or another most of the way." She and Andy both looked puzzled. "And we've always been traveling upriver. Why are we now traveling downriver but still headed west?" She and Andy exchanged confused looks.

"It's the mountains." I wasn't sure I understood it all well enough myself to explain it. "Water runs downhill, so on the east side of the mountains it runs east, on the west side it runs west. When we came through the pass we crossed the divide, so we're on the west side now." I wasn't sure if that all made sense or not.

Andy's eyes grew large with excitement and his shout was loud as thunder.

"Then we're there…or I mean here! We're in Oregon!" His face was near to splitting his smile was so wide. "We made it, we made it!" Skyhawk started prancing and high stepping as he felt Andy's excitement. I think Sandra knew better, but she enjoyed the moment and laughed good and strong. Guess I had to be the one to tell him.

"Whoa there boy." I couldn't help but laugh watching him. "Just you hang on a damned minute. If we was where we're headed I'd be the one yelling my fool head off."

"But we've crossed the mountains." He wasn't gonna give up easy. "You said when we crossed the mountains we'd be in Oregon. You said that Mount."

"What I said was that Oregon Country was on the other side of the mountains, and it is. I reckon there's a chance that we might be in Oregon Country, I'm not sure…but Oregon City, where your pa wants to go, is a far piece yet. A thousand miles or more I figure." His excitement was starting to fade as the truth sunk in. "But I figure we've gotta be more than halfway." That was supposed to make them feel better; it didn't work.

The first local from Fort Hall that we, or rather I, met actually happened several miles before the fort. The country had gotten real pretty, with the mountains moving in on us again from both sides. Beautiful pine forest with stands of birch or aspen scattered about. We were gaining height but the traveling was still easy along the trail. I didn't know we were as close to the fort as we were, so I was riding up through the draws to our north doing some hunting.

I crested a ridge and dropped down into a fairly steep gorge. At the bottom, in amongst some bramble and thorn bushes, I thought I saw an animal of some sort. As I got closer I realized that it was a mule lying on its side in the thicket. When I got up closer I saw that the mule had a saddle blanket that had slid partly off him. Next I noticed that mule had a human foot sticking out from underneath, nearly hidden in the weeds. I jumped off Goldfire and walked slowly around the mule and looked down into the thicket. An old codger, must'a been sixty years old was laying there bleeding from a hundred thorn pricks, his leg caught under the dead mule. The old feller was staring up at me like I was the devil come a calling.

"What the hell you starin at?" His voice was strong considering his situation. "Get the hell out'a here! I don't need no help." His eyes and mouth crinkled up and he looked a hundred years old.

"Your leg broke?" I'd had lookout till dawn and then ridden hard all day so I wasn't in the best of moods.

"Damned if I know, can't feel it no more. What the hell you care anyway?" He tried to spit at me, brown juice ran down into gray whiskers. "I said go to hell, and leave me alone. I didn't ask you for no help."

I slid down the embankment to where the ornery old chap and the dead mule lay. I reached down and wrapped my arms around that mules head, planted my legs, hauled back, and twisted. The mule slid off the old man's leg and rolled over. The old feller bent his knee and started rubbing life back into his leg. I knew it wasn't broke.

"Nope, you didn't" I said. I climbed out, walked back to Goldfire, mounted up, and rode down the draw towards the trail. I'd had enough hunting for the day.

By the time I got back to the Worthingtons I was feeling a little guilty about not tending to the old man, so I sorta forgot to mention seeing him. It wasn't two hours later we rode into Fort Hall.

Chapter Eighteen

Fort Hall, unlike the other "forts" we'd seen, at least looked like a fort's suppose to. It had log walls surrounding it with log buildings built into the wall on two corners. The wall had a few portholes just big enough for a gun to poke out. Fort Hall was in Blackfeet Country, and the Blackfeet didn't like it, so Indian attacks were frequent. Inside the bastion were several buildings, most built of rough-hewed logs with mud roofs and adobe brick chimneys. The main one was used as a trader's post and general meeting hall. The fort had been built in the early 1830s by a feller named Nathaniel Wyeth who was planning to get rich selling and trading with settlers and the Indians. Instead of getting rich he damn near starved to death and sold Fort Hall to the Hudson Bay Company back in '37. It sat on a real nice spot along the Snake River. The Snake ran north to south right there, draining down outta the mountains. The fort sat in a real pretty meadow, surrounded by rolling foothills that lead up to the mountains. The spring flowers were mostly gone and the grass wasn't exactly green anymore, but it was a pretty spot anyway.

We were welcomed at the front gate, and found ourselves in the main building surrounded by folks all wanting news from back east. We didn't have any. There were more people here than any of the other outposts. Being that Hudson Bay was a British outfit a lot of the folks talked funny, but were all nice enough. Captain Grant, the feller in charge, even made a point of saying howdy. There were even three kids around Andy's age, two boys and a girl. It didn't take but twenty minutes after we'd entered the fort and Andy was off playing with the other kids. The smile on his face as they ran outside was something to see. There were also several women, which Sandra was happy about.

We'd been in the meeting hall for a couple hours. Sandra was sitting at a table against the wall visiting with three local ladies. They were talking and laughing. Now and then looking over toward the menfolk, one of them would say something and they'd take off laughing and carrying on again. A couple times I caught them looking my way.

Mr. Worthington and most of the men were gathered around the counter in the store area of the large room. Someone had brought out a jug of whiskey and passed it around. I stood on the outside of the group, not taking part in the chitchat, but close enough to take my turn when the jug came around. The kids had been in having a glass of lemonade and were at the door headed out again when the door flew open, slamming up against the wall and damn near taking the lead kid with it.

"Get the hell outta my way ya little heathens!" This old feller stepped inside. The kids barely slowed as they ran around him and disappeared outside. "Damn kids. Ain't no call for younguns here." He stood and looked around, his gaze settling on the women over by the wall. "No call for womenfolk either," he said to no one in particular. He spat on the floor and started for the stairs off to his right. I hadn't recognized him until he started walking. Then, about the time I noticed his bad limp, I also recognized the saddle blanket thrown over his shoulder as the one I'd seen hanging off a dead mule a few hours ago.

Looking close I could see some leaves and sticks still tangled in his hair, hair which was mostly missing on top and down to his shoulders on the sides and around the back. It was gray, as was his two-week growth of whiskers. About the time I realized who it was, he saw me standing at the back of the group of men. Our eyes met and I nodded and smiled a greeting. He huffed, snarled, spit once more on the floor, and limped up the stairs. Yes sir, I was sure piling up the friends all along the way. There was a tall skinny gentleman standing beside me. He let out a disgusted little laugh.

"Don't pay him no never mind." He looked up at me. "That's Dale, folks round here call him 'Nugget' cause he's a prospector. He found a couple gold chips and some dust twenty years ago or so, and has been panning the same creeks ever since. Ain't found a damn thing, but he's sure the big nugget's out there somewhere waiting for him. I figure he'll die still looking for it. He cleans up around here and does other odd jobs to earn his keep." We watched Nugget make his way up the stairs and into a room two doors down. "He's got an old mule, some prospecting equipment, and the clothes on his back, and that's about it." The skinny feller finished.

"Reckon he'll be needin' a new mule," I said. I hadn't seen any gear other than the blanket, and he sure as hell didn't carry it back to the fort even if it had been laying in the brush somewhere when I pulled that mule off him. "Might need new gear too. Seems to be a cranky ole bastard."

"Don't know that he's got much to be happy about," he replied. I thought about it and damned if he wasn't right. Guess I'd be cranky too being in his boots. Boots I'd noticed that had as much hole as leather in them.

We'd come to the dog days of summer. The last couple weeks on the trail, and all the time we spent at Fort Hall it was hot as hell on fire. You could actually watch the flowers wilt and the grass turn yellow as you rode along. It was so danged hot I had squirrels and rabbits volunteering to be dinner just to get away from the heat.

We'd taken turns almost daily dipping in any clean running water we came across. Some creeks had dried up this late in the summer but there were still plenty running strong; this being rich drainage land. Twice between Fort Laramie and Fort Hall I happened upon Sandra while she was bathing, totally by chance of course. The second time I let her catch me watching just to see what her reaction would be. She couldn't look at me without blushing for a week. The only relief from the heat was now and again the good Lord would see fit to send a late afternoon thunderstorm by to wash the dust off.

We stayed in Fort Hall four or five days. The trip from Laramie to Fort Hall had seemed awful easy compared to the stretch from Kearny to Laramie; but that didn't make the ground any softer. It was sure nice to spend a few nights in a real bed. My feet hung over the end a little but that was okay. I slept like a bear in December every night.

I think if Sandra or Andy would've had their way we would've stayed at Fort Hall longer. They were both enjoying the company of the women and kids staying at the fort. But of course Mr. Worthington was all rambunctious to get back on the trail and on to Oregon City. I came walking up the hall heading to my room one evening when I heard raised voices coming from the Worthingtons' room. It wouldn't have been right to listen. I stood up against the wall so nobody'd see me, and so I could hear better.

"...been here long enough." It was Mr. Worthington. "There is no reason for us to stay any longer."

"But there is, Andrew. That's what I'm trying to say." Sandra sounded frustrated. "Andy is having so much fun playing with the children. Have you seen him? He is having such a time."

"A waste of time if you ask me." He was near to shouting. "What's the purpose of all that running around and carrying on anyway? Can you answer me that?" I honestly don't think that man had ever done anything just for the pure fun of it in his whole damned life.

"He's having fun," she started. "He needs to spend some time with others his own..."

"Don't argue with me woman!" Mr. Worthington interrupted her. "He needs to grow up and to prepare for manhood." His voice lowered and got real mean sounding. "Both of you have changed since we've left St. Louis. You would never have dared contradict me before." Then he said what I'd been waiting for; I knew it was coming.

"It's spending time around that guide of ours isn't it?" He couldn't even say my name. "He's been putting these ideas in your heads hasn't he?"

"Mount? Andrew, do you really think that Mount is..." I heard her laugh, but there was no humor in it. "Don't be ridiculous Andrew."

I heard several quick steps and then, what I figured was the bed squeak as he hauled her up off it.

"You watch your mouth woman!" I could've heard him in my own room now. I had one hand on the door handle, and if I heard him hit her I was going in.

Her voice was cold as a January morning. "Let go of me Andrew. You're hurting me." There was a pause, I assume he let go.

"You're right Andrew." Her voice was still cold. "Andy and I have both changed. Traveling across the country, being captured by Indians, and nearly killed several times I think would change any person. And yes, Andrew, having Mount with us has helped us change. He's taught us an incredible amount, especially Andy. And it's all been for the good, for both of us. And don't forget the fact that we would probably all be dead, or worse, if it wasn't for Mount." Her voice melted a little as she spoke. "We're growing into our own people, Andrew. We are not just Andrew Worthington the Second's wife and son anymore...and that's a good thing."

"A good thing for whom?" His voice hadn't softened much. I heard his footsteps coming and nearly busted my neck getting down the hall and into my room before he got to the door. He stormed out and stomped away down the hall. I lay on my bed staring, watching a spider at work up in the corner. I wanted to go to their room and talk to her, comfort her, see that she was okay, but I knew I couldn't. Could I? I fell asleep debating the issue.

Once again we were able to restock our supplies before leaving Fort Hall. This time our supplies included several bottles of whiskey, which I was mighty glad to see although I didn't know if I'd be tastin' any of it or not, with Mr. Worthington seeming to dislike me more and more as time went on. So I was surprised, and pleased as hell, when he handed me a couple of the bottles and asked coldly if I had room in my roll. I think it was more the fact that he simply didn't have any room on the packhorse, rather than

171

a friendly gesture. I really didn't give a hoot why, I just made room for the bottles.

Part of our restocking was clothes. I don't think I've talked yet about these city folks' love for clothes. I'm telling you, the Worthingtons changed clothes like the wind changes direction. When we first started out, and still had the wagon, there were whole trunks full of nothing but clothes. And it wasn't just Sandra's either, there were just as much for Mr. Worthington and Andy. After losing the wagon, then being captured by the Indians, they'd lost everything except what they wore. At Fort Kearny they'd gotten several changes apiece, and stocked up some more at Fort Hall. All those clothes sure took up a lot of room on the packhorse; room we could've used for food. Why a person would need more than one good set of clothes plumb evades me. Maybe it's because those store bought clothes, whichever fabric they're made of, weren't worth a damn anyway. The wool shirt and britches I'd gotten at Fort Laramie were already showing signs of wearing out, and it'd barely been a month. I needed to get me some deer hides and make some real clothes.

The morning we left Fort Hall there was quite a crowd gathered to see us off. There were even a few tears among the womenfolk; Andy and his new friends said goodbye by punching each other. No one had much to say to me. The more I had to do with people, the more I liked being alone.

It was fairly early in the morning and already getting hot. It promised to be a real scorcher. Once we'd left, again following the Oregon Trail, we followed the Snake River for several days then headed out across the great Columbia Plateau. Our next destination was Fort Boise, around 250 miles to the northwest.

I was glad to be back on the trail. Not only were we on the road again, but passing through some mighty pretty country. The river wound its way around the southern end of the Bitterroot Mountains with some other, smaller mountains, moving off to our south. Those first few days while we traveled along the river the grass remained green and the land dotted with flowers.

Once we moved away from the river, out on the plateau where water was scarce, the flowers mostly dried up except for dandelions and some larkspur; they'll grow anywhere. There was, of course, sage brush but the grass too was burnt. Off in the distance, to the north, we could still see pine forest; here and there sprinkled with different types of trees. The forest covered the distant foothills and stretched up into the mountains.

We were several days out on the Columbia Plateau. We'd been making real good time and had fallen into our daily routine. Mr. Worthington rode out front as usual. In the evening I looked for a hidden spot to make camp, and still posted a lookout at night. There hadn't been any Indian trouble but I wasn't taking chances.

The day it happened, mid-afternoon we'd come on a nice, strong running creek with some cottonwoods and cedars growing along it, and decided to stop early since running water was rare crossing the plateau. We set up camp up against an embankment that had washed out. I was coming back from seeing to the horses up above.

"Andrew please! You should be gathering wood or helping with the horses or something." I couldn't see and thought at first that Sandra was talking to Mr. Worthington and I started grinning. When I cleared the trees I saw she was talking to Andy who was sitting in the shade by the creek, boots off, and his feet in the water to his ankles. He was playing with some sort of puzzle made of rope and an iron ring he'd gotten at the fort. "Stop playing with that thing and help. I mean it now."

"Ahh, Ma" He didn't even look up. "I almost have it, hang on."

"You need to do what your ma says boy." I said as I walked into camp. I didn't even stop to think if my saying something was proper or not. Fact is, most of the time, I don't consider right or wrong before I open my big mouth. And besides, a boy just shouldn't backtalk his ma. "Go do what you were told."

Andy reacted just like most kids his age would. He stood up, threw down the puzzle he'd been working on, slipped on his boots, giving us that "I hate you" look the whole time, then stomped off muttering under his breath about how life just wasn't fair. Reckon he was right about that.

"Andy, now hold on a minute." I already felt bad, and started to go after him. He disappeared over the bank.

"It's okay Mount," Sandra called out to me. "Let him go. I think he could use being alone for a little while."

I thought about it, and decided she was right. We all had very little time alone, except Mr. Worthington who made a point of staying alone. I went over to where she sat and joined her. Oh Lord, why didn't I go after him right away?

I waited twenty minutes or so and couldn't stop thinking about Andy. We'd been getting along so well. He was like the little brother I'd never have; and I couldn't stop seeing that ugly glare he'd given me when I scolded him.

"Where's Mr. Worthington?" I asked.

"He went down the creek," Sandra answered. I could tell by the way she kept looking over toward where Andy'd gone that she was startin' to worry too.

"I'm going to look for Andy," I said as I stood up. I followed the game trail that he'd followed out of the creek bed and into the trees. It weaved through a stand of cedars, around a pile of deadfall, and past the cottonwoods. The trees thinned out there with only a few still along the creek. Off to my right the gently rolling hills began. The game trail angled left, following the creek, but I noticed some boot prints in the dirt headed onto the burnt grass and sagebrush covered hills.

As I topped the first knoll I began to hear a strange noise, an odd buzzing sound that seemed to be coming from all around me. It was familiar, but I couldn't place it. The sound got louder as I crested the hill. When I cleared the top, so I could look down into the next draw, I froze. The blood in my veins turned to ice, and I broke into a cold sweat. Panic grabbed a hold and started squeezin' my guts and numbing my brain.

Andy stood twenty feet away. He stood perfectly still, paralyzed with fear, and didn't make a sound even when he saw me step into view. Tears were streaming down his face. The reason I didn't recognize the unusual sound was that I'd only ever heard one snake rattle at a time. Andy had four big diamondback rattlers within five feet of him. All four coiled up, tail end up and rattling, business end up and ready for action. Behind Andy I could see five or six more snakes slithering among the rocks. Andy had walked smack dab into a den of western diamondbacks.

I had to fight off that first wave of panic. For a few seconds my mind just went plumb stupid, and all I could think to do was turn and run as fast and as far as I could. I didn't. Common sense, and my concern for Andy, overcame the panic. I had to take a couple seconds and clear my head so I could think. Andy's life depended on it.

"Okay now Andy." I tried to sound calm and confident. "You just stand right there for a little longer and I'll be right back. You're gonna be okay, just don't move a muscle."

I backed up slowly a few steps, then turned and sprinted back to the trees. I found a sturdy limb about eight feet long with a crotch near the end. As I ran back over the hill I took my knife and cut the ends so I had a fairly short Y at the end.

Nothing had changed when I got back, except Andy looked even more scared, if that was possible. I moved up to within six feet of the snake nearest me, and directly in front of Andy. Slowly...very slowly...I moved the Y at the end of my stick so it was directly behind his head. Then quickly...very quickly...I jabbed forward and down and used the Y to pin the rattler's head to the ground. He uncoiled and started whipping himself back and forth trying to get free. In one fluid motion, I raised the stick, slid it under his body, lifted, twisted, and threw him off to the right. He hit the ground five feet away and slithered off into the rocks. Two steps to the right and one forward and I was in position for the next snake. Slowly...very slowly...I moved my stick towards its head. It turned and struck. Andy let out a little squeak, but didn't move. I think I peed a little. The rattler hit the stick and settled to the ground. I was able to trap him before he could coil for another try. I scooped him up like the last one and threw him easily ten feet further; mostly because of fear. He too disappeared into the rocks. Sweat was running into my eyes and my hands were shaking. I wiped my eyes and took a couple deep breaths. The third snake went the way of the first two with no problem. I moved in to get the last one. I was within touching distance of Andy; the snake being to the right and behind him a couple feet. I glanced from the snake to Andy. Our eyes made contact; and that's when it happened. A sob escaped Andy's throat and his left foot shuffled no more than half an inch. I stabbed forward with my stick as soon as I realized Andy had moved, but I was too late. That snake struck with the speed of lightning, and my stick missed. The snake hit Andy about halfway up his calf; about two inches above the top of his boot, and just kinda hung there clinging to his leg. I actually had to knock it off with my stick. I pinned its head to the ground, pulled my knife from the sheath, bent, and sliced that son of a bitch in two just below its ugly head. The head died instantly, but the body kept squirming and twisting. I didn't waste any more time. Andy was in shock. He stood staring down at his leg where the snake was just hanging. He didn't make a sound, and couldn't seem to move. I checked the ground behind us for snakes then snatched Andy up and ran.

When I got to the other side of the hill and was fairly sure there were no snakes around I lay Andy down. He'd started to cry. I used the piece of rope I had for a belt and tied it off about midway up his thigh to try and slow the poison. Then I picked him up again and ran for camp.

They heard us coming. When I dashed over the bank down into the washout Sandra and Mr. Worthington were both standing and waiting. I didn't have time to be answering questions.

"Snake bite," I simply said. I lay Andy beside the fire and reached again for my knife. Sandra had fallen to her knees beside me.

"Oh God, no." Sandra's hands were clinched into fists at the sides of her face. "No, no, no. Mount please...no...no...Mount please." She raised her fists into the air and screamed. "Oh why God? Why my little boy?" She sank back to the ground crying. Mr. Worthington hadn't moved, he just stood and stared; a blank look on a ghostly white face. It was obvious, just like when I'd set Sandra's broke leg, he wasn't gonna be any help.

I left the rope tied around his leg, and used my knife to cut his pants open from the knee down. I set the knife tip in the fire while I looked for the bite marks. They were easy to find, it being one damn big snake. Andy had two deep wounds on the back of his calf. The leg was already swelling and the skin around the fang marks already changing color. Andy was lying on his side and crying softly. I could hear Sandra crying beside me. There was a piece of tree bark laying there; I picked it up and gave it to Andy.

"Bite down on this." He took it and bit down. I took the knife from the fire and quickly sliced across the snake bite. Andy screamed through the bark and tried to pull away.

"Hold him down," I yelled, not bothering to look up. Sandra, still crying, hurried around me and knelt behind him. She lay across his shoulders, and I could hear her talking to him. He still screamed as I cut. I slashed twice across each fang mark, started squeezing his leg from the top down, and started sucking poison blood from the cuts for all I was worth. I'd squeeze from where the rope was tied down, suck as much blood as I could, spit, and then do it again, over and over and over until I simply couldn't anymore. As I sank to the ground exhausted, I realized that I only heard one person crying. It was Sandra; Andy had passed out. I swished and spat out two mouthfuls of whiskey, then swallowed the next three or four.

Sandra sat on the ground holding Andy in her arms. She was staring up into my eyes. She didn't need to speak; her eyes spoke loud and clear.

"I don't know." I shook my head. "I've done all I know to do. He's in God's hands now."

We wrapped Andy in his blanket and Sandra insisted on staying on the ground next to the fire with him in her arms. Andy had fallen into a fitful sorta sleep. He moaned and groaned and tossed and turned so much Sandra had a hard time even hanging on to him; still she wouldn't let go. Mr. Worthington had disappeared.

I sat beside Sandra and Andy, now and then taking a pull from the whiskey bottle to make sure I killed any poison I may've swallowed. When Andy wasn't tossing and turning Sandra would rock him back and forth like a baby. Both of us jumped when we heard Mr. Worthington's rifle fire. After about the time it would take to tamp a new round, it went off again, then again, and again. Mr. Worthington was killing snakes.

Within an hour the worst of it had started. Sandra finally started to cramp up and was forced to lay Andy down so she could move around. Mr. Worthington had come back; after killing all the snakes he could find. He sat on the ground beside Sandra staring down at Andy. He'd talked very little, and hadn't given Sandra any comfort of any sort. I sat off a little ways wishing I could comfort her, or do something more for Andy.

Andy had started shivering uncontrollably and at the same time sweat poured off him. He puked over and over again until his body heaved but nothing came up. The worst part was when his eyes would open. They were watery, glassy, and unable to focus, but you could still see the pain, confusion, and fear reflected there; when his eyes opened I had to look away. His leg, from knee to ankle, was already damn near twice its normal size and an ugly shade of blackish purple. A yellowish fluid drained from the bite. At one point during the night Andy came around. I was nearly asleep sitting there when I realized Andy was talking.

"I don't wanna die, Ma." His eyes were focused and locked on his mother's. "Please Momma, I don't wanna die."

"You're not gonna die! You hear me!" She really did sound mad, even though I knew she was just really scared. "You hear me Andrew Worthington! You are not...you are not gonna...." She broke down and began to cry. It didn't matter, Andy's eyes had rolled back into his head and he was gone again. He began to shiver worse than ever. I put my blanket around him and got Sandra's for her. Even beside the fire on this summer night it seemed mighty cold.

Sometime after that I dozed off. When I woke up it was just starting to get light. The eastern horizon had a warm pink glow, promising a hot day ahead. Straight overhead the sky was a deep purple color as it got ready to change for the day. Off to the west I could see a couple of the brighter stars still hanging in the sky like they didn't want to give up the night; a fight I was pretty sure they'd lose.

With the mountains silhouetted off in the distance against the northern horizon, I swear, for the first couple seconds, still half asleep, I thought I was home at my cabin, and couldn't remember why I'd slept outside; but only for a couple seconds, then it all came back in a flash...a horrible disturbing flash. I sat up and looked around. Sandra had Andy in her lap again or at least as much of him as she could get. She was rocking slowly back and forth and crying quietly. My first thought was that the worst had happened, but then I saw that Andy was breathing and even seemed to be sleeping fairly peacefully. Behind them, Mr. Worthington lay wrapped in his blanket sound asleep. Sandra and I locked eyes and she smiled through the tears.

"I think he's going to be okay Mount." Her breath caught and she sobbed so hard her whole body shook. It took a few seconds before she could go on. "I really think he's going to be alright. He hasn't had any convulsions for quite a while now. That means he's okay right?" She forced a little smile onto her lips, but her eyes were still full of fear. "Right Mount...he's going to be okay...right?"

"Well Sandra, I just don't rightly know," I answered honestly. If the good Lord had owed me a favor I would've called it in right then so I could tell her everything was gonna be fine; but I couldn't. "I'm hoping them in Heaven have made their decision to let him stay, and now it's up to Andy. If that's the case, then yeah, I think he'll be just fine. He's a fighter." I looked at the ground between my feet. "Besides, he's got the most wonderful mother in the world to come back for."

I looked, and Sandra was smiling up at me, a real smile this time. The tears streaking her cheeks somehow made her even more beautiful. Her raven black hair was loose and fell off both shoulders and disappeared under Andy. Her dark brown eyes glistened with tears, still brimmed with fear, yet sparkled with her smile. Have I ever mentioned to you folks that Sandra was one mighty fine-looking woman?

"You know, you very well may have saved Andy's life…again." She had to pause for a moment. "Thank you Mount. Thank you more than I can say." Her eyes got that look again. The one that said she wouldn't mind if I took her in my arms and held her. Oh Lord, how I wanted to. With an effort I tore my eyes away from hers, and they landed smack dab on Mr. Worthington still asleep over yonder. The husband and father of the woman and boy that I had to finally admit I was falling in love with. I reminded myself once again, for about the hundredth time, that I couldn't let it happen. I thanked Sandra without looking back at her, got up, and went for a walk to clear my head.

When I got back it was full daylight. Andy was still sleeping wrapped up in his blanket. Mr. Worthington was tending the fire and Sandra was gone. She hadn't left Andy's side since I carried him into camp, so I imagine she was taking care of business. Mr. Worthington kept looking my way and I could tell he wanted to say something. Finally he came over to where I stood.

"I want to thank you for what you did for Andrew." There was no more emotion in his voice than if he were ordering up a drink at the saloon. He paused for just a second and then continued, his voice suddenly full of anger. "From now on I don't expect you to let Andrew go wandering off by himself. You need to keep a better watch on him." He turned and walked away.

First off I damn near went and hit him. My next thought was to call him back and explain a thing or two about being a father. What I did was sigh and remind myself the man was an idiot when it came to family, and let it be; besides I half blamed myself too. At least he said "thank you."

Andy drifted in and out of sleep all that day and the next night. I cut some heavy branches and built a little lean-to so Andy would be in the shade, and we cooled him with water constantly. The stomach sickness, shivers, sweats, and the like came and went. As the next day turned to night and the night wore on, the bouts of sickness got weaker and fewer. His leg was still badly swollen and now nearly solid black. Several times I opened the cuts in his leg and tried to drain as much out as I could. Andy wasn't out of the woods yet, but damned if it didn't appear the trees were getting a little thinner.

Next morning I was up early and off hunting. Everybody else was still asleep. Sandra and Andy lay beside what was left of the fire, Sandra's arm around him. Mr. Worthington was wrapped in his blanket down the creek a little ways. I figured it was time to get me a deer hide and start working on some new britches. These wool britches itched bad, and bound me up where a man don't like to be bound up.

I came back to camp a couple hours later with the intentions of getting a bite to eat, then going and skinning the big doe I'd gutted and had hanging from a tree back up the game trail a couple hundred feet. When I cleared the creek bank and entered camp I forgot about the deer; and everything else. Mr. Worthington was nowhere to be seen. Sandra was squatted by the fire stirring the large cooking pot. Andy was sitting up, propped against a saddle, with a cup of broth held firmly with both hands. Both were looking up at me with face-splitting grins.

"Howdy Mount," Andy said it like it was just another morning. His voice was a little weak, but sounded like music from heaven to me. "Have any luck? We heard a shot awhile ago."

I couldn't answer him. Damned if right then I didn't get a chunk of something in my eye the size of a walnut, and my throat must'a closed up with the pain because I couldn't talk. I think I managed a smile and nod, then went to my bedroll for my cup so I could get some soup.

Chapter Nineteen

We stayed put for four more days. It took two more full days before Andy's shivers and shakes and bouts of the pukes went away completely. Two more days before the swelling in his leg even started to go down. Even on the fifth day, when I helped Andy hobble up the creek to where the horses were, he was in an awful lot of pain. Sandra had followed us. Mr. Worthington, as usual, was pressing to get going. I'd seen Mr. Worthington talking to Andy the previous evening and knew the bastard had pressured Andy to travel. I think Sandra was fixin' to get riled up and demand we stay put until Andy had healed up some more and was a little stronger. Andy himself settled things by insisting he was okay to travel, and proved it by gritting his teeth, mounting up on Skyhawk, and riding around a little.

"See Ma, I'm just fine," he said from horseback. He even managed a brave little smile. "Let's get going."

Mr. Worthington was a couple hundred feet down the creek at camp packing. Sandra stood and stared up at Andy for a few seconds. There was still doubt in her beautiful brown eyes, but then she shrugged her small, delicate shoulders.

"Well okay, let's get going." She turned and started back to get her bedroll. I was the only one that saw the tears of pain that filled Andy's eyes after Sandra turned away, and the effort it took for him not to cry out from the pain in his leg.

"You ain't ready to ride yet," I said to him. "I'm gonna call another couple days' rest."

"No Mount, please don't!" His voice and eyes were both pleading his case. "Father is real anxious to get going and I don't want to slow us down anymore." He knew that excuse alone wasn't going to be enough for me. "And, I want to see if I'm tough enough to do it, really I do. Come on Mount, I can do it, let me prove it."

Why is it so danged hard to say no to a kid? I stared at him hard and decided, pressure from his pa or not, Andy really, truly did want to try.

"Okay, but you ain't gonna prove it for too long." I tried to make it sound like I was still in charge. "The first sign of your wearing out and we're stopping, that clear?"

"Yeah Mount, that's clear. Thank you." He smiled through the pain. We both knew who was really running things; it sure as hell wasn't me.

"Oh...and Andy?" He looked down from Skyhawk as I started walking over to where Goldfire stood. "Next time I say something that gets you riled up, and you go running off...watch where the hell you're going." I stepped up into the saddle and rode back down the creek to the camp site. Even through the pain, Andy's laughter followed me.

Once we got back to the main trail, which wasn't much of a trail out across that barren plateau, the sun had had a chance to climb into the sky and was doing a job of heating up the day. The creek we'd left behind was the last running water we saw till mid-afternoon the next day. We made less than ten miles and Andy'd had enough. He was sagging in the saddle, and I called a stop before he fell and got hurt more. He rode with his right hand holding the reins and his left hand rubbing his leg. He tried to put up a good front but the boy was hurting bad. Mr. Worthington made it clear by the expression on his face that he wasn't happy about stopping so soon, but he knew better than to say anything.

There wasn't a damn tree in sight, so I used three saddles for a base, then piled sage high up against them, and made enough shade for Sandra and Andy to be fairly comfortable. Sandra, with water from a canteen, kept a wet cloth on Andy's forehead while he rested. After a couple hour break, Andy wasn't able to sleep but the rest helped a lot, then some fresh made jerky, and Andy was ready to travel again; and again, he wore out fast. After another hour in the saddle the pain was just too much. We made camp for the day in a cutout between two sandstone shelves. There was no water, but we had shade from mid-afternoon on. We made Andy as comfortable as we could. I watched him lay there and try hard not to let the pain show. He could hide it on his face, but it was there in his eyes. It hurt to watch him. You could tell he was exhausted, but the pain wouldn't let him drift off to sleep. I wandered over to Goldfire and came back with a mug of water.

"Here's some water for Andy." I handed the mug to Sandra. "Have him drink it all."

Sandra took the mug and turned towards Andy. She froze, lifted the mug closer to her face, turned and looked at me with a shocked and questioning frown. I smiled a little smile and nodded toward Andy. "Have him drink it all," I repeated.

She paused, considered for a few seconds, then turned and handed Andy the mug. He'd been watching our eye talk, and he wasn't a dumb kid. He'd figured it out and took the mug with his own smile. He raised the mug to his nose and his grin grew when he smelled the whiskey. He looked over to where Mr. Worthington was tending a sore foot and not paying a bit of attention, then took a good healthy swallow. Now let me explain to you folks right here that it wasn't straight whiskey I was giving the boy. I'd just splashed a little in the bottom of the mug before filling it with water, figuring it would help with the pain, and hopefully allow him to sleep. Still, as weak as it was, he swallowed, shuddered all over once or twice and coughed like hell. When he recovered to the point that he could breathe again, just like I knew he would, Andy tipped that mug up and took a bigger drink. By the end of the mug he was hardly coughing at all.

I'm not sure Sandra was real happy with my way of doctorin', but she didn't have anything better, and she sure couldn't argue with the results. It didn't take but a few minutes and Andy was laying back in the shade with the most restful look he'd had since he'd been bit, and five minutes later he drifted off to sleep.

Later, getting on towards dark, I gave Andy another mug and had him take a couple swallows before I used some straight whiskey to clean the wound on his leg. I figured infection was about the only worry left. I ain't sure if the drink helped or not, he screamed like a banshee when I poured that firewater over his leg.

That became our routine for the next few days. Andy was good for a couple hours at most in the saddle then he needed to rest. At night I'd clean out the fang marks with whiskey, and slowly the swelling started to go down and normal color started coming back to Andy's leg. The third day we came up on some fresh running water. After that, for the next two days, we came across creeks pretty regular.

The mountains started moving in closer from the north, and the little hills to our south were growing up into some respectable peaks, both getting bigger by the day. It looked like there was a way through, but it was gonna get steep again. One day, late afternoon, we started climbing. We stopped for the night beside a nice spring that was running strong. The next morning we headed up. I don't rightly know if the trail we were following was the Oregon Trail anymore or just a damned goat path. Remember, we were a couple years ahead of the main rush of folks, and the trail hadn't been used much. I sure as hell couldn't see folks taking wagons where our horses sometimes had trouble staying surefooted. As the switchbacks took us higher and higher, Sandra's fear of heights got stronger and stronger.

"You okay?" I asked as we traversed the mountainside. Mr. Worthington was in front. Andy, still hurtin', was next followed by Sandra, then me. There was nearly a thousand-foot drop off our left side and a vertical mountain face on our right. Sandra remembered the trick she'd used before. Her eyes were locked on a spot right between her horse's ears. Her body was ramrod straight. You could smell the fear coming off her. Well, maybe that was the last three weeks on the trail. She didn't respond, so I asked again. "Sandra, you okay?"

Her lips barely moved. "Yeah" was all she managed.

"You want for us to stop?" I offered. "Maybe go back down?" It was real hard seeing her in such a state. I'm not sure she was this terrified when she was tied to a tree in that Indian camp.

This time she managed all of four words. "Is there another way?"

I didn't know. "I don't rightly know," I answered.

"Then we'll keep going," she said. The only thing that moved were her lips, like if she moved anything else, that whole damned mountain was gonna crumble right out from under her. Her eyes stayed locked on anything other than the drop to her left; and we kept moving slowly along.

Andy's toughness and resolve were sorely tested that day too. None of us wanted to spend the night on that mountainside. As hard as Sandra worked to keep her panic under control, Andy worked twice as hard just to stay in the saddle and keep moving. He too stared straight ahead, and you could see the muscles clench in his jaws from trying to hold back the pain. His leg was back to nearly normal size, but was still black around the bite, and although the pain had let up some, after riding as long as we had, Andy was in agony.

We didn't move fast but we kept moving. With those two city slickers showing a true mountain man's courage we made it up and across the face of that mountain, and came down the other side into one of the prettiest valleys you'll ever see. As we reached the valley floor the sun was just going down off in the distance setting the whole damned horizon ablaze. The clouds that stretched out across the sky ranged from brilliant yellow, to a red that seemed on fire, and then bright orange changing to a pale pink just above us. Halfway between here and there was a line of trees running north and south. I was damn sure hoping they'd be there, and was mighty glad to see them.

The next day we made it to that line of trees and met back up with the Snake River. It'd swung south of us, as we cut across the Columbia Plateau, then had worked its way back north to where we met it. We'd follow it now into Fort Boise.

Those next couple days along the Snake heading to Fort Boise were easily the best of this leg of our journey. Most important, Andy's leg was doing much better and hardly hurt anymore. The color had come back except for about three inches all around the bite, which I doubt will ever heal. Sandra had been in an exceptionally good mood since we'd reached the valley.

The Snake River was awful pretty rolling down that valley, making its way through some beautiful meadows and lined on both sides with different types of trees. The river was a mighty welcome traveling companion; and we were eating really good too; with all the jerky from the deer I'd butchered at snakebite camp, plus we still had supplies from Fort Hall. Added to that it was getting to be prime berry season, and that meant chokecherries, huckleberries, wild raspberries, hawthorn berries the size of a crab apple, and more. Food wasn't a problem.

Ole Mr. "gotta get there" Worthington, as usual, rode ahead of us like that was gonna get us there faster. I followed up behind, and couldn't help but smile as I watched Andy riding stronger and feeling better all the time. I also caught myself smiling a time or two while I simply watched Sandra ride.

By noon of the third day along the Snake I wasn't feeling nearly as at ease. I'd seen Indian scouts three different times since morning, watchin' us from the hills. We were riding out in the open away from the river, beside the trees. The Indians hadn't done anything, and I hadn't seen more than the three, or maybe the same one three different times, so I hadn't said anything to the others.

It'd been an hour or so since I'd seen the last one and I was just starting to relax a little when I saw two Indians directly to our right, maybe a quarter-mile away, trying to stay hidden up a little tree-filled draw. As we passed I saw one back out, turn and ride hell bent up the draw and out of sight. I knew. I don't know how I knew, but I just knew. Thank the good Lord I did.

"Ride!" I shouted. Sandra in front of me and Andy in front of her had both been daydreaming and off in their own little worlds. At my shout they sat up and turned to look at me. "Indian attack! Ride! Ride!" I shouted and kicked Goldfire into action.

Sandra and Andy paused for only an instant before taking off like the wind. There wasn't an Indian in sight but the urgency in my voice, and just the word "Indian" was enough to convince them. Mr. Worthington heard the commotion and stopped to wait for us.

"Ride Pa!" Andy was the first to reach Mr. Worthington. "Indians Pa, ride!" Then he was past. Sandra rode past her husband at a full gallop without saying a word. Twice she'd turned to look behind, and I was able to see her eyes. Pure panic; in her eyes was pure panic. They were big and glassy, her mouth open in a silent scream, and she hung on to her horse for all she was worth.

I had to hold Goldfire back a little to stay behind Andy and Sandra, but I was still moving fast as I approached Mr. Worthington.

"What the hell's wrong with you?" I shouted. "Ride!" I pulled Goldfire back to a walk.

"I don't see any Indians," he shouted back as I moved past him. "Where are they?"

As if in answer to his question, out of the next draw ahead and to our right came a thunderous Indian war cry followed immediately by what looked to be a small raiding party. Probably thirty or so Indians were riding full out heading to cut us off. I don't remember urging Goldfire at all; suddenly we were just back up to a full gallop. Mr. Worthington was finally convinced, and I heard him yelling and swearing at his horse to follow.

As I watched those Indians coming across that meadow heading for where we were gonna be, I heard more commotion behind. I turned and saw another twenty or so Indians that'd come outta the draw behind us, and were now cutting off any retreat we may've had. Mr. Worthington was up to a full gallop and coming hard. When I turned back to the front my blood ran cold, and my heart skipped a couple beats. There were three Indians from the pack that'd pulled out ahead of the others, and it was clear they were gonna get to the trail in front of us. I had to do something.

"Fly Goldfire! Fly like the wind!" I shouted. Kicking him wasn't necessary. The tone in my voice and the smell of fear coming off me in waves was plenty. From a full gallop, he took off like a shot, so fast in fact that I damn near didn't keep up, and nearly spilled off the back. When I got back firmly in the saddle and was able to look ahead, we were gaining on Sandra and Andy fast, but I wasn't sure if it was gonna be fast enough. The three lead Indians were gonna get to the trail before we passed them, and there was no turning back. I urged Goldfire on even faster, and again…somehow, he responded.

As I passed Sandra, the Indians were maybe three hundred feet to the right of the trail and coming fast; as I pulled beside Andy they were less than a hundred. My rifle hung from my saddle, useless as a buffalo robe in a heat wave. I saw the lead Indian reach for an arrow and notch it in his bow. I had no weapon other than my horse and myself. I turned Goldfire into the path of the Indian pony and just as he let loose with the arrow we slammed into him, our horses meeting chest to chest. There was no doubt who was gonna win that battle. That little Indian pony buckled and went over sideways taking its rider with it. Goldfire stumbled with the impact and then plowed right into the second horse that was directly behind the first. Our momentum was less, and the second horse was bigger. Goldfire still got the best of the collision but as the Indian horse went down Goldfire lurched and went down on his front knees with his head nearly touching the ground. I tried my damndest to stay up but couldn't, and shoulder rolled off to the right.

I rolled once and came up onto my feet. I turned and saw that the third Indian rider was just feet away from Sandra, as she and Andy rode side by side. Two running steps and I threw myself into the side of that charging horse and grabbed for the Indian. You'd think there'd be a little give in horseflesh; there ain't. Slamming into the side of that horse was like running full on into a moving mountain. I was thrown backwards but managed to grab that Indian's legging as I fell. I couldn't hang on, but I felt him coming off his horse, and was delighted to hear him scream out in pain.

I couldn't see a thing for a few seconds, as I was busy rolling and bouncing across the ground. Before I came to a full stop I was up on my feet and running. Sandra and Andy had passed, and Mr. Worthington was just going by. The first Indian we'd hit was still on the ground and wasn't moving. The one I'd just ripped off his horse by his leg was laying there screaming like a mad man with his leg sticking out at a real funny angle from his hip. The Indian that'd been on the second horse, had made it up to one knee, and was staring at the ground and shaking his head trying to clear it. Three or four quick steps and I kicked up and into his face as hard as I could. The top of my boot covered from mid nose to his forehead. The sound was sorta like swinging a big pole into a wet melon, followed by a loud crack that was the melon's nose breaking. That Indian went over backwards like he was meaning to stay there awhile.

I never even stopped running. Goldfire was standing twenty feet away waiting on me. His eyes were wide with fear and he pawed the ground nervously; but he was waiting. A few more steps and I was up on his back. It took Goldfire all of five steps and he was up to full speed. I finally was able to look around. The rest of the Indians were just reaching the fallen braves. A couple stopped to help, the rest came running; screaming even louder than before.

In front of me the Worthingtons had a good head start and were moving fast. As I watched, Sandra turned and looked back at me, our eyes met and I saw her concern. Even in her panic she'd needed to look and see if I was okay.

Hell no, I wasn't ok! I had nearly fifty angry Indians chasin' my ass. And worst of all, I knew that with Goldfire under me, if I was gonna get caught the Worthingtons would get caught too. I couldn't bear to think about that.

I saw a couple arrows fly past wide of the mark before I was out of range. Goldfire was so smooth and so fast, even under these circumstances I couldn't help but admire his strength. I gained on the Worthingtons and the Indians fell back. Problem was, when I caught up to the Worthingtons I'd have to slow down. I could only pray to God that we didn't have to slow down too much.

When Goldfire and I caught up with the Worthingtons, Mr. Worthington and Sandra were nearly side by side in front with Andy right behind. I pulled up beside Andy and slowed to his speed.

"We can outrun them! Keep riding!" I tried to shout loud enough for all three of them to hear me.

"Where are we headed for Mount?" Andy yelled as we rode side by side.

"Don't know!" I yelled back. I turned to look, the Indians were still a fair piece back, but it looked like they were gaining ground.

"Well, what are we going to do?" He couldn't hide the panic in his voice. I wished to hell I had a better answer for him.

"Don't know!" I kept my eyes forward so I wouldn't have to meet his stare.

We rode in silence for a couple minutes; each of us lost in our own nightmare. I dropped back a few feet and turned to look again. We still had a two or three hundred yard lead, but there was no doubt those bastards were gaining on us. I looked out ahead and saw a little rise was coming up. If it slowed us down much we were gonna be finished.

And it did slow us some. Our larger horses were getting tired and were no match for those smaller, faster Indian ponies. Except for Goldfire, of course, who I believe could outrun any other horse alive. As we came up over that rise those Indians were less than a hundred yards behind us. We could hear their war cries. That was the bad news. The good news...the really damned good news...was that there in front of us, less than a quarter mile away, was Fort Boise. I wasn't sure at the time if it was Boise or not, and damn sure didn't care, as long as whoever it was would help us.

Andy and I both let out war cries of our own when we saw the fort. The horses found a final burst of energy and stayed about the same distance ahead of the Indians clear to the fort. I lagged behind a little just in case something bad should happen. For once on this adventure, it didn't.

They had the main gate open when we got there. The four of us rode through at full speed and the gate was shut and locked with a lock pole nearly six inches around, before we even got stopped. We didn't see, but were told that those Indians turned tail as soon as they knew we were making it to the gate.

As soon as we stopped, I jumped down off Goldfire and went over to where Sandra and Andy were dismounting. Sandra wrapped Andy in her arms and gave him a good squeeze. When she let go they both had tears in their eyes. I looked at Andy and through the tears in his eyes were shining like a full moon on a clear fall night. There was pure joy in those eyes, the kind only a kid who'd just escaped a pack of Indians could conjure up.

"We did it Mount!" he nearly shouted with excitement. "We outran them."

"We surely did Andy." My grin nearly matched his. "That was some mighty fine riding you did. Good job."

"And you knew this fort was here didn't you?" He looked at me with a knowing kinda expression. "You knew we could make it here when they started chasing us didn't you Mount?"

"Sure I did Andy." I lied, and gave a little laugh while I looked at my boots. "I knew it was just over that rise all along. Hell, I wasn't ever worried a bit."

"I'm thinking that's a tall tale, Mount." Sandra laughed. "I'm thinking you were just as terrified as we were."

"Probably more," I admitted. I looked over at Sandra. Our eyes met, and in that instant I think everything that'd happened sank in for her. I saw the joy in her eyes at being here and being safe, but I also saw the fear still left over, and I saw something else too. She stepped up to me and put her hand on my arm. Her eyes started brimming over again. Tears rolled down her cheeks. Her hair had come loose and was a wild tangle, sticking up and out everywhere. She was sweating and had dirt smeared across her forehead, nose and right cheek. She never looked more beautiful.

"You saved our lives again Mount. Thank you." She smiled, and her bottom lip trembled. "You threw yourself in front of a charging horse for me Mount, how do I thank you for that?"

I was ready with a real clever answer, something like, "ah hell, I just tripped and fell in front of that horse." but I never got the chance to use it. Just as I was opening my mouth to answer Mr. Worthington brushed past me.

"Come along Sandra, Andrew," he said. He took ahold of Sandra's arm with one hand; grabbed Andy's arm with the other, and led them toward the main building. Sandra pulled her arm free and glared up at him. They paused for a second, he said something I couldn't hear, and she followed him through the door. She did look back at me with a sad little smile as they entered the trading post; I went to see that the horses were being taken care of proper.

Chapter Twenty

Fort Boise was built back in '34 by the Hudson Bay Company. The British built it to compete with the American Traders' Fort Hall for the fur trade. Problem was by the '40s the beaver were getting scarce, the fur trade dyin' out in a hurry. A feller named Thomas McKay ran the place and was real friendly toward us while we were there.

The first evening we were at the fort they put out a feast fit for a damned king or somebody. We sat down to a table overflowing with goose, duck, bacon, salmon, buffalo, elk, deer, boiled potatoes, turnips, and cabbage, with wild berry pie to finish it all off. I don't believe I've ever eaten so much at one sitting. There wasn't one thing on that table that wasn't about as good as it could be; and all the preparing was overseen by one person, one of the few womenfolk at Fort Boise. Her name was Maude Peplow.

Now, I ain't met many men that can look me eye to eye, being tall as I am, and I sure as hell ain't never met a woman that came close...until Maude. That woman was looking down at six foot and appeared to be as strong as any man I've ever seen. Her shoulders were wide and square and she narrowed some toward her waist. Her hips widened back out, with long muscular legs reaching clear to the ground. Her arms were big and strong and her breasts were simply big. Now, being a fairly ugly character myself I ain't in the habit of talking bad about another's looks, but I gotta tell you folks, Maude was not a good looking woman. I'm pretty sure she could scare a buzzard off a bloody carcass with just a glance.

Several times during the meal I noticed Maude staring my way. She had a smile on her face and a glint in her eye that made me real nervous. When I was done eating Maude was still at the serving table helping folks. I went over to thank her for the food and to tell her how good everything had been, because it was the proper thing to do. I mentioned I especially liked the wild berry pie. Her face lit up like high noon.

"Why, I could make you one," Maude exclaimed. "I could make you one of your very own in no time at all."

"Thank you Maude, but no thanks." I wanted to be nice, but not too nice. "A whole berry pie to myself would probably lay me up for days." I grinned hoping she'd just laugh it off. She didn't. Her eyes got this far-off look; she smiled a funny little smile, and kinda rolled her head off to one side.

"I'd take care of you if you got sick Mount." She looked me square in the eyes. "I'd take care of you no matter how long you were sick." Her face turned red, she looked down at the floor and giggled like a little girl.

I mumbled another "no thanks" and nearly ran outside. On my way out I noticed the Worthingtons at their table. Mr. Worthington was looking down at his plate like there wasn't anybody else in the room. Sandra and Andy were both watchin' me and sharing a good laugh.

For damn near the first time on this trip, Mr. Worthington and I agreed on something. He was, as always, in a hurry to restock our supplies and get back on the trail. I agreed the sooner the better, and Maude was only part of the reason. It was getting on towards the end of September and we still had a month or more traveling ahead of us. That was if everything went smoothly, and I knew that sure as hell wasn't gonna happen. In this country winter can hit anytime after the berries ripen. The last thing in the world I wanted was to get caught out on the trail by an early winter storm.

We took a day to rest up and restock. I spent most of it trying to avoid Maude. She spent most of it trying to be where I was. She'd see me and angle my way; I'd see her comin' and angle the other way, suddenly getting real interested in one thing or another. The couple times I was trapped into talking to her, I made it as quick as I could and excused myself claiming work to do. After I'd made sure of everything I needed for the trail, I took a long walk along the river to waste some time.

It was real pretty country, with mountains to the north. The pines covered the foothills, then climbed the side of the mountain in steps, with granite cliffs or sections of slide rock separating each step until it got too high for the trees to grow. The mountain continued up a couple thousand feet above tree line. To the south, stretching off as far as I could see, a beautiful, lush river valley, full of stands of cottonwood, aspen, and birch. I began to really missing my own home in my own valley.

That evening I had Andy go to the kitchen and get me some sandwich makings and I had my evening meal in my sleeping room. Some folks may think it was to keep away from Maude, but I just had a hankering to be alone; ain't nothing wrong with that.

Next morning I was up and gone before the sun, and waited for the Worthingtons a couple miles out from the fort. Some folks may think that was to avoid Maude too, but as the guide, it was my job to scout up ahead…well it was.

Another mile down the river from where I met the Worthingtons was a river crossing, and a wooden ferry to help people across. The Oregon Trail continued on the west side of the Snake River, down through something they called Hell's Canyon, then northwest till we got to the Columbia River. Then we'd follow the Columbia until we got nearly to Oregon City.

"Easy as that," is how one feller at Fort Boise put it. I pointed out that nothing had been easy this whole damned journey.

We were a hundred yards away from the crossing when Sandra moved up beside me. Her voice was filled with fear.

"Those look like Indians, Mount," she said. She reined her horse to a stop. Andy and Mr. Worthington stopped behind us. "Oh God, Mount, those are Indians aren't they?" She started to turn her horse around, and a glance back told me Andy and Mr. Worthington were ready to bolt too.

"Now hang on a minute." I nearly yelled it out. "Those Indians ain't the same that chased us into Boise. These are here to help us ferry across the river."

"And just how do you know that?" Sandra wasn't taking any chances where Indians were concerned. "How can you tell from here that they are friendly?"

"I don't trust them." Andy couldn't hold back any longer. "They're Indians." He said that last word like it tasted real bad.

"These are Cayuse," I tried to explain. "They told us about them back at the fort, remember? For a little prepared jerky and a bottle of whiskey they'll ferry us across the river, otherwise we swim for it." I knew they didn't like that idea. "The Indians that chased us into Fort Boise were most likely Arapaho or maybe Blackfeet. The Cayuse, so far, have no fight with the white man."

"They're Indians," Andy repeated. My explaining didn't make the word taste any better to him. Talking wasn't gonna get anything done.

"You folks wait here," I said as I nudged Goldfire forward. "If you see any of those Indians acting up you hightail it back to Fort Boise. I'll be right behind you."

"No Mount!" Sandra's concern was obvious. "Don't go down there, Mount. You don't know for sure."

"I thank you for worrying Sandra." I couldn't help but see Mr. Worthington's glare before locking eyes with Sandra. "But I do know. Believe me I wouldn't ride down there if I thought there was any chance of them turning on me." I gave her my bravest smile, and rode off at a trot.

Not only were those Indians friendly, they were also drunk. Apparently they were celebrating some special Indian holiday because it was still early morning and they were nearly to the bottom of their second bottle of whiskey. The first bottle was planted upside down in the soft dirt beside the river, and one particular Indian, I figure the one that did the planting, was pointing and laughing, like an upside down bottle in the dirt was the funniest thing he'd ever seen. The other three Indians were laughing at the first one laughing at the bottle.

When I got close, and the Indians became aware someone was coming, they took to singing and dancing and carrying on like they were plumb loco. The good thing was that their carrying on was seen by the Worthingtons and it should have been clear, even to them, that these Indians were no threat to anybody but themselves. The Worthingtons started slowly riding in.

The Indians saw the other horses coming and got even wilder. They were dancing in a circle around that damned planted whiskey bottle when the family got there. I was smiling myself and watching Sandra when I realized the Indians were suddenly quiet and still. As they rode up, Sandra had taken off her hat and brushed some loose hair back behind her ears. Those four Indians were standing, mouths hanging open, and staring. For them, any white woman was something to stare at, and they'd never seen a woman nearly as beautiful as Sandra. I found myself staring at her too, and feeling a little jealous despite myself.

"Have you negotiated our crossing?" Mr. Worthington broke the trance Sandra's beauty had put us in. "Are these savages even capable of getting us across?"

The Indian closest to Mr. Worthington answered before I could open my mouth.

"I assure you sir; we are most capable of getting you fine people across the river." Other than the fat tongue caused by the whiskey, he didn't have even a hint of Indian accent. "And who sir, are you calling savages?" At that, they were off again, laughing, dancing and carrying on.

Turned out the talkative one's name was Towahnah and he'd been raised by some white folks up Chicago way. Seems he'd been found nearly froze to death early one spring by some trappers up north, with all the rest of his people lying dead around him. The trappers had nursed him back to life and kept him until they crossed paths with a couple scouts heading to Chicago to report to their employer. The scouts took the Indian youngun with them, and he ended up being raised by a wealthy French Canadian family. Not long before we saw him, he'd returned to the west, and his own people. I heard the story while "Tow" and his crew ferried us across the river. The Worthingtons knew there was nothing to fear from these Indians, but all three of them stayed as far away as the ferry would let them get. Two bottles of whiskey paid for our crossing.

It took two more days to reach Hell's Canyon. We were all feeling fairly good. Andy's leg was as healed as it was gonna get. There was some dead flesh around the bite that he had no feeling in, and probably never would. We all had become trail hard a long time ago. Sleeping on the ground and eating off the land was everyday life.

I'd finally gotten a couple of deerskins cured and was able to make me a new pair of britches, using supplies I needed for sewing and such at Fort Boise. They were a whole bunch more comfortable than those damn store-bought pants.

The second day out from the fort, the Snake River picked up considerable speed, as it began heading downhill. We came up over a couple different rises and with each one the river dropped a little deeper. Then we came over the last little rise and I wanna tell you that river dropped off, must'a been a mile down into the canyon. The sight was incredible, one of the good Lord's very best. The Snake River really did look like a snake as it wound its way down through the valley below. On both sides the mountains rose up nearly from the very banks of the river. The Seven Devils Mountains, as they were called, towered off to the east. Very little grew up on the mountains. There were some scrub pines about midway, following the different drainages that cut the valleys down to the Snake. The slopes to the west were a little less steep and covered with bunchgrass and shrubs. Again, some pine and fir trees marked where the drainages were. Even this late in the summer waterfalls cascaded down both sides in several places. Standing there looking down into that canyon, it was a beautiful sight, but even thinking about making our way down through it all set my nerves to singin'. There was no more than a game trail leading down, and then even that disappeared.

"Are we going down there?" Sandra asked, with more than a little fear in her voice. She stared off down that canyon like it was the very road into Hell itself.

"Well." I studied the land around us. "I sure don't see any way around it. It looks like it's down through the valley or back to Boise. We just need to be slow and careful and we'll be fine." Seemed like anymore I was always saying shit I didn't know, if I believed or not. Without another word I nudged Goldfire over the rim and we headed down.

It took all of about a hundred yards until the route got downright dangerous. It was real steep with loose rock and shale covering the ground. The horses had such a devil of a time keeping their feet that we ended up dismounting and walking them down the steepest parts. I tied off the pack horse with a real long lead onto Goldfire, so she couldn't get lost, but both of them still had plenty of room to move.

So we slipped and slid, stumbled and staggered, tripped and tumbled our way down into the bottom of that canyon. Sandra took the first tumble. She was leaning uphill with her feet sideways trying to slide just a little bit at a time, when suddenly her feet went out from under her and she landed on her butt, spun to the right, and started to roll. She'd only gone fifteen feet or so when she run up against a Juniper bush and came to a stop. I was concerned for a couple seconds because it was quite a tumble, but I knew she was okay when she started pulling herself up out of that tangle using language that definitely wasn't very lady like. Andy and I started laughing till we saw the look on Sandra's face as she waited for us to make our way down.

It wasn't nearly as funny a couple hundred feet further down when I took my fall. There'd been enough room that we were able to do small switchbacks to make our way down, but then it narrowed as the mountainside moved in on us, and there was just barely room for us and the horses. I went first with Goldfire and the pack horse behind me. After about my second step I realized what a stupid idea that was. The thought of those two horses coming down on top of me wasn't a pleasant one. They didn't. As a matter of fact, the whole way down that treacherous mountainside not one horse fell. But I did. About the time I was wondering about the horses, I stepped on a fist-sized round rock that rolled out from under me. My left foot rolled, my left ankle twisted, I came down on the side of my foot with all my two hundred plus pounds. I think all that saved me from a broken ankle was the fact that it was so damned steep. Before my ankle could give way, I started sliding. Then I was tumbling and bouncing down the mountain.

After I cleared the narrow chute I was in, the slope widened out and flattened enough that I slowed a little. By digging my fingers and toes into the ground I was able to get myself stopped. My ankle screamed in pain, and I could feel my heartbeat in the end of my fingers. I looked, and six of the ten were bleeding. The third finger on my right hand had the fingernail hanging by just a piece of skin, blood was dripping steady. I rolled over and tried to stand. I screamed out in pain when I tried to put weight on my left foot. I quickly lay back down.

"Stay put Mount." It was Sandra's voice. "We'll come get you." I turned on my side and was able to look back uphill. It wasn't more than thirty feet back up to where the Worthingtons stood at the top of the narrow chute. Goldfire and the pack horse had slid down through and now stood off to the side grazing on what little grass there was. I was barely able to hear Sandra's call due to the roar of the river beside me.

Turned out it wasn't even all that hard for the rest of them to come down. Sandra had somehow controlled her fear and slid down through that narrow spot like she'd been mountain climbing all her life. If it wouldn't have been for that damned rock I would've been fine. It took just a few minutes and the Worthingtons and all the horses were gathered around.

It took another ten minutes till I could put any weight on my foot. Andy found a deadfall limb that was big and sturdy that I could use for a crutch. With it, and a little help from Sandra and

Andy I was able to keep going. Mr. Worthington went ahead, and now and then glanced back at me with fire in his eyes, like I'd twisted my ankle on purpose or something.

The sun had set early down in the valley and it was getting dark by the time we got to the bottom. Most of the way down we were able to do our little switchbacks to keep our feet under us. Sandra's horse went down onto her front knees once, but other than that they did real good. I went real slow, my ankle and my nail-less finger pounding with every heartbeat, but I made it without much trouble. We set up camp as soon as we got to some flat land and slept like the dead.

Chapter Twenty-One

Next morning we woke to a glorious day. The sun wouldn't reach down into the bottom of the valley for quite a while yet, but it was slowly working its way down the mountainside to our west. Where the sun reached the mountainside it was ablaze with liquid fire, the colors intensified even more by the dew that covered everything. It was so bright you damn near couldn't look right at it.

As the sunshine slowly slid down the mountain towards us, we got the morning started. Andy had a fire going and Sandra was preparing breakfast. I was sitting on a fallen log working on my swollen and stiff ankle. I worked it with my fingers, which by the way hurt like hell too, and tried to turn my foot one way or the other. I didn't think anything was broke, but it was gonna hurt for a while.

Mr. Worthington had gone off back into the underbrush to do his morning duty. I looked up as he cleared the undergrowth. He stopped, gave me the usual hateful glare and then motioned for me to follow. Since the only communication we'd had for a while now had been his nasty looks, I was curious what was going on. I picked up the makeshift cane I'd been using because of my injured ankle, and hobbled towards where he stood. As I got close he turned and stepped back into the foliage. I noticed he walked with a little hitch in his get along and was scratching at his backside. I followed him around a large willow patch and as I stepped into the clearing he reached for his belt and started undoing it.

"What the hell you think you're doing?" I asked.

"Shut up," he answered through gritted teeth. I noticed a little red in his cheeks, bleeding through his considerable growth of whiskers. "A couple minutes after leaning back against that log over there I started itching." He turned and pulled his shirt up and his pants down. I had a real time of it keeping myself from busting out laughing. His lower back and butt were covered with a rash, a poison oak rash. The look in his eyes when he looked back at me didn't encourage laughter. "What the hell is it?"

I laughed. I couldn't help myself. He glared at me with hate in his eyes as he hitched his pants up and continued scratching his backside.

"It's poison oak," I answered. We walked over to the log he'd pointed at and I pointed out the leafy vines growing around it. The leaves, in sets of three, were a shiny green with some berrylike buds at the stem. "Leaves of three let it be. That's a little saying my pa taught me a long time ago."

"What do I do?" he asked.

"You itch and burn," I answered. "For a few days I'm guessing. You might try taking a dip in the river; it might give you some relief for a little bit. "

I made my way back to the camp while Mr. Worthington headed for the river. There was a small inlet just downriver where you could walk right into the water and it wasn't rushing by fast enough to take you with it. In fact, it was such a good place that all of us ended up taking a bath before we headed out that morning. I made sure I was real busy tending to the horses while Sandra was bathing so I wasn't tempted to wander that direction. There was some rustling in the tall weeds beside the river while I was taking my turn. I ain't saying one way or the other, but it damn sure wasn't something little like a rabbit or something, and I didn't see any deer or other critters to account for it. Sandra didn't meet my gaze when I returned to camp.

Making our way down through Hell's Canyon was probably the most beautiful country we'd seen yet. Probably the prettiest I'd seen since leaving my mountain cabin. The river was rushing past to our right, sometimes dropping ten to fifteen feet at a time. On both sides, the mountains rose to majestic, bare granite peaks. The hidden spots, in the higher mountains to the north, were dotted with small snow fields. Yes sir, it was beautiful country alright, and probably the hardest sixty or seventy miles we did on the whole damn trip.

Even after we reached the valley floor, most of the time there was barely room beside the river for the horses to pass, except when there wasn't any room at all. Also, there were creeks, big and small, joining up with the main river every few hundred feet or so. Whether they had water in them or not they were a real struggle to cross. Sometimes we had to work our way forty to fifty feet up the side of the mountain until we could find a place. The going was awful slow. I reckon we were lucky if we made ten miles a day.

I believe it was the afternoon of the fourth day in the canyon. We'd come to one of the very few wide spots in the canyon floor. Along the river for a quarter mile or so there was a couple hundred feet of fairly flat, grass-covered ground, then in a soft upward sweep it became the side of the mountain, rising several thousand feet. We decided to make an early camp since it was such a good spot.

After camp was set up, I took a walk along the river to give my ankle some exercise. I'd thrown away my walkin' stick only the day before, and my ankle was still plenty sore. I was down around a bend in the river, and truly enjoying the afternoon. As I rounded a couple big fir trees I sensed movement off to my right. As I watched, at least fifty feet in front of me, coming up from the river, was a little black bear cub. He'd been born that spring so was nearly six months old I figured. He stood maybe waist high at the shoulders. He rolled from side to side as he walked, and was watching two yellow butterflies dancing in the breeze.

I reckon there ain't a lot of folks that know bears as well as I do...so I admired the little bear cub for maybe half a second before looking for his Ma. I didn't need to look long because that sow bear was damn near right alongside me, partially hidden by a berry bush not twenty feet away. About the time I figured out that I was between her and that cub she looked up and saw me. It didn't take her nearly as long to figure out that I was on the wrong side of her baby. She stood up on her hind legs, pawed the air with her front legs, let out a roar that blew my hair back even from twenty feet, and charged.

Now growing up with Pa there'd been several times we'd seen bear in the wild, both black bear and grizzly. We'd even had a grizzly put a fake charge on us one time. Pa and I surprised him while fishing the river. Pa whispered for me to stand perfectly still, and somehow I did. That grizzly charged right at us for ten feet or so, then pulled up, sniffed and snorted, turned and walked away.

This time I ran! I ran for two reasons. First off, I knew damn good and well that this wasn't no fake charge. That sow was planning on taking me apart chunk by chunk. Second, and to be honest, I don't remember making the decision one way or the other. That bear roared and charged, and I was running…well, at least with my right foot I ran. Every time my left foot hit the ground I sorta lunged ahead trying to get my right foot under me again as fast as I could, while pain shot up my leg clear into my guts. As I ran I screamed a warning "Bear! Bear!"

As I cleared the trees and lurched, staggered, stumbled into camp all three Worthingtons were waiting. Andy and Mr. Worthington had their muzzleloaders ready. In that instant I was angry at Andy for not running, surprised that Mr. Worthington would be there, and when I saw Sandra standing behind them, fists clenched to her mouth, well I suddenly felt sorta the same thing that mother bear was feeling. There was no way in hell I was letting that bear harm that woman. I turned to face her down and take my chances. I struggled to get my knife from its sheath.

I'm not sure when that momma bear gave up the chase but turned out that when I ran into camp I was alone. Thank you Lord. Although I assured the Worthingtons that we didn't have anything to fear from the bear overnight, now that her cub was safe, I'm not sure if they believed me. The next morning it was obvious none of them had gotten much sleep, I got to admit I slept with both ears and one eye open myself.

It took us a full seven days to make our way through that canyon. The morning after my little bear adventure the

Worthingtons weren't sure it was safe to even continue. I tried to get through to them that unless we wandered between that sow bear and her little one again, we were safe, that mamma bear didn't want to meet up with us any more than we wanted to meet up with her. Despite my assurances, they rode like they were expecting that she bear to take us all any second. It wasn't until we cleared that open stretch and got back into the narrow, hard going that they relaxed.

The rest of the way through Hell's Canyon was fairly uneventful. Damn hard work, but uneventful.

"It's an awfully good thing it's so beautiful," Sandra said one afternoon as we took a break following an especially hard drainage crossing. "I don't know if I could work this hard if I didn't have that view to enjoy." Despite how tired she had to be, she had a smile as she scanned the mountains on either side of us. And despite being dirty and sweaty, with her hair partly up in a knot but mostly flying everywhere, her clothes filthy, her boots muddy, Sandra was still the most beautiful woman I'd ever laid eyes on. These months of travel, the hard work and all she'd been through, had only made her more beautiful. All that hard work had only made me kinda skinny, and real shaggy looking.

"How much further do you think we have to go Mount?" Andy asked.

Sandra's jet black hair, the part that was loose and flying, framed her face, and her dark brown eyes were lit with a glow that the sun alone couldn't account for.

"Mount, how far do you think until the end of the canyon?"

...even that little tear in her shirt, there on the front of her shoulder made her....

"Huh? Did you say something Andy?"

"I asked, how long till the end of the canyon?" Andy repeated himself. "You sure were daydreaming or something."

"Just enjoying the view," I answered honestly. Sandra blushed, and gave me a knowing look. I hadn't realized she'd been watching me watching her. Mr. Worthington sat on a fallen log twenty feet downriver with his shirt hiked up, scratching at his backside and looking the other way.

My ankle had nearly healed up, and Mr. Worthington's poison oak rash should've been getting better after five days, but, I guess, it still itched like hell.

"They told us back at Boise," I continued. "we'd need a full week going through Hell's Canyon, if we made it at all. If I'm remembering right, today is day six, so I'm guessing late today or maybe tomorrow."

Damn...I guessed that one right for a change...and around noon the next day the Snake took a hard turn to the left and the mountains to our west just sorta rolled back, and the mountains to our east kept going straight. The river slowed down and flattened out, and we were out the other side of Hell's Canyon.

I believe they'd called it the Imnaha River back at Fort Boise. Whatever it was called, it came from the west and emptied into the Snake moving a whole bunch of water for this late in the year, and it was the canyon's farewell annoyance. We had to move upriver a quarter-mile or so till we found a place to cross. Then downriver along the Snake a few miles further, the Salmon River, coming from the east, met up. What a beautiful sight. And what made it the most beautiful was that it was coming in on the other side of the river, and we didn't have to cross it.

Of course, because I'd celebrated the fact that we didn't have to cross the Salmon, the good Lord saw fit to put me in my place with the Grande Ronde River, a day's ride downriver. It wasn't much worse to cross than any of the others, and with no serious problems we made it, but I just didn't, don't, and never will like swimming a damn river. In all the crossings we'd made since I'd been riding Goldfire, he'd never given me any cause to fret, but I still did, every time.

Shortly after crossing the Grande Ronde we left the river and followed the trail due west. Our next goal was a place called the Whitman Mission. Seems a Dr. Marcus Whitman and his wife,

Narcissa, had come west a few years earlier and set up in a spot the Indians called Waiilatpu. Dr. and Mrs. Whitman were a part of a group from New England that was bound and determined to bring the good Lord's word west to the Indians. Sometimes the Indians listened, and sometimes they took your scalp, depended on the Indians, and their mood that particular day.

The Indians listened for nearly eleven years before they decided to kill the Whitmans. The way I heard it, the Whitmans and other missionaries set up in three different spots out west, and did a lot of good from '36 till '47. In 1847 there was a great sickness, some say measles, that hit the Cayuse tribe, wiping out hundreds. Somehow the Indians determined that it was the missionaries' fault, and a small band attacked the mission, killing the Whitmans and several of other folks.

When we were there in '41 there were maybe ten Nez Perce Indians at the mission. Again, the Worthingtons were real leery of them and kept their distance, but they were as nice and friendly as the Shoshoni Indians that stopped by now and again back home.

It took two days after crossing the Grande Ronde to get to the mission. The morning of the second day, we woke up to a light frost covering everything; each breath was a cloud of fog. It was getting mid-September and in the mountains summer was preparing to give way to fall.

"It feels like it's gonna snow," Andy managed thru chattering teeth. He was wrapped in his sleeping blanket and the extra blanket I'd pestered Mr. Worthington to buy. "Is it gonna snow, Mount?"

"Nope." I studied the sky. "It'll be too damned hot by afternoon."

"And just how can you tell that?" Sandra asked. She too was shivering inside her blankets. Mr. Worthington was a few feet away, wrapped up with his blanket even over his head like a hood. He pretended not to listen, but I knew he was.

"I agree with Andy," Sandra continued. "It feels like snow."

"Sky ain't right," I answered simply. "These clouds are gonna burn off in a couple hours." I was right; by noon we were squinting into a sunny sky and wiping sweat off our brow.

What I didn't talk with the Worthingtons about was that every night from here on it was gonna get cold. And one of these days it wasn't gonna warm up. If we didn't make Oregon City within the next couple weeks, or before the first snow, we could be in serious trouble.

That evening we got to the mission. Dr Whitman and his wife welcomed us like family. There was also a younger couple there name of Spalding. They ran another mission at Lapwai, but happened to be visiting the Whitmans. They were all real nice, God-fearing folks, and treated us like long lost friends. We had a feast that evening of fresh venison, fried potatoes, several garden-grown vegetables, and apple pie that was still just a little warm in the middle. The Indians I mentioned ate the same as us, but luckily for the Worthingtons, in a different room. There were beds for everyone, and mine even reached nearly clear to my feet.

Before we retired that evening we gathered around the fire in the stone fireplace, and shared some tea, talk, and prayer. I was quickly and firmly reprimanded by both Mrs. Whitman and Mrs. Spalding when I mentioned how "damn" cold it'd been that morning. They made it real clear language like that wasn't allowed at the mission.

Those folks at the mission even offered to let us stay through the winter if we wanted since the feel of fall was definitely in the air. Sandra was the only one that would've even considered it. Mr. Worthington, Andy, and I all wanted to move on, and the sooner the better, as far as I was concerned.

Before that first evening was up I let slip a "hell," as in "hell of a canyon," when talking about passing through Hell's Canyon. Also, shortly before bed Mrs. Whitman caught me out in the supplies taking a little taste from the whiskey bottle. I think by morning the mission was okay with us, or at least me, leaving so soon. Although they fed us a good breakfast, and a big send off, no one, especially the ladies, had a whole lot to say to me. Just a very short "goodbye and God bless."

There wasn't any frost on the ground that morning, but there was a chilly nip in the air that promised more to come. I figured we had a two or three day ride till we met up with the Columbia River. Once we got headed down the Columbia, or so I'd been told, we'd leave the snow behind and get into a little warmer and a lot wetter country. Now if we could only get there before the snow started flying.

We didn't make it.

Chapter Twenty-Two

It never did really warm up much that first day out from the Whitman Mission. It was gray and overcast and cool all day. As evening approached cool turned downright cold. We made camp in a stand of pine trees. I was worried about Indians, but I was worried about freezing to death worse. We built up a good healthy campfire. Andy and I gathered a big pile of firewood, and between the four of us we kept wood on the fire for most of the night. At some point before dawn we all fell fairly sound asleep and the fire was gone when we woke up, just as the eastern sky began to lighten. The cold had turned to damn cold. Each of us was wrapped in two blankets and they weren't nearly enough.

At my suggestion, we had a quick, cold breakfast, loaded up the horses and got on the trail. By the time we'd started riding, it'd started snowing. It was just a little flurry at first. Except for the cold, which you gotta get used to again every year, I kinda enjoyed the falling snow. Andy looked up into the sky and studied it like he'd been reading the weather for years.

"So, I think this one's gonna blow over pretty fast." He sounded like he was fifty years old and had lived in those parts all his life. "That the way you figure it, Mount?" He and Sandra looked at me with hope and anticipation in their eyes...damn.

"I don't think so Andy," I replied. "Sorry to say, these clouds look like they could settle in and hang around a spell, and drop a hell of a pile of snow before they leave." Both their faces went hound dog sad. "I could be wrong...hope I am," I added.

The snow commenced falling faster and heavier. The temperature rose enough that wrapped in a blanket while riding we were all fairly comfortable. The snow fell heavier and heavier as the hours crawled by.

When we stopped for our midday meal, I gathered wood, made a fire, and we put together a stew. I had a time finding burnable wood and knew it'd probably be impossible by nightfall. We needed the fire's heat and the hot stew working from the inside.

We got back on the trail as quick as we could. The snow was deep enough that the horses were working hard breaking trail. I took the lead so Goldfire could do most of the work. It was just warm enough that the snow had some weight to it, not the dry, fly-away kind you get when it's really cold. The snow was already two feet deep and piling up quick. We rode with our blankets wrapped around us and pulled up over our hats, our heads down, lower face and ears wrapped in a bandana, bandit style. None of us spoke for most of the afternoon. We were somber and sullen. That meant Mr. Worthington was his normal self. It was like there was four of him. Damn, now if *that* ain't an alarming thought.

As the afternoon wore on and the snow piled up, I was hoping we would reach the Columbia that day and start leaving the heavy snow behind. I couldn't see them, but I knew the mountains were getting smaller behind us. The country we were traveling through was plenty rough, but easier than traversing the mountains. The later it got the more it became apparent we were spending the night in one hell of a snow storm. At least, thank God, the wind wasn't blowing.

Just as it started to get dark the wind picked up. We kept riding until we nearly couldn't see at all. It was snowing even harder, and now it was coming at us sideways. Luckily it was blowing from behind us and to our right.

I had the Worthingtons group up, backs against the wind and snow, and wait for me while I looked for some sort of cover to spend the night. I found a deep-cut gully not far to the south. Or was it west, hell I couldn't see nothing. It took several minutes and a couple circles to find the Worthingtons, then more than several to find the gully again. Hell, I'm not even sure it was the same one.

Once we got up into the back of the ravine the wind was howling over us like a pack of coyotes gone loco, but for the most part, we couldn't feel it. But damn, we could sure feel the cold, and it was getting colder every minute.

I put the Worthingtons in the most protected spot in the ravine and told them to leave everything on the horses except the blankets they used to wrap up in. I went down the gully to some big pine trees. The lower branches were nearly on the ground from the weight of the snow. I shook them clean and used my knife to hack off eight of the branches. While I was working on the last couple I thought I heard raised voices, but wasn't sure. As I was trying to pick up as many of the branches as I could, I jumped a foot when suddenly someone yelled behind me.

"Mount!" It was Andy, and I figured that explained the voices a couple minutes ago. "Mount, let me help you!" His hat was pulled low, his bandana tied tight, and his blanket wrapped around his shoulders and tied in front so his hands were free. I didn't take time for talk.

As I handed Andy some pine branches I looked up to see a ghostly form moving through the snow towards us. I grabbed Andy and shoved him behind me to protect him just as Sandra emerged from the swirling snow.

"Andy, don't you ever run off like that!" she yelled over the wind. Even muffled by the storm and her bandana I could hear the panic in her voice; the fear of losing her son again.

"But I thought Mount might need help Ma." He was sounding more like a mountain man all the time. "Besides, I couldn't get lost in the gully."

"I told you not to go!" Sandra yelled.

"Mount?" Andy turned and yelled to me for help. Bad move.

"A boy needs to listen to his ma! We've discussed this before, remember!" Yelling was the only way to be heard. I figured that was enough of a lesson for now. "Now take a couple of these branches and head back up!"

Andy stepped up and I filled his arms with three of the big pine branches. As he turned and began dragging the branches up the ravine, Sandra stepped up and held out her arms, and actually smiled up at me. I couldn't see her mouth, but her eyes sparkled and crinkled up around the edges like they do. I suddenly felt considerably warmer.

"I might as well carry something back with me!" Her voice still muted by the bandana and wind.

"Since you're here and all!" I yelled back as I filled her arms. "You're quite a lady, Sandra Worthington!" That last was out before I realized I'd yelled it out loud. Even in the snow and cold I could see her frozen cheeks turn a darker red.

I was able to get the rest of the branches and made my way back up to the rest. Taking one of the branches, I made my way into the back of the gully, up against the shale rock walls. Using the branch like a big, awkward broom I cleaned away as much snow as I could.

A couple of driftwood pieces that had washed down with some spring runoff worked as my frame, and the pine branches made up the walls and ceiling of our lean-to.

I took the horses down to where the pines trees were, found the most protected spot I could find, and hobbled them. All except Goldfire, because I knew there was no need. When I made my way back to our shelter the Worthingtons sat under the branches, each wrapped in their own blankets; each shivering uncontrollably. It wasn't just cold, it was "sink clear down into your bones" cold, and I knew there was no chance of getting a fire started. I pulled the last couple branches in place to close us in.

"Give me your blankets!" I shouted over the wind. All three Worthingtons sat and stared at me like I was crazy.

"We need to bunch up!" I shouted. "Use each other for some warmth! Now give me your blankets!" Sandra and Andy unwrapped themselves and handed me their blankets. Mr. Worthington paused just long enough for me to start towards him then handed his over too.

I took three of the blankets and spread them out underneath us. The other five we wrapped over and around ourselves. This required that we damn near sit right on top of each other inside our pine branch tent, which already was covered with a couple feet of snow that had both fallen and blown in. We sat hip to hip, Sandra on my left and Andy to my right, and took turns either sitting Indian style with our legs crossed under us, which ain't easy when you're almost six and a half feet tall, or two at a time could put their legs out straight. Then we covered ourselves with the blankets. It didn't take long and we could notice the change. I ain't gonna say it ever got comfortable, but it stayed warm enough that we didn't freeze to death. We even had a supper of sorts, a couple bites of jerky and cold beans; no one had much of an appetite.

At some point during the night, which seemed like it lasted several days, the wind died down, and all four of us actually got a little fitful sleep, leaning against each other. Sandra leaned against Mr. Worthington when she slept.

When dawn finally came we had to dig our way out of our shelter. My pine branch lean-to held up, there was very little snow on our blankets, but there was four feet or more on top of the branches and it had also drifted in front of us. When we took the blankets off we couldn't see anything. It was like one of those snow houses I've heard the Indians up in the far north live in.

After kicking the branches outta the way, it didn't take much to wade through the drift in front of us, and when I did and was able to stand up and look around, a beautiful scene greeted me. It took some muscle rubbing and stretching before we all could stand straight and move around proper. Other than the drift at our door, and some drifting along the low side of the gully, there wasn't a whole lot of snow down in our little ravine, but the rest of the world appeared to be covered in about three feet of pure white. A white so pure it hurt your eyes to look and the sun hadn't even cleared the horizon yet. At the horizon there was an indistinct line between the pure white snow and the dirty white of the sky. It took some squinting before we could keep our eyes open to really appreciate the view.

Looking down out of the little valley, the flat land right in front of us, the hills beyond that, and the larger hills behind those, were all blanketed with snow. Where the shorter stands of shrubs, brush, and bushes were there were just funny shaped mounds of snow. Where the trees stood you could see their trunks, but branches and leaves were covered with snow. Two hundred feet down, the horses stood amongst some trees where the snow was not even a foot deep, and looked like they'd burrowed down enough to find food. All in all it was a magnificent sight.

"This is beautiful." Sandra stood beside me looking down the ravine. "I've seen snow before, but never this much, and never did it look this pure or clean or...oh, I don't know how to explain it."

"I know what you mean Ma." Andy stood on the other side of me. He was staring back behind us at the snow-covered hillside. "It's...whiter than white."

Mr. Worthington was rolling up his blankets and grabbing up the bag of jerky. As far as I know he never did even take a second to gaze around and enjoy the beautiful scene. Not that I expected it mind you.

"It's cold, let's get going," is all he had to say as he walked past and headed for the horses.

The drift along the gully edge extended out a few feet and was spread out in front of us. As Mr. Worthington started to wade through he lifted his leg to step, but didn't lift it quite high enough to clear the snow and went down face first, nearly disappearing into the snow.

"Goddamnit!" We could hear him before we could see him. "Goddamn snow!" He was mighty lucky the ladies from the mission weren't around.

Mr. Worthington tried a couple times to stand, but just fell, cussing like a cowhand, back into the snow.

"Goddamnit all to hell!" Why...hell...even I was gonna get embarrassed pretty soon. He ended up crawling out of the deep snow on hands and knees before he could stand up.

Now, I'll admit I kinda enjoyed this whole thing, but I didn't necessarily find it all that funny. I was grinning but didn't laugh. Andy and Sandra, on the other hand, both had to get real busy gathering their things so Mr. Worthington didn't see them giggling. He stood up, shook the snow off his shoulders, most of which went down the inside of his shirt, and stomped off toward the horses. We got our stuff and followed.

Mr. Worthington didn't see, or pretended not to, when I threw myself down into the drift and made a real show of digging out. Sandra and Andy were howling with laughter before I was done.

He tried to complain when I said we should eat something before we mounted up.

"We need to get going." He'd regained his arrogant composure. "We need to get out of this snow and into that Columbia Valley like they said back at the mission."

"And how far is that from here?" I asked. "How long is it gonna take?"

"I don't know." It was the only answer he could give.

"I don't either," I answered. "But I know I'm damn sure not gonna make it without something to eat. The snow is less than a foot deep right here, and it's two, three, or more out on the trail. We eat here before we head out." I started digging out the food.

We had a splendid meal of cold jerky and cold beans while stomping our feet and swinging our arms around trying to keep warm.

Chapter Twenty-Three

We started out that morning riding with our blankets wrapped around us, hats pulled down tight, and bandanas tied over our nose and mouth. By the time the sun was full up and started traveling across a flawless light blue sky, we'd undone the bandanas. By mid-morning we'd loosened our hats, and by noon put the blankets away. The snow even started melting a little by early afternoon, but that perfectly clear sky promised a cold night.

By mid-afternoon we dug the blankets back out. As the sun set we pulled our hats back down tight and put on our bandanas to protect our faces. The snow that had gotten soft in the afternoon refroze and was crusty and treacherous for the horses. Luckily it was mostly flat land and with Goldfire leading the way we rode till well after dark; with the fresh blanket of snow reflecting a nearly full moon in a clear sky, we had no trouble seeing as we rode. We spent that night huddled together, inside a circle of horses, under a stand of cottonwoods. Nobody got much sleep. On the bright side...again, nobody froze to death.

The next day started pretty much the same, mighty cold, and warmed as the sun got higher. By mid-afternoon we rode with just our coats on. The snow was melting and with every mile there was less and less.

As the sun started setting we began to hear, off in the distance, what only could be the sound of a rushing river, a big rushing river. It had to be the Columbia. Shortly after dark we reached it. It came down from the north and about where we met up with it, it took a right turn and headed west.

We spent the night in some pines on the hillside not far from the river. I was able to find enough dry wood, mostly dead branches still on the trees, to have a campfire and I wanna tell you it felt awfully nice after being cold for the last three days.

"How much farther, Mount?" Andy asked. We sat around the fire enjoying the warmth and a hot meal. Even Mr. Worthington sat by the fire, although he may as well of been miles away. Sandra was dipping into the stew pot for the third time.

"Well, seems to me they said it was five or six days after we reached the Columbia until we reached the Willamette, then south for a day." A couple of the menfolk at the Whitman Mission had been this way before. "So, provided we don't run into any trouble, it should take a week. With our luck so far...I'm guessing a month yet." I laughed, but was only half-joking. Sandra and Andy laughed too, but not very loud.

Luckily it'd been an early October winter storm and not an early January winter storm, or we would've been in real trouble. As it was, by the middle of the next day we were mostly out of the snow and the temperature was getting bearable.

You could still feel that little bite of fall in the breeze that blew just enough to rustle the leaves. Leaves, that without my noticing had, I believe overnight, turned a whole passel of different shades of red, yellow, orange, gold, and every possible combination of all them. The land went from pure white winter one morning to a beautiful autumn afternoon by the next day. Another of the Lord's small wonders.

The trip along the southern bank of the mighty Columbia wasn't a whole lot easier than traveling along the Snake River had been. The northern bank was a pretty flat plateau and looked like it'd be easier traveling, but we weren't about to try and cross that mighty river. So it was climb up and over a ridge then drop down into the ravine, then climb up the next ridge and drop down into the next gully, then climb up the next ridge and then drop down into...you get the idea. There weren't any trees to speak of once we got going, but there was plenty of sagebrush and juniper bushes to get in the way. Then to make it a real challenge, the first day alone, we had to cross four different tributaries coming from the south down to empty themselves into the Columbia. The gullies these streams cut were deep and steep and a real son of a bitch to get across. Andy and Mr. Worthington both took bad tumbles while crossing when their horses lost footing. In Andy's case, Skyhawk pitched forward and sent him rolling off the front. Being a kid, he rolled a little, bounced off a couple trees, then bounced up laughing and jumped back into the saddle.

For Mr. Worthington, his horse's rear legs slipped out from under, and it sat down real fast like. Mr. Worthington fell back against his bedroll then rolled off to the left. He hit the ground and took off like a twig over a waterfall. It was steep enough that he took a couple real young saplings plumb outta the ground going past. When he finally stopped, up against a downfall log in the bottom of the ravine, he was bumped and bruised and bleeding in a hundred different spots, but he wasn't hurt seriously. It hurt me to watch Sandra mend his cuts and rub liniment oil into his bruises. He limped around, pretty sore, for the next couple days.

It was late morning of the second day along the Columbia and we were crossing an easy stretch along the river where a fairly wide valley came down and opened up as it neared the river. The grass was long. The weather was nice and warm. We were letting the horses have their head and travel at their own speed. If they wanted to stop and graze some of the sweet grass we'd let them. For the most part, they did whatever Goldfire did. He stopped now and again for a couple mouthfuls, but kept moving and making time. About halfway across the valley we were surprised as hell to hear shouting. As we stopped and looked off to the south, up the valley, two horses cleared the trees and came towards us at an easy lope.

"It isn't Indians is it, Mount?" Andy nearly shouted, as both he and Sandra started to turn their horses, ready to run. Mr. Worthington had been in front of us and was stopped looking from the horses to us and back again, I guess watching me to see what he should do. I had a sudden urge to yell at him, "Run, run for it!!" Just to see how far he'd go, but I didn't do it. I squinted into the sunlight.

"Can't rightly tell what they are, but they sure ain't Indians," I answered. "They're wearing too many clothes for Indians, and they sit their horses like white folk." They were now moving at a fast trot. "The one on the right looks like it might be a kid."

We kept our mounts and waited for the strangers to reach us. As they got closer we saw that it was an old feller and a youngun. The man looked like a mountain man with long hair, a full beard, and deerskins top and bottom. He was topped off with a Daniel Boone type coonskin hat. The kid had some deer skin britches and what looked like an elkskin robe wrapped around him. He had an old beat up cowboy hat pulled down low over his eyes. As they rode up and stopped the old fella jumped down off the brown mare and ran up to us, a grin the size of the Rockies spread across his face.

"Well hang me high if it ain't some real live white folks!" He looked from one to the other to the other. His gaze froze when he noticed Sandra. "Well if you ain't a pretty one." He started to walk towards Sandra. I jumped off Goldfire and cut him off, stepping in front of him and offering my hand.

"Name's Mount," I said as we shook hands. I squeezed just a little tighter than I had to and was pleased to see him try to hide a grimace. Sandra and Andy dismounted and came to stand behind me. The youngun with the elk robe was already down and standing beside him. Mr. Worthington stayed where he was and no one seemed to notice.

The old fella turned out not to be that old…he just looked it. I ain't any good at such things, but I'd guess mid-forties, and like I said, used hard. I figure he was about six feet and looked to be powerfully built under his deerskins. The kid was hard to see with the robe around his neck and the hat covering his eyes. He stood looking at the ground. The coonskin hat and the feller still looked at Sandra.

"Sloane." He said it like that was all we needed to know. "Edward Sloane's my name, but folks just call me Sloane." He said all this without taking his eyes off Sandra and I was about ready to give him something more painful to think about. He seemed to sense it and turned to look up at me. He nodded his head at the kid. "That's Teri." He looked me up and down. "Damned if you ain't a big one." He looked from me to Sandra, paused a second or two then moved on to Andy. "So what you folks doin' out here in the middle of nothin'?" His gaze returned to Sandra, then back up to me.

"We're on our way west." I didn't see any point in telling him too much till I found out a little more. "Where you headed, and where you coming from?" I asked. Andy had moved up beside me, and I noticed he and the kid were looking each other over.

"Ain't you full of questions?" He laughed, and as he answered he went to his saddle and undid a water bottle and took a swig. "I was up in Granger at the fall Rendezvous a while back. I sorta lose track of days and weeks and such." It felt like home somehow hearing him mention the Fort Granger Rendezvous. From where I stood I could smell the whiskey from his jug. He paused; looked upriver, then downriver, then back at Sandra, then back to me. "I guess we're headed west too. I ain't never been west of here before."

I nodded at the kid. "That your son?"

Before the word "son" had completely cleared my lips there was a flash of movement and my left shin exploded in pain. As I yelled out, grabbed my shin, and started hopping around trying not to fall over, I was barely aware of Andy leaping forward, wrapping his arms around that other kid and taking him to the ground. As my eyes cleared, a second later, Andy was on top trying to punch the other kid. The kid was doing a fair job of covering up. Sandra stood mouth open, eyes wide and too shocked to react. Sloane stood and watched with his arms crossed and a little smile on his face.

I stepped up to grab Andy and suddenly Andy wasn't there anymore. The kid had grabbed his right arm and pulled and at the same time grabbed his left leg and pushed. Suddenly Andy was on his back and the kid was on top sitting up high on Andy's chest and doing a much better job of punching Andy then Andy'd been doing punching him. I took another step, leaned over and wrapped my arm around the kid making sure I pinned his arms too. Then I stood up and held him to my side so he couldn't do much damage with his feet.

"Now just hang on there a damned minute." I shook him just a little. "You need to settle down young fella. Nobody needs to be fighting here." That kid twisted, fussed, wiggled and finally slipped from my arm.

I thought he'd go after Andy again, or maybe me this time, but he didn't; instead he stood toe to toe with me, looked up, pulled off her hat and declared "I'm a girl! I ain't no son!" A whole bunch of light brown hair fell past her shoulders. She wiped some dirt and sweat from her cheek, spat once towards where Andy still lay on the ground, looked over at Sloane, then back up at me. "And he sure as hell ain't my pa."

Andy lay on the ground with both hands over his left eye, which was swelling up fast, his good eye staring up at that girl in disbelief. Sandra stood, still with her mouth and eyes wide, but now she was staring at the girl too. Even Mr. Worthington had made his way closer during the commotion and was staring. Sloane stared at her too with that same smile and a look of pride in his eyes. I started laughing.

"Well excuse me young lady." I offered my hand. She looked like she might bite it but she took it and gave it a good hard shake. "If you're so proud of that fact, you shouldn't hide it so good. I guess we just figured you was a boy."

"Besides, you got a boy's name." Andy had gotten up and was standing beside me. Well...maybe more behind me. "Terry is a boy's name."

"Ain't either!" she fired back. "It can be for both. I spell it T-E-R-I and that's for a girl." She stared at Andy with her chin stuck out just daring him to disagree.

Andy turned his back and kicked at a rock "Dumb name for a girl if you ask me," he mumbled, just loud enough for everyone to hear. Teri started to say something but she wasn't fast enough.

"Andrew Worthington the Third!" Sandra had gotten over her shock and using his whole name like that meant Andy was in big trouble. "How dare you talk to this young lady like that! Now you apologize right this instant." Andy knew better than to do anything other than what his ma said.

"Sorry." If you listened real close you could almost hear him.

"Andrew!" It just took that one word. Andy turned around, faced the girl, and spoke very clearly.

"I'm sorry; Teri isn't such a dumb name for a girl." It took a lot for Andy to do that, but he'd plumb run out of choices.

"Ya thanks." Teri looked at Sandra then at Andy. I saw a nasty gleam grow in her eyes as she turned and headed back to her horse. From over her shoulder we heard. "What the hell kinda name is Andrew Worthington the Third anyway?"

"Well hang me high." Sloane laughed. "It's good to see the younguns are gonna get along." He followed Teri to the horses and they started unloading their gear. Don't know why, but except for Sloane's staring at Sandra like she was a prize cut of steak, I liked these two and decided that was as good a place as any for our midday meal.

"We'll take a break here too," I said. "Let's unload and cook up a hot meal."

"Ahh...Mount, do we have to?" Andy whined like the wind through the trees. "Shouldn't we be moving on while the weather holds?" He tried to sound like a wise ole trail hand. He even followed it with a knowing look up into the sky, then off to the horizon.

"I think we've left the real bad weather behind us." I didn't want to disagree with Andy, but I was hungry and it was nice having company; even if half the company was a wise-ass, arrogant little girl. "I'm sure we're okay to take a break for some grub."

Andy gave me a dirty look, gave his ma a dirty look, gave Sloane and especially Teri a dirty look, but then started unpacking his stuff all the same.

It didn't take but a few minutes, in fact even before the pot was boiling, Sloane had Sandra and Andy in the palm of his hand. He was just a damned likable fella. I figure he'd probably spent some time on both sides of the law. I didn't care for the way he kept looking Sandra up and down like she was in a display glass at Uncle Joseph's store, and I was pretty sure most of his stories were pure buffalo droppings...but, all that said...there was just something about the ole bastard that made you like him. You know, one of those folks that other folks just take to right off; except for Mr. Worthington, of course.

"Well that is one fine lookin' coat you got there Mr. Worthington." Sloane smiled and even tried to help him with the saddle he was uncinching. Mr. Worthington slapped his hand away like he was a little kid reaching for trouble, glanced down at his coat, then wrinkled up his nose.

"It was the best they had at Fort Boise," he said. "I prefer European." Sloane looked from Mr. Worthington to me and back again. He grinned.

"Ya, me too." He looked around at all of us. "Why, I'm usually spendin' my time in fancy hotels and ridin' around in a white wagon pulled by pure white horses. This here deerskin shirt? It's made from the very finest deerskin ever growed by a deer." Sloane kind of snorted in Mr. Worthington's direction, walked away, and didn't try talking to him again.

As we cooked and ate we learned all about Edward Sloane. More than we necessarily wanted to know as a matter of fact. He'd come west in his mid-twenties and had been a trapper, a hunter, a prospector, a scout, and a farmer at different times during the last twenty years, and those were just the things he'd admit up to. To hear him talk, and it didn't take a whole lot of persuading, he'd been damn near the best too…at all of those things. He had more stories then a spring meadow's got flower petals.

Sloane told them that he'd taken charge of Teri in Fort Granger. Teri had been living with the elderly proprietor of a general store there; where the old feller had gotten her from, no one seemed to know, and Teri never had said. Teri earned her keep by cleaning up around the place and cooking for her keeper.

When Sloane showed up at the fort, he and Teri just seemed to hit it off. Within a couple hours the mountain man and the young girl were friends, laughing and joking with each other. The day before he left, the proprietor asked Sloane if he would be willing to take Teri with him.

"I ain't got much time left on this earth." The proprietor spoke with very little emotion. "I'm old as granite, and my lungs and heart are dueling to see which will give out first." He looked Sloane in the eye. "I'm afraid of what might happen to that little girl here without me to look after her. I think she'd be better off with you."

"She's likely to starve or freeze to death along with me," was Sloane's first response. "Hell, I ain't sure I can keep myself alive most of the time." Then Sloane spent a couple minutes thinking about it, and had to admit that having Teri along would certainly liven up a usually boring trail. The more he thought about it, the more he liked the idea.

According to Sloane, that's how he ended up traveling south with a feisty young girl as company. All the time Sloane was tellin' his story, Teri sat staring into the fire with an expression on her face that said she was remembering things best left forgotten.

As the day passed midday and headed into the afternoon it started getting colder. We stoked up the fire real good, then all moved in a little closer; five of us around one side and Mr. Worthington on the other. There wasn't any wind to speak of so the smoke whirled around pestering everybody at different times.

I was sitting beside Sloane, and when he got up and grabbed a piece of driftwood to put in the fire I noticed for the first time an ugly scar that looked like it ran all the way around his neck. As he sat back down he noticed me noticing. He laughed a dry laugh without any humor.

"Had me a small misunderstandin' with the folks in a small town back east about whether this snake of a man there deserved to live or not." He didn't look at any of us, just stared into the fire as he remembered. "I figured he didn't, most of the rest of the folks figured he did." Again the dry laugh. "Well hang me high if those townsfolk didn't try to hang me high right there in the middle of town."

Even though it was fairly cold out, Sloane had broken out in a sweat like he'd been working under an August sun. "Ole Sloane ain't so easy to hang though...no sir, he ain't." He glanced up from the fire and noticed our questioning looks. "Ain't sure what happened...when they kicked me off the back of that wagon I tensed up my neck and shoulders as hard as I could. I remember swingin', everything going' black...and next thing I knew I was wakin' up on the ground, and there wasn't a soul in sight. I lay there in the street till I could breathe, then made my way to the stable and rode outta town; I headed west and ain't turned around yet." Like I said, most of Sloane's stories were so much hot air, but this one I believed. If you could've seen that scar around his neck and his eyes as he talked, you would've believed too.

While Sloane talked Teri had finished eating and walked away upriver. Nobody really noticed. As we cleaned up I realized Andy was gone too. I was just tying down my roll behind my saddle when the screams started. They came from upriver. Even Mr. Worthington joined us as we ran. I ran through some willows and entered a grassy clearing that went to the edge of the water where a backwash eddy had cut its way into the bank ten feet or so. There, not three feet from the water, were Teri and Andy on the ground with their legs wrapped around each other and fists flying; both screaming like banshees.

I was the first to get to them. At the moment Teri was on top. As I bent down to pick her up Andy's leg flailed up and around and hit me square in the crotch. At the same time Teri's fist, on the backswing, caught me square on the nose. I stood up with one hand holding my bleeding nose and the other clutching my stomach cause there was a woman present. As Sandra, Sloane, and Mr. Worthington ran up, pretty much together, I stepped forward and using my right leg shoved both kids off the embankment and into that backwash.

It was deeper than I thought it'd be. Both kids disappeared under the muddy water and came up three or four feet out in the swirling pool. Their eyes were full moons, they were sputtering and gasping for breath, and their lips were already turning blue. They came up, bobbed once, wrapped their arms around each other, and went under again. Ignoring Sandra's screams and Mr. Worthington's yells, I ran around to the downriver side of the pool, which was where the kids would be washing out into the main current of the river. They came up again just a couple feet in front of me. I reached and grabbed Andy by the shoulder and pulled both of them from the water, the two of them clinging to each other with both arms and legs.

"What the heck you doing, Mount!" Andy was the first to recover enough to start the yelling. His arms were wrapped around himself and he was shivering. "What the heck you doing anyway!" It'd seemed like a good idea a few minutes ago, and like I said I didn't think a side pool like that'd be so deep.

"Well I..." I started to answer.

"Yes Mount." Mr. Worthington was suddenly in front of me. "What the hell were you thinking? You did that on purpose! We all saw you!"

"Well I..." I started again.

"Now hang on a damned minute." Sloane had stepped up beside Mr. Worthington and was staring up at him with pretty much the same expression that Mr. Worthington was using on me. "The way I see it, damned if Mount didn't solve the problem." He looked down at the kids; both looking like drowned rats; real cold drowned rats. Sloane started laughing. "He sure enough stopped 'em from fightin'!"

"Well I…"

Sandra stepped up. I hadn't dared look her way yet. I turned and met her glare. My heart stopped and my stomach suddenly hurt worse. She looked at me with what could only be described as hate in her eyes. In fact it showed in her whole body; her rigid stance, her blazing eyes, the set of her mouth. She didn't say a word, simply stepped past me and helped Andy off the ground. She gave me one more smoldering glance then wrapped him in her arms and they walked back to the horses and dry clothes.

Teri got up off the ground, gave me a look that could start a grassfire, punched me hard in the stomach, and headed back too.

"Well I think you handled the situation just fine Mount." Sloane slapped me on the shoulder as I was bent over holding my stomach and rubbing my privates, which still hurt like hell; my nose had quit bleeding at least. I stood up straight, feeling low as a worm's belly, and there was Mr. Worthington.

"Well I…" nothing interrupted me, but I didn't know what to say. "I didn't think it was that deep," was all I came up with. I thought he might take a swing and wasn't sure if I'd stop him or let him whoop on me; he didn't take the swing. He just looked at me with a funny one sided grin and an expression mixed with disgust and joy, shook his head, turned, and followed the others. There was no doubt that Mr. Worthington didn't mind the idea of everybody else hating me…too.

Chapter Twenty-Four

Don't rightly know when, or even if, the decision was made that we'd all travel together. Guess it was just natural since we were going the same direction and all. It was a good thing for me because at least I had Sloane to talk with, and for the next couple days he was the only one that even acknowledged I was alive. The other four went about their business as usual, and visited among themselves, but didn't so much as look my direction. Mr. Worthington made it real clear how much he was enjoying the situation. It was the only damn time on the whole journey that he was in what I'd call a good mood.

Now, Mr. Worthington ignoring me was normal, in fact, I preferred it that way. But Sandra and Andy acting like I wasn't there hurt worse than I can explain. For the entire trip, and everything we'd been through, the one thing that hadn't changed was my friendship with the two of them. Sure, I'd made both of them mad a bunch of times and I'd been fairly riled myself a time or two, but we'd remained friends through it all. I don't think I even realized how much those friendships meant to me till I'd lost them.

Sloane and I rode up front taking turns telling each other stories. I pretended nothing was wrong and talked and joked and laughed as we rode. Sometimes, even I could tell that I talked too loud and laughed too hard.

Sandra rode behind us, beside Mr. Worthington. Mr. Worthington was worse than I was at talking and laughing extra loud, making sure I heard how happy he and Sandra were. I knew what he was doing but it didn't help. I felt slimier than swamp mud.

Teri and Andy rode all over the place when the land would allow. They'd become great friends, of course, and were inseparable. They ate together, slept side by side, and never stopped wandering and exploring as we rode along. When we were stopped they ran and played and even did chores together. The one thing they didn't do was have anything to do with me, not so much as a glance. I did notice Andy and Sandra both staring at the ground a lot when I was around, both with those sad hound dog eyes. I was thinking they weren't liking being mad any more than I was, but I couldn't bring myself to say anything first; leave it to a kid.

It was evening of the second day after meeting up with Teri and Sloane. I was sitting alone beside the river wrapped in my blanket. It was chilly down by the water, but it was chilly sitting beside the campfire too. I was wondering what in tarnation I could do to mend things between me and Andy and Sandra. I heard someone come up behind me. I turned and Andy and Teri were standing there.

"Hey Mount." Andy was obviously nervous.

"Hey back." I wasn't sure if I was talking to a friend or not. They both looked at me, then at each other, then at the ground, then into the sky, then at each other again. Finally Teri was the one to start.

"We're sorry Mount, we...," she said, and that was all the encouragement Andy needed.

"Yeah Mount, we're sorry," he interrupted. And once he got going there was no stopping him. "We're sorry we were fighting...and we're sorry that we hit you...and we're sorry that we've been acting mad at you. Heck, I wasn't even really mad all along. It's just that you shouldn't have dumped us in the river like that...but we're glad you did, because if you hadn't we wouldn't have become friends...so thanks. And we're sorry if we..."

"Hang on there Andy," I interrupted him. "All I wanna know, is does this mean you and I are friends again?"

"You bet Mount!" He was grinning ear to ear and a tear welled up in the corner of each eye. "Heck, you're the best friend I've ever had."

I had to pause a few seconds before I could answer; I believe some spit went down the wrong pipe or something. I had to turn away for a bit. When I could, I turned to Teri.

"And how about you young lady?" I smiled and reached out my hand. "You and I friends too are we?"

"Sure." She smiled and shook my hand. "Andy says you're the smartest man in the world when it comes to living off the land. Is that true?"

"Well I don't know about the whole danged world." I had to laugh. I suddenly felt like singing and dancing; luckily for everyone I didn't do either. "Probably just the smartest in the Rocky Mountains...well, maybe the United States of America."

They both sat down and we spent the next half-hour or so talking about living off the land. We talked hunting, fishing, trapping, eating plants, and eating bugs. Andy looked around for a grasshopper to eat for Teri, but it was too late in the year. When they'd sat about as long as two kids can sit, they took off running and laughing towards some cottonwoods. Feeling really good for the first time in two days I walked back to camp and the warmth of the fire.

As I walked up towards camp Sandra came from the other direction. When I saw her my good mood vanished like smoke in a thunderstorm. Rather than walk past her, I switched directions and started over to where Goldfire and the other horses were tethered; I studied the ground as I walked.

"Mount."

I paused in mid-stride. Did I really hear her call my name? Did I dare look up? I looked up...and my heart nearly leapt plumb outta my chest. A tingle, like a magic spell, went through my whole body, and my spirit soared. Sandra was standing there looking at me with friendship again reflected in her eyes and a warm smile lighting up her beautiful features. Her hair was down, around her face and over her shoulders, the way I liked it best, and as usual, I had trouble catching my breath.

"Andy and Teri talked to me." Her smile grew. My heart started skipping beats. "I know you didn't mean to put the children in danger Mount." She looked at the ground, then back up at me. "It's just that...I was so scared. I've come so close to losing Andy so many times in the last months." Her voice caught, and she choked back a sob. Tears started running down her flushed red cheeks. "I was scared Mount."

"I'm sorry Sandra." I stepped towards her. "I'd never put those kids in danger on purpose. I honestly didn't think it was that deep, and even when they went under I knew I'd be able to haul them out before they got into the current." I knew I was babbling out of control, like Andy had been a few minutes ago, but couldn't stop; I had to explain before Sandra went back to hating me. "I knew there was no undertow because the cut in the river wasn't right...and I knew it was cold, but I knew we were just a little ways from the fire and warm clothes and all...and I knew..."

"Okay, okay, Mount." The tears were gone and Sandra was rocking back and forth with laughter. "I'm convinced that you didn't mean the children any harm. You're forgiven...and I'm sorry for the way you've been ignored the last two days." She took two steps forward, stood on her toes, put both hands on my shoulders, pulled me down, stretched up, and kissed me on the cheek. She held me there for an extra second and whispered. "Your friendship means the world to Andy and me, Mount. It truly does."

Somehow my arms got around her waist and I hugged her back. When she looked up and I looked down, our faces were just inches apart. Without thinking I leaned down to kiss her. She came up to meet me, and I swear I actually felt her lips touch mine when Sloane yelled.

"Well hang me high if it ain't gettin' cold out." I didn't remember moving, but suddenly Sandra and I were four or five feet apart. Sloane was staring at us from the willows with a knowing grin, then stepped aside for Mr. Worthington who was following behind him. From the look in Sloane's eyes I knew he'd yelled to warn us; I gave him a slight nod that said thanks.

Sandra gave me a guilty look, then a quick glance towards Mr. Worthington, and she headed into the willows towards the river to get ready for the night. I decided to go check on those horses anyway. I needed some time alone to think, and wasn't sure I could look Mr. Worthington in the eye without him knowing.

The next four days were some of the best of the trip. The further west we went, the ridges coming from the south, that we had to climb over, got less steep, and the ravines we had to crawl down through weren't so deep, and the travel got considerably easier; it wasn't easy, just easier. Also, as we got further west the trees returned. The hills became covered with mostly pine, along with stands of birch, cottonwood, and maple. These last three were still wearing their finest fall colors. The weather held, and it was shirtsleeve weather during the warmest part of the day. You could definitely feel the fall bite in the air every evening. In the distance the mountains started coming in view. We could see Mount Hood off to the south, and further away and to the north Mount St. Helens sparkled bright in the sunlight.

Mr. Worthington had gone back to his normal self now that Andy and Sandra and I were friends again. He rode either out front, when the leading was easy, or back behind us, when the leading was hard and we needed Goldfire to pick the way. He sulked even more than usual, and didn't have much to say to anyone.

The rest of us ignored him. With Sloane telling stories and making jokes, Sandra again talking to me, everybody, except me, singing traveling songs, and the kids carrying on, It was a pleasurable time on the trail. I knew there had been very little trouble this far west with Indians but I worried cause of the ruckus we sometimes made as we traveled along. I worried, but I didn't stop it. I was having fun; and there hadn't been nearly enough of that.

Late evening of the third day traveling with Sloane and Teri, we came to the mouth of the Willamette River. We'd been told back at the Whitman Mission that a feller name of Etienne Lacier, a French gentleman, had a cabin around here somewhere, but we didn't see it. We backed off the river aways and set up camp.

We were done eating and cleaning up, I'd had a couple pulls off the last bottle of whiskey I had, and was laying back staring into the fire when it hit me, hit me like a wall of flood water, this would be our last camp. If our information was right, Oregon City was less than a day's ride south.

For the last seven months all I wanted was for this cross-country trek to be over. When I realized that it damn near was, I was surprised to find that the thought depressed me, and it wasn't just me. Sandra sat by the fire looking forlorn. I even saw her wipe away a tear when she thought no one was looking. Sloane was with the horses, taking his time tending to them, like he purposely was leaving everyone alone. Even the kids were subdued. They sat side by side near the fire and for the first time since they'd become friends they were quiet.

Of course, since everyone was in a somber mood, Mr. Worthington was in rare fine spirits. He wouldn't lower himself to talk to any of us, but he whistled and walked with a spring in his step as he went about his business. We all turned in fairly early.

"Come on, come on, and let's get moving." It was Mr. Worthington, and it wasn't even daylight yet. "If we get an early start we can be in Oregon City by noon."

"Andrew Worthington you just calm yourself down." Sandra's voice came, surprisingly strong, from inside her blanket. I could tell where she lay because the blanket covering her was a shade darker then the night. "You either lay yourself back down and finish sleeping, or go off somewhere so the rest of us can. We'll get to your precious Oregon City soon enough." The Mrs. Worthington I'd met seven months ago would never even consider talking like that to her husband, and he wouldn't have put up with such disrespect. As I peeked outta my blanket with one eye, I saw

Mr. Worthington stand and stare at Sandra for only a couple seconds, shake his head in disgust, then walk off towards the river. I liked this Sandra much better than that Mrs. Worthington.

When we did get up and going, we all took just a little more time with our morning chores and duties than normal. Part of it, at least for me, was the fun of watching Mr. Worthington chomping at the bit. He wanted to yell at us to hurry so bad he was about to bust, but he knew it wouldn't do a lick of good. Heck it might even slow us down.

When we did finally get on the trail the subdued moods continued. Heading down the Willamette Valley was mighty pretty. Even this late in the year, most everything was still green and lush. No mistaking it, this valley was created to grow things.

The coastal mountains were to our right and the Cascade Range was to our left as we traveled south along the Willamette River. Once we'd cleared the southern hills and could see for a ways, there was Mount Hood, now off to the east. It must've been forty or fifty miles away, but was standing up clear and tall and majestic. It already had a good start on the winter snowpack. On a beautiful, clear, sunny day it was a sight to behold. Even the beauty of Mount Hood didn't do much to raise our spirits. Mr. Worthington rode out front, most of the time way out front, trying to hurry us along. We took our time.

I also noticed Andy and Sandra now and again talking in hushed whispers to Sloane or Teri, but neither of them even so much as glanced my way. I caught Sandra looking once and she damn near broke her neck turning around. I knew they weren't still mad at me, so I could only assume they were feeling the same mixed emotions about the end of the trail that I was.

Sloane'd been riding alongside Sandra in front of me. The kids were roaming the valley, making sure to stay in sight. They'd started enjoying the day a little more, but were still pretty quiet and calm for a couple of rambunctious kids. Sloane slowed down and waited for me to catch up.

"You know Mount, it ain't none of my never mind, but...," he said. "Well, you can hang me high if I don't think that lady up there is plumb crazy in love with you." He stared over at me. I looked everywhere except at him. "I see I ain't telling you no secrets."

I had to swallow hard and start over a couple times before I could talk. "She's a married woman."

"Yes sir, that she is." He made sort of a snorting noise. "And Mr. Andrew Worthington the Second has got to be the worst excuse for a husband or father there is on God's good earth; and you know that Mount." He was getting worked up. "I've known the man for not even five days now. That woman and that boy ain't but possessions of his. They ain't no more to him than a pretty saddle or a nice rifle."

I looked over at him. He was still staring at me. He smiled and his eyes twinkled like there was a star in there shining bright. "You'd be ten times the husband and father that man is Mount, and you know you'd enjoy it too." He reached over and slapped my shoulder. "Why, that lady is dang near the prettiest thing I've ever seen. Nearly as pretty as this Indian Princess I was married to for a spell. Ya see, her pa was the Indian Chief of all the..."

I let Sloane's story of the Indian Princess sort of fade away; I had important things to ponder. I loved Sandra, I couldn't deny that anymore. Before we left St. Louis she was perfect on the outside; now, after seven months across country, she was perfect on the inside too. The thought of raising Andy as my son set my heart racing and my imagination running wild with the possibilities.

But I couldn't get away from the fact that Sandra was a married woman. Hell, not only was she married, but she was married to one of the richest men in the country. A man that was only gonna get richer as folks started flocking out here to Oregon Country. All I had was a cabin in the mountains, and one really nice palomino horse. How could I ask her to give up all she had for the very little I could offer?

As we'd been riding, each in our own little world, the clouds had snuck up over the mountains to our west, and it started to rain. It seemed to fit the mood perfectly. I hadn't looked ahead for a while because all I'd see was Sandra, twenty feet in front of me and Mr. Worthington a couple hundred feet ahead of her. When I finally did look, off in the distance, I saw smoke rising into the sky; chimney smoke. That smoke could only mean one thing, Oregon City. We were there.

Chapter Twenty-Five

I believe we even slowed down more as we neared Oregon City. As soon as he saw the smoke, Mr. Worthington had taken off. Sloane and Teri, you could tell, were anxious, but didn't hurry any. Sandra, Andy, and I were creeping along like turtles headed to their own hangin'.

As slow as we went, that damn town kept getting closer and closer until we were there; early afternoon on a cloudy, rainy, gloomy day, we rode into Oregon City. My cross-country journey with the Worthingtons was over.

Oregon City was established by Dr. John McLaughlin back in 1829. The power of the Willamette Falls was used to run a lumber mill just outside of town. To the north of town the Clackamas River joined up with the Willamette after running down from the Cascade Range. The town itself was on a grassy shelf beside the river. It all was overlooked by a tall bluff to the south. In the distance, to the east, you could see Mount Hood. All in all, it's a mighty pretty valley.

The town itself was mostly one long muddy street that was fronted, on both sides, by all the businesses. There was a general store, an assessor's office, combination saloon and hotel, town meeting hall, and combination dry goods and tack shop. The other side of the street had a grocery store, a hardware store, a large warehouse, two churches, and one more saloon. Maybe three hundred feet further down the street, sitting off alone was the stable and corrals. Back behind the line of businesses, spread out in no particular order that I could see were the houses for all the townsfolk. There was everything from crudely fashioned huts made from what looked like some kind of adobe brick, to nice sturdy, well built log cabins. I don't know how many people lived in Oregon City back in 1841; it looked to be in the hundreds. It had to be one of the biggest settlements west of St. Louis.

When the five of us rode into town there was a small group of people standing under an awning that covered the wood walkway that ran in front of the businesses. They were in front of the land assessor's office. Mr. Worthington was standing with the group. We tied our horses to the post in front of the office. Sandra and Andy dismounted and stepped up onto the walkway, Sloane and Teri went next door to the saloon. I stood by Goldfire, in the light rain, watching and waiting.

"Mr. Brocknell, you remember my wife." Mr. Worthington stood beside a tall distinguished looking feller that I took to be the business partner we'd come all this way to see.

Mr. Brocknell took Sandra's hand and damned if he didn't actually bow towards her. "Mrs. Worthington, it is such a delight to see you again." Yep, this was one of Mr. Worthington's kind all right. "I trust your trip west was not too much of a hardship."

Sandra glanced back over her shoulder at me. I could tell she was uncomfortable from where I stood. She looked at me for only a second, then she looked back at Mr. Brocknell and gave a short dry laugh. "We've had our moments Mr. Brocknell...we've had our moments." She paused, then squared her shoulders, stood a little straighter, and added. "Please, call me Sandra."

Now it was Mr. Brocknell's turn to be uncomfortable. For Sandra to be so forward as to ask him to use her first name was just not done in their social group...by a proper lady, anyway. Mr. Worthington glared at her, then tried to move on as if maybe they'd misunderstood her or something.

"Mr. Brocknell, I don't know if you ever met my son." Mr. Worthington took Andy by the arm and pulled him up in front of Mr. Brocknell. "This is Andrew Worthington the Third."

"Hello Andrew." You could tell by his bored tone and the look in his eyes that Mr. Brocknell didn't give a damn about Andy, or probably any kid. They couldn't make him any money. He was already turning away as he added absently, "Welcome to Oregon."

"My name's Andy," Andy replied.

Mr. Brocknell stopped and turned back to Andy with this unbelieving look in his eyes, his mouth half open in shock. "Pardon me?"

"I said, my name is Andy, not Andrew." Andy stood up tall with his chest and chin both sticking out. "I don't go by Andrew." I could've busted with pride.

Mr. Brocknell was so taken aback by Andy's brashness he didn't know what to do. Imagine a boy having the nerve to tell you right out like that...like he was a person or something, instead of just a child. In Mr. Brocknell's world, children, if allowed to speak at all, were to simply agree and be polite and respectful.

"Andrew Worthington you'll mind your manners if you know what's good for you." Mr. Worthington stepped up and loomed over Andy...he shrunk back. Sandra reached a hand out to lay on Andy's shoulder, but a look from Mr. Worthington and she pulled it back and stood staring at the ground; maybe not all that much had changed after all.

I wanted awfully bad to step up onto that walk and send Andrew Worthington the Second flying into the horse trough, then maybe Mr. Brocknell in on top of him. I could even picture it happening in my head. Instead I stood in the mud and the rain and watched as Mr. Worthington took Andy's arm in one hand, Sandra's in the other, and lead them inside the office. As they went through the door one by one, all three of them glanced back at me. Sandra and Andy both looking like they might cry. Mr. Worthington with a look mixed with hatred and triumph. I stood there another couple minutes, then took the horses down to the stable and made my way up to the saloon.

"Well hang me high if that ain't a near drowned mountain man." Sloane was leaning against the bar with a whiskey bottle and a glass in front of him. By the slur in his voice I could tell he'd already had several. Teri sat beside him eating a piece of apple pie that looked like it'd been bigger then her when she'd started.

"Come on over and have a glass of what's good for ya." Sloane leaned over the counter and helped himself to a second glass.

"Damned if I don't enjoy a little nipple of whiskey after a long time on the trail." Teri looked up and giggled around a huge mouthful of pie. "A nip..." Sloane realized his slip of the tongue. "I enjoy a nip of whiskey." He laughed till I thought he'd fall over.

I was still feeling pretty low. I kept seeing Sandra and Andy walking through that door, looking back at me. Hell, I didn't even know if I'd ever see either one of them again. We'd all three been busy avoiding each other because we didn't want to think about saying goodbye. Now the thought that I might not get the chance nearly drove me crazy. How could it end like this, without even a chance to say goodbye?

I joined Sloane at the bar. "I ain't got any money." I didn't want to get in that trouble again.

"All bought and paid for," Sloane answered as he filled the second glass. "I've had myself a stretch of luck lately. I sold some pelts and hides for top dollar at the Rendezvous, won me some money gambling, and a little girl playing cards." He glanced down at Teri, but she was still focused on her plate. He then looked around the room and leaned in closer so he could whisper. "I even pulled a couple fair-sized gold nuggets from a creek way up north." He laughed. "I ain't in your friend Mr. Worthington's class yet, but for a wandering no-good, I have more money than I've got a right to." I emptied my glass and Sloane filled it up again, and then again, and then again.

At some point I, through a foggy haze, I remember Sloane falling off his stool. I think I helped Teri carry him to their room, then made my way down to the stables. I woke up the next morning in the loose hay beside the stalls with an empty whiskey bottle beside me; I was still depressed and now my head hurt too.

I didn't see any point in hanging around Oregon City. I didn't have any money, and would rather sleep on the trail than in a stable. I couldn't stand the thought of leaving without seeing Sandra or Andy, so I tried my best not to think of it at all. I fed, watered, and loaded Goldfire up for the trail. As I worked I tried to concentrate on home; the beauty of the mountains, the beauty of the valley, the beauty of the tree-lined creek running beside my beautiful cabin. Trying to think of anything other than the beauty of the woman I was about to leave behind, never to see again, and her son who I loved like he was my own. There was a noise behind me.

I turned, and there stood Andy. Our eyes met, he let go a strangled cry, ran across the floor and threw himself into my arms. He hugged me hard, and his whole body shook with sobs. I hugged him back hard and tried to fight back my own tears. We just stood and held each other for a long time, Andy's feet dangling about a foot off the dirt floor. Finally Andy quit squeezing me, I put him down, and he stepped back a little. He looked up at me, tears streaming down his cheeks.

"Are you...really...gonna go...Mount?" He had a hard time talking around the sobs. "I don't...want you to...leave Mount. I'm gonna...miss you terribly." Suddenly his eyes lit up and a hopeful grin fought its way across his face. "I bet you could work for dad and Mr. Brocknell, Mount!" It was amazing how fast he could go from sad to excited. "I bet they'd give you a job doing...doing...well something. You could do whatever they needed, Mount. I know you could."

I had to laugh at Andy's enthusiasm, and the thought of me working for those men was damn funny too. I wanted to cry thinking about leaving. "Andy, all I am is a mountain man. I know hunting, and trapping, and being in the mountains. Your pa don't have no need for me and I don't have no desire to work for your pa anymore." I looked at my feet because I couldn't look at Andy. "It's time for me to go home. I'm gonna..." I had to take several deep breaths. "I'm gonna miss you too Andy."

I expected him to start crying again. Instead, he got even more excited. He was actually hopping up and down. "I'll come with you!" he nearly shouted. "I'll come with you back to the Rocky Mountains to live!"

"You know you can't do that Andy." I still had a hard time looking at him. "Your pa wouldn't allow it, and you can't leave your ma; you couldn't leave your ma, Andy."

Andy looked me in the eyes for a second then it was his turn to look at the ground. "You know she'd come too…if you asked her, Mount." His feet shuffled nervously. "She'd come with you in a second."

"I can't do that Andy." I also looked at the ground and shuffled my feet. "You know I can't do that." It took a couple more deep breathes before I could add. "Goodbye Andy."

I came down on one knee and Andy threw himself into my arms again. His arms were around my neck and he squeezed so hard I thought it might break, but I didn't care. I didn't want to ever let go.

He pulled away suddenly. "Goodbye Mount." He sobbed as he turned, and without another look ran from the stable. His crying faded away quickly as he ran up the street.

"Goodbye Andy," I whispered. I wiped my eyes and turned back to Goldfire.

I'd just barely checked my tie on the bedroll and cinched up the saddle when I heard footsteps again. My heart hoped it was her, but my common sense told me it was probably Sloane, or maybe the stable hand. I turned around.

"Hey Mount." She was more beautiful then she'd ever been. Was it the fact that I knew I was leaving? "I saw Andy. By the way he was crying I guess you two have said you're goodbyes." Our eyes met for only a second then we both had to look away. I looked at the ground; Sandra looked up into the ceiling beams. We glanced at each other again for another second and I looked up into the rafters and Sandra looked down at her feet.

"I didn't know if I was gonna get to see either one of you again." I couldn't look her in the eye so I stared out the open side doors and across the street; I didn't see a damn thing. "I was hoping you'd come."

"I had to come see you, Mount." Her voice was soft, almost a whisper. "Andrew didn't want me to, but I couldn't let you leave without seeing you...without...I..." Her voice broke.

We were both quiet for a full minute or more, both real busy not looking at each other. My mind started wandering back over the last seven months and everything that'd happened. Stuck wagon, falling tree, broke leg, killed dog, Indian attack, snake bite, nearly drowning, nearly starving, nearly freezing, and those are only the things that flashed through my mind in that brief moment.

I laughed a little short laugh. "We did have us a time of it didn't we? Guess we should thank God Almighty that we all got here alive." I didn't look, but I heard Sandra step closer.

She laughed the same laugh. "We sure did Mount, and I've thanked God in my prayers every night." Her voice dropped back to a whisper. "I thank you too, Mount. If not for you, none of us would have made it even halfway." Did she shuffle a step closer? "Not only did you save our lives Mount, but you helped all of us grow up." She laughed again. "...and I mean all three of us. Andy's become a man because of you Mount. I'm a stronger, more independent woman because of you Mount." Another little laugh. "Even Andrew has grown and learned from you...mainly that his money can't buy everyone. You've helped all three of us in a hundred different ways Mount, and for that I thank you."

I turned to look just as her arms reached up around my neck. I wrapped my arms around her waist, picked her up, and hugged her to me. At the last instant, just as our lips were about to meet, we both turned our heads slightly, and we kissed each other on the cheek; both very red cheeks. The fact that we both turned at the last instant said a lot.

A very tight squeeze from both of us, and she was back standing in front of me and we were both busy looking at our feet again. I think we both knew right then that it would never be; knowing didn't make it hurt any less.

I turned to Goldfire and started to redo my bedroll just for something to do. I knew I couldn't look at Sandra and still talk. "Andy's fine on the trail, but you'll need to keep an eye on him here in the city. There are things around here way more deadly than a rattler."

"I will Mount." I could tell Sandra was struggling to control her voice too. "And you be careful on your way home. Watch out for Indians and stay away from those momma bears." She tried to laugh but it turned into a sob.

I turned around and looked her straight in the eye. She met my gaze. "Don't let him run you." I could tell she knew what I meant instantly. "Just because he's your husband doesn't give him the right to hurt you; with words or his fists." I couldn't stop a tear from slipping outta my left eye. "You're a strong woman Sandra; don't let him beat you down."

She stepped up once more, rose up on tip toe, I leaned over a little, and she gave me one last, very gentle, kiss on my cheek. "I promise you Mount." She smiled that smile that melted my heart. "Seven months ago I wouldn't have even considered it, but now I know I can stand up for myself, and Andy, if I have to." Her smile started to turn upside down and her eyes filled up again. "I promise I will Mount...goodbye Mount."

I stared deep into those incredible brown eyes for the last time. "Goodbye Sandra." I started to say something more, but my voice caught and wouldn't work. Hell, I don't even know what I was gonna say.

Sandra turned and started walking towards the doors. She got about halfway across the stable when I heard a choked sob, her hand flew to her mouth, and she broke into a run. Through the doors, a quick turn to the right, and she was gone.

Goldfire had wandered over to a bucket of oats that was against the wall. I walked over, picked up the reins, and heard steps again behind me. My heart raced. Was she back? I turned. It was Sloane and Teri.

I couldn't hide my disappointment. "Well it's good to see you too, ya damned ole mountain man." He and Teri both laughed. It just took a couple seconds for me to join them.

"Sorry Sloane."

"No ya ain't." He still laughed. "We saw Sandra leaving. You'd be a fool if you'd rather see the likes of us rather than her back again."

I looked past them out into the street. It took a couple deep breaths till I could answer. "She's a married woman, and she ain't married to me. That's all there is to it."

"Well she likes you well enough to give you twenty dollars" Teri blurted out. They were both grinning now.

"What you talking about Teri?" I asked.

"Sandra stopped us in the street." Sloane took over. "Seems she forgot to tell ya while she was in here." He was like a kid with a secret he couldn't wait to tell. "Damned if she didn't arrange for twenty dollars credit in your name at the general store."

I was still confused. Sloane saw it in my eyes.

"Damn it mountain man, you can get twenty dollars worth of goods at the store and it's already been paid for."

"Why?"

He looked at me, then at Goldfire. "Maybe she figured a damned horse; no matter how nice, ain't near enough payment for guidin' 'em clear across the country."

I took Goldfire and we made our way up the muddy street to the general store. I tied Goldfire up out front. I cleaned my boots the best I could on the wooden walk, and went in.

The proprietor was behind the counter and there was a boy putting goods up on the shelves. Besides them, there were only two other customers, a couple of workmen from the mill I guess, looking at some tools up against the wall. The proprietor confirmed the twenty dollars credit.

I stood in the center of the room not knowing which way to go. "Twenty dollars huh?" I shook my head. I'd never had any money to speak of, and now suddenly I was rich. Okay, maybe not actually rich, but twenty dollars was more than I'd ever had before...way more.

"You look plumb lost Mount." Sloane and Teri were again, or still, laughing at me. "Me and Teri can sure help you spend some of that money if you can't handle it."

I came outta my spell and commenced to stocking up for my ride home. In under a half-hour I had more then I was comfortable putting on Goldfire. I had jerky and bacon, salt and pepper, coffee, sugar, even a new cooking pot. Anymore and I'd of needed a pack horse. I even bought Sloane and Teri each some gloves, with winter coming on and all. They didn't want to take them at first, but I wouldn't take no for an answer. Hell, I even had enough left that I was able to go next door and buy three bottles of whiskey for the ride home.

Sloane, Teri, and I stood outside by Goldfire. Everything was packed and there was nothing left to do but ride. I offered Sloane my hand.

"I got me a nice little cabin in a beautiful valley in the Rocky Mountains. Sweetgrass Creek runs past the cabin and down to the Yellowstone River." I finished shaking Sloane's hand and gave Teri a slap on the shoulder. She had a smile and a tear in the corner of one eye. "The two of you are welcome there any time." I stepped up into the saddle. "Don't matter if I'm there or not, you're welcome." Enough talking...I started down the street.

"Well now," Sloane yelled after me. "All the valleys in the Rockies are beautiful Mount, but I'll surely try to find yours. We will Mount, that's a promise."

I waved back over my shoulder. It'd stopped raining but it was still a cloudy, gloomy-looking day, which was sort of the way I felt. The second I turned away from Sloane and Teri, I thought of Sandra and Andy and my heart sank.

As I passed the assessor's office the door opened and out came the Worthingtons. Andy saw me and ran down the steps into the street. Sandra stepped down onto the bottom step. Mr. Worthington stood by the door. I looked over at him first. Our eyes met, and dueled for a second, then he turned and hurried inside, slamming the door.

"Goodbye Mount." Andy was running beside me. I could tell he wanted to say something more, but there wasn't anything to say. "Goodbye."

"Goodbye Andy." I smiled down at him. "You take good care of Skyhawk." It was all I could come up with.

I looked back to where Sandra stood. Our eyes met, her hand came up to cover her mouth, and she stepped down into the street. I was nearly turned completely around in the saddle looking at her. Damned if I could come up with one word that seemed proper. I smiled at her, gave a little wave, turned around, and rode away.

For several hundred feet I held my breath waiting. Would she call out? Would she yell for me to stop? Then maybe confess her love for me to everyone, and proclaim that she and Andy wanted to come and live in my mountain cabin.

She didn't call out; I didn't stop riding.

Epilogue

It took me nearly three weeks to get home. I followed the Willamette River back up north to the Columbia, then the Columbia back to the east and then north again for a piece. I picked a spot, left the river, and made my way back east through the mountains. It had to be December by now and winter was setting in up in the mountains. It was a hard, bitter cold ride.

I had plenty of food and good protection from the cold. As good as you can get in this country anyway. If you're camping out this time of year, you're gonna be cold, that's just the fact of it. I was able to find dry wood and have a fire most nights.

Goldfire continued to impress me. Damn near every day that horse did something to amaze me as to how smart or how strong he was. It was almost like the good Lord meant us to be together. I swear, that horse and I could read each other's thoughts and feelings. Most of the time I didn't even hold the reins, I'd just tie them off so they didn't dangle, and let Goldfire have his head. I'd lean back against my bedroll, which was huge because of all my supplies, and daydream the afternoon away, while Goldfire picked our trail. Hell, a couple times I even fell asleep while riding.

Once I'd made my way over the divide and the water was running the proper direction again, I knew I was close to home. I followed a river I don't know the name of down outta the mountains and came to what had to be the Missouri River where it came down from the south and before it turned and headed east. Once I'd crossed the Missouri I knew the Yellowstone and home weren't far away.

The good Lord saw fit to welcome me home with a bit of late summer. After crossing the Missouri, and as I made my way through the hills and finally along the north bank of the Yellowstone, the weather just got nicer and warmer every day. There had been a blanket of snow once or twice already but most of it melted off, leaving only the mountains with their brilliant white cover.

I still spent a good portion of everyday thinking about Sandra and Andy. When I did, I'd start feeling sad and gloomy, but riding through country as beautiful as I was, with the weather showing off like it had been, it was hard to stay depressed for long. I'd try to clear my mind of thoughts of Oregon City and the folks there, and then could relax and enjoy the ride. When I was able to do that, my spirits would soar, and I'd fill to nearly busting with love for the mountains, the valleys, and my way of life. I knew deep down that I'd made the right choices.

The day I got to Sweetgrass Creek and made my way up it to my cabin was truly a glorious day. The creek was running strong from the snow that was melting in the upper meadow. I swear that creek even played a happy tune to welcome me home as I rode beside it.

When I came around the bend in the creek that hid my cabin, and I saw it there just like I'd left it, I'm not ashamed to admit I got a little hitch in my breathing and my eyes watered up a bit. Then with a hoop and a holler, Goldfire and I galloped the last couple hundred feet to the cabin and I was home. I was really home!

Before I even went into the cabin I walked up on the hill under the big cottonwood and looked down on Ma's grave. It just seemed right to say howdy and let her know I was home.

When I went into the cabin I knew right away that someone had been there. I could feel their presence, I could smell their smell, and the little furniture I had had been moved around. Both straight back chairs I had were over by the fire pit. The place was clean, if a little dusty, and nothing but a little firewood was gone, so whoever had stayed had been a friend. Friends are always welcome.

It's been a couple weeks now since I got home. Except for some hunting and trap setting I haven't wandered far from the cabin. It's so good to be home. I'm behind on my stack of firewood for the winter, so that's been taking up most of my time. I need to get a hard winter's worth stacked by the cabin before the real snow comes and covers everything over. It could happen any day now. The weather has stayed nice the last couple weeks, but it's staying quite a bit colder during the day.

I still think about Sandra and Andy several times a day. There's an empty place in my heart that hurts a little whenever I think of them. There is also a place in my heart and my spirit soars sky high every time I think of them too. I remember the good times we had, I remember the laughing, the singing, making fun of Mr. Worthington behind his back, all the good times. The bad times I already barely remember, like a dream that's mostly faded away.

Who knows? Maybe in a couple years, I might get a hankering to do some travelin' again. If I do, I just might have to make my way back to Oregon City and look up some old friends.